D0683548

"In exploring themes of cultural identity and women's friendship, Barrientos covers the same ground as writers Julia Alvarez and Denise Chávez—adding her own unique brand of unconventional wisdom. . . . Her sassy voice . . . shines through the entire work. . . . An interesting addition to the (regrettably minuscule) body of work by Latina writers in the United States."
—*The Philadelphia Inquirer*

"I've never been anywhere near the Texas/Mexico border, yet felt quickly at home walking Barrientos's Frontera Street, an intricately stitched story of a family formed by the hand of compassion."
—Suzanne Strempek Shea, national bestselling author of *Around Again*

"A host of memorable characters . . . an insightful exploration of what it means to live in this evolving culture."
—*San Antonio Express-News*

"Straightforward, entertaining. . . . Barrientos does a wonderful job letting the reader get to know both women. . . . Superb. . . . It leaves you with a pleasant, hopeful feeling that people of all races do need each other." —*El Paso Times*

"Anyone who's ever struggled with a secret, found a new friend, or wondered about how the people on the other side of the tracks live will cherish a visit to *Frontera Street*."
—Jennifer Weiner, *New York Times* bestselling author of *Good in Bed*

"A vivid tale of hope and healing that will lift the heart of anyone who has ever needed a friend. The women of the barrio are as strong, colorful, and unpredictable as the bordertown neighborhood that surrounds them. Stop and linger on *Frontera Street*. It is a place you will never forget."
—Lisa Wingate, author of *Good Hope Road*

"Strongly detailed . . . renders the life in a small west Texas bordertown very well indeed."
—*Kirkus Reviews*

Written by today's freshest new talents and selected by New American Library, NAL Accent novels touch on subjects close to a woman's heart, from friendship to family to finding our place in the world. The Conversation Guidelines included in each book are intended to enrich the individual reading experience, as well as encourage us to explore these topics together—because books, and life, are meant for sharing.

Visit us online at www.penguin.com.

ALSO BY TANYA MARIA BARRIENTOS

Frontera Street

Tanya Maria Barrientos

FAMILY RESEMBLANCE

CONVERSATION GUIDE

NAL
ACCENT

INCLUDED

FICTION FOR THE WAY WE LIVE

NAL Accent
Published by New American Library, a division of
Penguin Group (USA) Inc., 375 Hudson Street,
New York, New York 10014, U.S.A.
Penguin Books Ltd, 80 Strand,
London WC2R 0RL, England
Penguin Books Australia Ltd, 250 Camberwell Road,
Camberwell, Victoria 3124, Australia
Penguin Books Canada Ltd, 10 Alcorn Avenue,
Toronto, Ontario, Canada M4V 3B2
Penguin Books (N.Z.) Ltd, Cnr Rosedale and Airborne Roads,
Albany, Auckland 1310, New Zealand

Penguin Books Ltd, Registered Offices:
80 Strand, London WC2R 0RL, England

First published by New American Library, a division of Penguin Group (USA) Inc.

First Printing, July 2003
10 9 8 7 6 5 4 3 2

Copyright © Tanya Maria Barrientos, 2003
Conversation Guide copyright © Penguin Group (USA) Inc., 2003
All rights reserved

FICTION FOR THE WAY WE LIVE
REGISTERED TRADEMARK—MARCA REGISTRADA

LIBRARY OF CONGRESS CATALOGING-IN-PUBLICATION DATA:
Barrientos, Tanya Maria.
Family resemblance / Tanya Maria Barrientos.
p. cm.
ISBN 0-451-20872-2 (alk. paper)
1. Fathers and daughters—Fiction. 2. Parent and adult child—Fiction. 3. Identity
(Psychology)—Fiction. I. Title.

PS3602.A837 F3 2003
813'.6—dc21   2002043139

Set in Adobe Garamond
Designed by Ginger Legato

Printed in the United States of America

Without limiting the rights under copyright reserved above, no part of this publication may be reproduced, stored in or introduced into a retrieval system, or transmitted, in any form, or by any means (electronic, mechanical, photocopying, recording, or otherwise), without the prior written permission of both the copyright owner and the above publisher of this book.

PUBLISHER'S NOTE
This is a work of fiction. Names, characters, places, and incidents either are the product of the author's imagination or are used fictitiously, and any resemblance to actual persons, living or dead, business establishments, events, or locales is entirely coincidental.

BOOKS ARE AVAILABLE AT QUANTITY DISCOUNTS WHEN USED TO PROMOTE PRODUCTS OR SERVICES. FOR INFORMATION PLEASE WRITE TO PREMIUM MARKETING DIVISION, PENGUIN GROUP (USA) INC., 375 HUDSON STREET, NEW YORK, NEW YORK 10014.

The scanning, uploading and distribution of this book via the Internet or via any other means without the permission of the publisher is illegal and punishable by law. Please purchase only authorized electronic editions, and do not participate in or encourage electronic piracy of copyrighted materials. Your support of the author's rights is appreciated.

For my husband, Jack,
who knows what it took

ACKNOWLEDGMENTS

As always, my parents must come first. And then, Judi Kauffman, Suzanne Strempek Shea and Lil Swanson, for the depth of their friendships. A giant thank-you to Annette John-Hall, Karen Outen, Jeff and Chris Gammage, Ellen Ridyard, Lauren Cowen and Stephanie Nachum for being buoys in a choppy sea. A special thanks to Dr. Jay Cowen, for his medical assistance. To Amy Myers, the ladies at the Jenkintown and the Elkins Park libraries, as well as the folks at the Philadelphia Free Library, who opened their hearts to my first book, and their writing rooms for the making of the second.

My deepest gratitude to friends and colleagues at the *Philadelphia Inquirer,* especially Nancy Cooney, Neil Goldstein, Mike Rozansky and Linda Hasert for patiently standing by me while this book was completed, and to the Pew Fellowship in the Arts for giving me the priceless gift of time. *Gracias* to my agent, John Talbot, and to copy editor Bill Harris. A special hug to Genny Ostertag, who makes my work better every time it crosses her desk. Finally to Jack, to whom this book is dedicated, thank you.

CHAPTER 1

$\mathcal{I}$ used to know my father's friends by what they drank and how they argued.

Dr. Carver sipped vermouth before dinner and chilled Madeira after. He was chairman of the philosophy department and almost legally blind, so when he spoke he tilted his square head toward the ceiling to focus his weak and watery eyes through the thickest portion of his glasses. With his chin jutting toward the chandelier, he built a wall of reason by stacking one brick of human nature on top of another, and then challenged the others to make it topple.

It was Beefeater all night for Dr. Lansky, the high-strung sociologist who anesthetized his rivals with numbing statistics, and ice-cold Stoli for Dad's closest friend, Randy Stevens, who looked more like an aging tennis pro than a scholar. Long limbed and perpetually tan, Professor Stevens would swirl his vodka while the others spoke, waiting for the most strategic moment to make his point.

That is how it went once a month, when the professors would leave their wives and children at home and come to our house to drink and smoke and expound at what my father liked to call his full-moon dinner debates. Sometimes, the guest list swelled to as many as nine or ten but, over the years, it was the core group of Carver, Lansky and Stevens who never faltered. Their wives would work out a menu of rump roast or pork chops or baked lasagna and send their husbands to our door cradling a host of hors d'oeuvres, a main dish, two sides and a clever dessert. My job was to set the table, pull out the liquor bottles and fade into the background.

The evenings began with idle office chat—complaints about paperwork, the university's meddlesome administration and slipping student standards. My father would play Herb Alpert on the stereo, turning the volume up just loud enough for the sass of the trumpets to saturate the room, and by the time the men sat down for dinner they were warm with drink and ready to spar.

There was always a place for me at the table, but the conversation rarely swayed my way. I'd quietly pass platters while my father and his friends considered topics to discuss. I'd refill their glasses as they winnowed down their choices, and nestle my chin in the heel of my hand when they finally settled on one subject to chew on all night.

The first time I watched them battle they frightened me. Instead of debating the way I expected college professors would, they bellowed and railed and shouted at one another. They slammed their palms against the table and pounded their feet against the floor. They baited one another like junior high bullies begging for a fight.

I'd never heard my father rant like that before, and it made my stomach ache. I was twelve, and almost everything about our lives had changed in the eight months since my mother was killed; for all I knew, the way my father behaved around company was one of them. That first night, I was on the verge of tears when Dad calmly excused himself from the table and asked me to follow him into the kitchen so I could help him pour the coffee. Arranging cups without saucers onto a metal tray, he told me the bluster was just sport. It was a game these men played the way other men might toss a ball. All the yelling and stomping, he insisted, was nothing but theater.

But why would grown-ups attack one another that way? I wanted to know.

It was a discussion, Dad explained, an exercise for the mind, and when it was over the men would still be friends. I had my doubts—the emotions I'd seen were close to boiling—but by the time we returned to the dining room with a dozen lemon squares and six cups of Maxwell House, the fullmooners had peacefully shifted from politics to Hollywood and were happily reviewing Woody Allen's latest.

After that night, I actually began to look forward to the long and noisy evenings. From my corner of the supper table I would secretly keep score as each professor set up his argument, pitched his theory and let the others take their swings. Occasionally, my father would shoot a gleeful wink my way, checking, I suppose, to see if I was having a good time. And then, at ten o'clock sharp, Mrs. Stevens, who had been my mother's best friend, would telephone to remind me it was time for bed.

That is why I dial her number first.

"It's time to pack up his things," I say, pausing for a moment to let the sweep of my statement register. I tell her the neurologist believes it is unlikely Dad will ever return to Texas, or live by himself again. It comes as no surprise to either of us, but repeating the grim facts into the phone, listening to words like "global aphasia" and "emboli" tumble out of my own mouth, depletes me. Four months have passed since my father's stroke, and while a daily regimen of physical and occupational therapy has helped him reclaim partial control of his right arm and leg, the permanent damage to his brain is proving to be severe. He has a difficult time swallowing, can no longer read or write, and his vocabulary consists of no more than a dozen words, which he struggles to pronounce. It is painful to watch him try. He begins with focused determination, pushing his reluctant lips to make two or three undiscernible sounds before getting so lost in the thick weeds of jumbled language that he simply surrenders.

While his former colleagues enjoy retirement in the bright Dallas sunshine, the once brash and brilliant professor Diego DeLeon is living at a nursing home in Philadelphia, straining to recite the letters of the alphabet.

"You can get into the place, right?" I ask Mrs. Stevens, even though I know that a copy of our house key has dangled from a cup hook inside her pantry since the day Mom died more than twenty-five years ago. I can picture it now, lying flat against the yellow flowered wallpaper, attached to a simple silver key ring none of us ever bothered to embellish. Carla Stevens knows my family's house, and everything inside it, as well as she knows her own.

"I'll start tonight," she says. "Is there anything I can do for you right now?"

I roll my desk chair to the corner of my office that faces the road and raise the window an inch or two. A stiff gust billows the dotted Swiss curtains, reminding me that, in Philadelphia, March is still the heart of winter, not the beginning of spring. The street is damp and the color of tin. The sidewalk is littered with bits of broken branches that the old oak near the curb has shed. Dead leaves lay strewn across the lawn and the spindly branches of the naked azalea bushes quiver in the wind.

In Texas, the azaleas would be just about to bloom, promising a fireworks display of tiny pink explosions against a cloudless turquoise sky. Folks would be making plans for boating weekends and family barbecues along the shores of the man-made lakes outside of Dallas.

"Could you look for the rest of his papers?" I think back to the panicked state I was in when I rifled through Dad's mahogany desk looking for the health insurance documents I needed to get him transferred to the nursing home in Philadelphia. We made the difficult trip ten days after the stroke. Dad's doctor pronounced him stable enough to travel, but it still took two airline employees in Dallas and in Philly to lift him into and out of his wheelchair, and a special van to drive us from the airport to the nursing home.

"Sure." Mrs. Stevens pauses for a moment, and then asks, "What about you, Nita? What do you need?"

I smile. "A miracle? Could you arrange for that?"

Of course I don't expect an answer. I know that what I'm feeling is the same emotional weariness that my clients battle. Death, illness, divorce, they're all part of the package, and any good counselor would point out that my ride isn't any more painful or any less haphazard than anybody else's. Still, you lose perspective when the troubles land at your door, and in my case I'd like to know when enough will finally be enough.

I look at the clock that hangs over the doorway. It is almost six and I have one hour to eat dinner and get prepared for my next appointment. No time left to wallow.

"I'm all right," I say. "It's not what anyone would call a surprise."

Mrs. Stevens hears the change in my inflection and picks up on her cue to finish the conversation. "I'll go right over," she says. "And I'll call the fullmooners to give them the update."

"Tell them to write," I add, giving her the address of the Rose Tree Assisted Living Center, which I know she already has. "I'm not certain how much he takes in, but I'm sure he'd love hearing from the old coots."

They, after all, are the closest thing to uncles I've ever known, the men who helped my father raise me.

After I hang up with Mrs. Stevens, I close the window and walk across the braided throw rug that is positioned like a puddle in the center of my office. At its edge, near the door, is a chintz love seat that faces two wide-bodied leather chairs, the kind you'd imagine Englishmen would sit in to read the evening paper. They are the only good pieces of furniture in the entire place since the family counseling practice I opened in my home a year ago is still, essentially, a start-up affair.

I check the answering machine perched on a small desk in the outer alcove, where I hope one day a live receptionist will sit. I call the area my reception room, although there is nothing particularly inviting about it. Clients who arrive early are subjected to a rock-hard futon covered with a worn Indian blanket. I have no nerve-soothing tropical fish in an aquarium to amuse them, no carefully tended exotic plants, and the issues of *People, Cosmopolitan* and *Newsweek* stacked on the bleached pine coffee table are dated and tattered. Still, I tell myself, nicer things will come with time and I should be grateful that I got the house.

It's cliché, I know, but I fell in love with the suburban Tudor the moment I saw it. Its spacious side suite is lined with wide windows and swims in natural light, and I instantly pictured it serving as a guest room for all the friends from Texas I was certain would come to visit Aaron and me. I also expected it to become the nursery. With its private entry off the side yard, its own washroom and little sitting area, it seemed perfect for those first sleepless weeks of infancy. Of course, after I repeatedly failed to get pregnant, it became Aaron's study. Then his bedroom. And, finally, the place where he stacked his things before he moved out.

There are no messages on the answering machine, which means the Taggerts will be on time for their weekly session. I grab a *Cosmo* and head for the kitchen, where I throw a Lean Cuisine into the microwave and pour myself yet another cup of coffee. On the magazine's cover, beneath a tarty photograph of Nicole Kidman in a red satin corset, is a headline that shouts: LIVING SINGLE—AGAIN. I punch the timer on the oven and find the article. The writer recommends nurturing your "inner girl" after a breakup. She suggests leaping, feet first, into the deep end of femininity by placing vases of fresh flowers on every available surface and redecorating your place in soothing shades of sherbet. She says you should eat your meals off the *good* china, and listen to lots of Streisand. It's pop psychology at its bubblegum best, and I keep reading. But, I wonder, what are you supposed to do with the vacant space in your bed? Or the married friends left to choose who to stay in touch with?

Buy shoes, the magazine says. And handbags.

My supper spins in the microwave for a final minute while I walk to the front door, flip on the overhead light and run my toes over the little mountain of mail the postman has dropped through the brass slot. Too tired to bend over and pick up the grocery store circulars and white-sale catalogs, I sort through the junk with my foot, like a horse pawing dirt. There isn't a single handwritten envelope in the mix, just two more Spanish-language credit card pitches addressed to "Srta. Juanita DeLeon."

They don't waste any time, do they? Someone in the marketing-by-mail business must actually hold the job of sifting through divorce records at the county courthouse and plugging the names of the newly single into a giant database. It is an insultingly blunt, but brilliant, tactic. Aren't divorcées perpetually short on cash?

I haven't received mail addressed to "Juanita" since I tried to trade on my ethnicity to get financial aid for graduate school. Nobody, not even my own father, calls me that. But, to be honest, it's not Juanita that sounds so strange to my ear. It's DeLeon. I am going to have to get used to hearing that name again. I'll have to fall back on the tiresome practice of stopping people in midsentence to say, "It's Da-LEE-on, like the boy's name Leon. Not Del-YONE."

How many millions of times did I do that as a kid? Yes, it's Spanish, I'd say. Yes, other people pronounce it Del-YONE. But not my family. We say Da-LEE-on. Accent on the LEE. As a kid, I never questioned why we pronounced it differently, but looking back I realize it was just one of a million things my parents did to fit in. Their English could never lose the sound of the Spanish they'd spoken before they moved here, but they worked hard to make every other aspect of their lives, and mine, ultra-American.

That's probably one of the reasons I happily switched to Nile on the day I married Aaron. Nita Nile. Who wouldn't love a name like that? So mainstream. So morning television. Mom would have been proud.

In fact, I was so eager to let the world know I'd become Nita Nile that during our seven-hour honeymoon flight to France I needle-pointed a new passport holder for myself, joyfully stitching two tomato-red N's into a field of navy blue with little white stars along the border. When we landed in Paris, I proudly presented my new identification to the immigration officer. He took a long look at the Nita Nile in the passport photograph, and an even longer look at the real woman standing before him, and with a quick smack of a rubber stamp declared me genuine.

The microwave buzzes. Dinner is served.

During the session with Frank and Joy Taggert, my concentration flounders. I find myself staring at the wide diagonal stitches running through the braided rug, thinking of the messy nest of papers I left strewn across Dad's desk. His filing system was always incomprehensible to anyone but himself. He stuffed manila envelopes with deeds and owner's manuals and grocery store receipts that had nothing to do with one another and stashed them wherever it felt convenient. God only knows where Mrs. Stevens will have to look to put her hands on a few months' worth of bank records or last year's tax return. It occurs to me that I have, essentially, asked her to hunt through every drawer and closet in the house.

"Excuse the hell out of me, Doctor, but are you even listening?"

I smile calmly at Mr. Taggert and his wife, who are seated on opposite ends of the love seat across from me.

"Frank, whether I'm hanging on your every word isn't what's important in the long run, is it? What's critical is whether you and Joy are making yourselves heard—really heard—by one another." I use a tone dangerously close to sarcasm, hoping to hide the fact that I haven't absorbed a thing he's said in the last minute.

Mr. Taggert sneers, clearly insulted by my condescension. This is not the first time he has taken a gibe at me. He knows damn well that my degree is in family therapy, not medicine, and still he loves to slather a thick coat of disdain over the word "doctor" and slap me in the face with it every chance he gets. Usually, I take the blows like a champ, never giving him the pleasure of seeing me flinch. But this time he's caught me daydreaming, and he knows he has me on the ropes. So he keeps plugging.

"Hear? I'll tell you what I hear, *Doctor.* I hear lots of nothing. I hear us fighting about the same goddamn things we fought about last Wednesday, and the Wednesday before that. I *hear* my wife droning on and on about the same crap she's been harping about for months, the same stale stories, word for word, like she's singing along with the bouncing ball."

"And what about you, Frank?" I ask, sounding more irritated than I'd like. "What's your favorite song?"

There are ten minutes left in the session, and I'm grateful it is almost time to stop.

Joy Taggert reaches for the box of Kleenex that I keep on a side table and crumples another pink tissue into the wad she is already clutching. After months of painful stalemate she is still trying to push the boulder of her marriage uphill, and I don't know how much longer her strength will last.

During the Taggerts' first appointment, it took me less than an hour to figure out that Frank has something going on the side. His wife knows it, too, in her gut, if not yet in her head. After that initial session, I pulled Frank aside and asked if he wanted to schedule a few meetings with me by himself, but he refused. So it's clear that he isn't really interested in changing his behavior. He's showing up just to go through the motions. Which makes me wonder who he is trying to impress—his wife or his girlfriend?

It isn't my place to pronounce the Taggerts' marriage dead. My job is to help them work to save it. But tonight that feels virtually impossible. The dismissive tone in Frank's voice, the hostility in his body language, tells me he has already detached. And, as hard as Joy may try, she won't be able to pull him back. It is, I tell myself, just a matter of time before Frank calls it quits. I wish I could take his wife out for a drink and advise her to get ready. Being alone isn't easy, I'd say over a stiff vodka tonic, but at least you'll be able to let go. Of course, I can't do that. All I can do is wait, and be here for her when it happens.

Frank looks at his wristwatch and rakes his long fingers through his salt-and-pepper hair.

"Homework!" I chirp, rubbing my hands together and trying to sound upbeat.

Frank keeps his eyes on the ceiling and sighs impatiently as Joy pulls a ballpoint pen and a palm-size memo pad out of her pocketbook.

"This week I want you to spend three minutes a day facing one another, holding hands and looking directly into each other's eyes. You can talk, or you can choose not to speak. But I want you to maintain eye contact for the full three minutes. Set an egg timer."

"Jeezus," Frank grouses. "You're writing that down?"

Flustered, Joy looks at me with a sheepish smile and stops writing. The Taggerts gather their things and I rise to say good-bye.

"Oh!" I touch Frank on the shoulder before he steps out of the office. "No sex, okay, Frank? I mean, don't let the three-minute thing turn into sex."

His eyebrows lift and the corners of his mouth slide into an amused grin. "Don't worry about it," he scoffs.

After the Taggerts leave, I punch the love seat's cushions back into shape. I scoop up the two throw pillows they wedged into the corners and place them inside an antique steamer trunk I keep against the far wall. There are more than a dozen other pillows already stored inside the trunk, most of them needlepointed during the two years I was in graduate school. At first glance they look like duplicates of the two I just put away, but they aren't. I have needlepointed a different scene into the center of each. There is one with dark clouds and fat gray raindrops falling at a fierce angle over a field of golden wheat. There is another with a Grandma Moses family of four standing at stick-figure attention in front of a barnyard filled with wide-eyed sheep and flat-eared cows. There is an entwined couple kissing under the leafy umbrella of a weeping willow, and a triangular orange cat sitting as serenely as a Buddha in the middle of an ornate Persian rug.

I use them as silent messages to my clients, although I am sure it has never occurred to Mr. Taggert that I select the gray clouds for him each and every Wednesday. Nor does it register with his wife that, when they began their counseling, I optimistically graced her side of the sofa with the kissing couple, but quickly switched to the red bird flying out of a golden cage, and most recently have settled on the tapestry showing a collection of old-fashioned traveling bags with the words BON VOYAGE marching across the bottom. How much more blatant can I get?

No, there's no sign the subliminal messages are getting through. But I keep making the pillows and setting them out, for my own amusement, if nothing else. The one I am stitching now is a woolen version of the classic optical illusion that at one moment looks like a wine goblet and a few moments later appears to be the profiles of two people. I am recreating the design in simple black and white and it is, I think, taking shape nicely.

The telephone rings and I'm not surprised to hear Mrs. Stevens's voice on the other end of the line. As fast and efficient as ever, she tells me she's already unearthed the most recent bank statements belonging to Dad's checking and savings accounts. But then she says she's come across something curious.

"It's an old address book. You wouldn't believe where I wound up finding it. Folded right into the middle of that tablecloth your mother used to set out on Christmas Eve."

I raise my eyebrows as she forges ahead.

"You know, I don't think your father ever touched that piece of fabric after your momma passed. But I wanted to take a look at it for old times' sake. And I'm telling you, you could have knocked me over with a feather when this little notebook tumbled out."

It's a surprise to both of us because Dad is not the sort of man who would keep names of acquaintances in an address book. The only alphabetized item on his desk is a clunky Rolodex filled with index cards on which he's scribbled telephone numbers for the dentist, the plumber, the accountant. He's never mailed Christmas cards or birthday greetings with precision. He has no extended family, and no close friends other than Mrs. Stevens and the fullmooners.

"Why would Dad have saved it?"

"I'm pretty sure it didn't belong to him," she answers. "Everything inside it is written in your mother's hand. It's all in Spanish, too. Addresses and phone numbers. Looks like they might be names from when they lived in Guatemala, Nita. Nobody I recall them speaking of."

"Well, I appreciate you taking the time."

"No problem, doll. The strange thing is that I found a letter stuck between the pages. No envelope, just the letter. I can't make heads or tails of it, but it's signed by your aunt Pancha."

"Pancha?"

"Uh-huh."

"My father's sister, Pancha?"

"I'm supposing that's the one."

"Didn't she die before my parents moved here?"

"That's what your momma told me. But, honey, your parents came to this country in 1963, and this letter is dated July second, 1976."

Which, Mrs. Stevens doesn't need to mention, was two weeks before my mother died.

CHAPTER 2

On the morning of Mom's funeral, Dad put away her pearls, her good gold watch and her orange opal pendant, telling me he planned to give them to me when I got older. He said they were precious reminders of her, heirlooms that I'd cherish one day. But the jewelry meant nothing to me. It did not smell like my mother's gardenia-scented bath soap. It did not match the kind of clothes she liked to wear. It was cold and utterly useless in my shattered twelve-year-old world.

Mom was an artist, an accomplished potter, who lived most of her life wearing oversize men's shirts caked with globs of glaze and clay. When she wasn't spinning pots on her wheel, she was sketching the geometric patterns she would carve into the bowls, or mixing chemicals to devise the perfect glaze. The only time I'd seen her put on the pearls was when she and Dad would go out. She would lift her thick black hair off of her neck and dip her chin while Dad's big hands secured the tiny clasp. She'd rest her square-tipped fingers on the sleek beads and ask him how they looked, knowing Dad would say what he always said—beautiful.

But on regular days, Mom wore no jewelry at all, and that is how I remembered her. So, when Dad wasn't looking, I slipped into her closet and took what I considered to be her most sacred possessions—four of her work shirts, her red umbrella, her wedding album and the de-coupaged lunch pail she used as a handbag. I hid them in my own closet and gazed at them every morning while I got dressed for school. Before I went to bed at night, I cracked the closet door open and looked at them until I fell asleep. I took them to college with me, and I still have them today.

I know, without having to look, that inside the lunch box there is one tattered houndstooth wallet, four ballpoint pens, two tubes of Avon Tuscany Rose lipstick and a Cover Girl compact, medium beige. There is also a book of 7-Eleven matches, although she did not smoke, a plastic yellow paddle comb, two paper clips, and a still un-signed permission slip allowing me to visit the planetarium with the rest of the sixth grade. There are fourteen dollars in bills, two pennies, four dimes and a quarter. I've kept a faithful inventory for more than twenty-five years.

These days, I store Mom's wedding album on the magazine shelf un-derneath the coffee table, next to my own collection of formal wedding photographs, which I do not know what to do with. Do you throw some-thing like that away after a divorce? Do you stash the pictures in the back of a file cabinet with your old tax returns? Do you set them on fire?

After hearing about Mrs. Stevens's odd discovery, I pull out my mother's ivory leather album and telephone my best friend, Lauren. It's impossible to count how many times I've turned to this photo album when I've craved my mother's comfort. I've looked through it so many times that I've memorized every feature on every face in every snapshot. I feel as if I know each of the smiling young women in dainty dresses, and the earnest young gentlemen in narrow ties and boxy suits who cel-ebrated my parents' good fortune. I don't know their names because my mother died before I thought to ask, and my father considered the issue closed after telling me once that they were "just people we invited." But, I've peered into their eyes so often that, in a way, I believe they know me, too.

Lauren screens her calls, so I wait for the beep at the end of the taped message before I begin to speak.

"Hey, it's me. I just got the strangest news from Mrs. Stevens . . . goose bump kind of strange."

I wait for her to pick up.

"She found a letter in Dad's house that she says is signed by my aunt Pancha. But Pancha's been dead since the forties or something."

No answer.

"She died from malaria, or maybe it was typhoid. Are you there?"

I hear her machine record my breathing.

"Are you at work? If you—"

An ear-piercing beep cuts me off.

I consider dialing Lauren's cell phone, but there's no point. If she's not home by now it means she's out on an assignment for the newspaper. She could be anywhere, taking pictures of anything from a classical music concert to a raging three-alarm fire.

I call her house again and wait for the message to play.

"Call me if you don't get in too late."

I set the album on my lap and open it slowly. The first page is dedicated to a photograph of the newlyweds and their families, and I know Pancha is not there. I search my memory for any stories Mom or Dad may have told me about her, but I can only remember that she was Dad's younger sister, and she died young. That is all.

I look at the picture again and see a small, round-faced, ample-hipped woman in a flowered hat standing at Dad's side. It is my grandmother Olympia, whom I have never met, never spoken to and never seen another photo of. My father told me we didn't stay in touch with her because that was what she wanted, and the one and only time I asked my mother why Grandma would want such a thing, her answer was simply: "Because."

In that same photo I see my mother's mother, Yolanda Acosta, a slim, regal woman with long shapely legs. She is dressed in a satin suit with pretty cap sleeves and is holding Mom's elbow as if she is not quite ready to let her daughter go. Standing next to her is my grandfather, Arturo Acosta, with his hands clasped firmly in front of him. His white shirt cuffs peek out of his dark suit and his smile is tinged with melancholy. They were killed in a fire before I was born, and because my mother was an only child, I have no cousins.

On the day Mom got married, she was twenty-six, more than a decade younger than I am now. I study her face for similarities. Most of my life I've been told that I resemble my father, but who else did people have to compare me to? If they could take one long look at this picture they would see that the fullness of my mother's chest and the thickness of her hair is identical to mine.

I turn the page and see my parents standing next to their best man and maid of honor, turn another page and see them kneeling at the church's altar. Then I come upon the images of the young and moneyed crowd that was my parents' social circle in Guatemala. I see women smoking cigarettes through sleek ivory holders and men winking at the camera with cocky self-assurance. There are entire tables of smiling well-wishers holding uplifted glasses of champagne, and there are a couple of photographs of three somber men wearing sunglasses and keeping themselves apart from the rest of the crowd.

My favorite picture is on the final page. It shows my beautiful mother dressed in her going-away suit, complete with a pillbox hat and matching gloves. She is climbing into the backseat of a long wide car. Next to her, smiling into the camera, is my father, the newly minted groom, with his chin held high and his arm raised over his head to shield himself from rice being thrown by the guests. The shot looks like something that might have appeared in *Life* magazine, a perfect portrait of that tidy and tailored era, a scene so universal that it could have been any couple anywhere. But this couple happened to be my parents, and the wedding happened to be in Guatemala, a tiny nation in such turmoil that before I was born my parents had to flee. They never told me the full story of why they packed their things and left their friends and family for good. They said the government was crazy and had, essentially, left it at that.

I'm hypnotized by the scenes in the album, drawn so deeply into a world I've pieced together in my imagination that when the telephone rings it startles me.

"I was in the shower," Lauren says.

I hear two quick clicks and a long drawn breath, which means Lauren has lit a cigarette. I picture her in a long flannel robe with a damp towel draped over her shoulders and strands of still-wet hair fanned out like fringe. To me that first hour after a shower, when the fruity smell of shampoo still lingers and my skin is buffed and tender, is complete bliss and I can't imagine sullying it by sitting in the middle of a cloud of cigarette smoke. But I don't say a word. Lauren has made it clear she's not interested in quitting, so, for the time being, I've stopped nudging her.

"What's this aunt's name?"

"Pancha."

"Mmm. Never heard you talk about her."

"There's not much to say. She died."

"Well," Lauren says, inhaling and then making me wait two or three seconds until she exhales and finishes her thought, "apparently she didn't."

I roll my eyes, knowing somehow the expression will translate over the line. "I'm sure Mrs. Stevens just read the date wrong. She said the whole letter was written in Spanish. It's coming by overnight mail, so I'll see for myself tomorrow."

"You don't read Spanish."

"Yeah, but I do know how to read a date."

We both chuckle.

Lauren asks what I know about my parents' lives in Guatemala and I tell her the truth, which is that the first time I even thought about Guatemala as an actual place was when I was in the third grade. My teacher assigned us to find out where our ancestors were from, and I had to be shown where Guatemala was on the map. Below Mexico, my mother told me as she ran my finger over the plastic globe on the desk in my bedroom.

Sliding both our hands toward the equator, she stopped in the middle of the long necklace of land that stretches between the continents. That, she told me, was once her home. It was, she said, a nation known for its Mayan ruins, its coffee and its active volcanoes. I reported those facts to my class, and if anyone were to ask me to tell them more about the place today, I doubt that I'd be able. Neither of my parents talked about Guatemala at home. We never celebrated whatever holidays the little country observes. Everything I know about it is in the wedding pictures my parents brought to the United States with them. To me it is a country filled with people I'll never know, living lives forever disconnected from mine.

"I know someone who can read the letter for you."

"You do?"

"A new guy at the newspaper. He's Hispanic."

Lauren's answer chafes, and I know she can hear the irritation in my voice. "That doesn't automatically mean—"

"Nita," she interrupts. "I covered a Puerto Rican thing with him at Christmas. That's how I know he speaks Spanish. Not just because he's Latino. Okay?"

I don't answer, but she knows statements like that push all my buttons. I've lived my entire life knowing that when people look at my brown skin and dark hair they instantly make assumptions. That I speak Spanish, which I don't. That I grew up poor, which I didn't. That my family is big and loud and joined at the hip, which is opposite of the truth.

"Maybe," I say, pushing the conversation back to our regular topics—the tyrannical photo editor Lauren works for who is bucking for a promotion, our plans to someday have brunch at the French bakery that opened last month.

We chat for another half hour and, when we're done, I close the wedding album and set my parents' history back where it belongs, on the shelf where it has rested for two and a half decades.

CHAPTER 3

The receptionist at the front desk of the Rose Tree takes a quick swig of coffee and dabs her mouth with the corner of a napkin as I approach. Without being asked, I present my family identification card and sign my name in the center of what the people there like to call the guest book. As soon as I put the pen down, the young clerk turns the book around to inspect what I've written, and that alone tells me she must be new. Linda, the regular receptionist, knows me by sight.

A narrow plastic tag pinned to the new receptionist's pink blouse says "Marnie" and I notice that she is wearing the style of snug black pants that the college girls have adopted as a uniform these days. Student nurse, I think to myself, or a sociology major.

"He's just finished breakfast," she says, removing a telephone headset from her ears and pushing her rolling chair away from the desk to a stack of red and yellow file folders behind her.

It is just after eight thirty in the morning, which means Dad is getting ready to begin a schedule that never changes. He gets an hour of speech therapy, followed by half an hour of occupational therapy. After lunch it's a few rounds of range-of-motion exercises, and then a nap. In the late afternoon he is ushered into the common television room to watch talk shows, and then there is dinner and the evening news.

Marnie hands me a "family" badge attached to a stainless steel chain.

I slip it around my neck and begin down the central hallway. Several of the more active residents greet me with friendly smiles.

"Where's Linda?" I ask a bifocaled lady dressed in a red sweat suit and red house shoes. She steps toward me and leans into my shoulder, indicating that what she is about to tell me is delicate information.

"Kidney stone," she whispers.

"Oh." I nod. For a long moment we stand facing one another, her eyes searching mine for a more satisfying reaction to her comment. Mine searching hers for more information.

"Come on, Fran," one of the other old women finally calls out to her. And without another word, she turns and walks away. I proceed through a set of swinging doors that leads to the hospital wing and my father's room. From the doorway I watch an aide named Beth slip a fat-handled hand mirror into the palm of his good hand.

"All set, Mr. D?" she asks as he peers into the glass.

My father is a handsome man. Despite the crippled muscles on the right side of his face, his features are majestic—a straight sloping nose, a right-angled chin and a gently curved forehead. His dark eyes, which are not perfectly oval or perfectly round but some ideal shape in between, lie beneath a pair of vigorous black eyebrows. He looks like a museum painting, an artist's vision of the beauty of Man.

I step inside and plant a kiss on his cheek.

He smiles, but only the left side of his face responds.

"Beth," I say, "can we have a few minutes?"

"You can have five," she answers firmly, "but then it's therapy time."

I take the mirror out of Dad's grasp and set it on the little tray that stretches across the armrests of his wheelchair. He is dressed in what has become his daily outfit, a pullover sweater and dark wool trousers. A pair of leather slippers I ordered from a catalog hug his stocking feet.

"Dad?" I ask, sitting on the edge of the bed so I can look squarely into his face. "Didn't Pancha die a long time ago?"

He cocks his head to let me know he isn't following.

"Pancha," I say again, but still the name does not register. "Your sister, Pan-cha."

He looks at me with hollow eyes.

"Nee-ta," he says, with half a smile. "Ree."

"I can't read to you right now, Dad. You've got therapy."

He nods and takes my hand and gives it a gentle pat, which means his concentration is already starting to sway.

"We'll talk about it later, okay?" I put the mirror back into his good hand and grab his comb from the dressing table. Standing behind him like a barber, I skim the plastic teeth through his waves. He is completely gray at the temples, but there is still more pepper than salt in his crown.

Beth comes back into the room and claps her hands together to get our attention.

"Ready to go?" she chimes. "Say bye!"

I move away from the chair so she can push it into the hallway. My father raises his left wrist and mumbles.

Beth and Candide, my father's daytime and evening aides, are two of the best caregivers on staff. But I wince whenever they carry on as if Dad is an oversize infant in a stroller. I realize the line between compassion and condescension is fuzzy in cases like his, but making him wave bye-bye strikes me as one step over the line.

After they leave, I look around my father's room. The wallpaper is a languid shade of sand with a subtle seashell motif cascading diagonally across it. Some architect must have picked it in an attempt to soften the austerity of the quarters, which consist of nothing more than a single bed, a boxy dresser, and an easy chair next to the window.

One of the first things I did after transferring Dad from the hospital in Dallas was tack posters on the walls. From what I could see, the other residents favored rural landscapes by sedate painters like Andrew Wyeth and Thomas Eakins. But my father's taste runs in the opposite direction, so I filled the walls with the rebellious lines and noisy colors of Picasso, van Gogh and Matisse. When it was clear he was going to be staying for months instead of weeks, I had the posters framed. I also brought in a small television set with a built-in video player and now, every few days, I rent one of his favorite movies—Hitchcock, Jimmy

Stewart, Henry Fonda—and watch it with him. The dialogue in my earliest selections seemed to wear him out, so I recently switched to silent comedies by Chaplin and Buster Keaton. Last week we both laughed out loud at *Modern Times.*

Neatly stacked on the nightstand are the three books I have been reading to him since he arrived. Early on, when he was showing absolutely no sign of comprehension, I plowed through *Breakfast at Tiffany's* and most of *To Kill a Mockingbird.* Ignoring the fact that every time I looked into his face his expression was locked in a tense and troubled scowl, I read several chapters every day to keep myself calm. I relied on the steady cadence of my own voice to hold a rising tide of panic at bay, and prayed that the style and timbre of my speech might help Dad salvage a sense of who he is and what had happened. But he did not respond. Not to me. Not to the therapist. Not to anything.

Five weeks after the attack, one of the neurologists gently suggested that Dad's condition may never show significant improvement, that the permanent damage might be too severe for him to find his way back, and that certain doors in his brain might be locked for good. That was it? I asked. That was his entire prognosis? Doors? Locks? I glared at him and said he would have to come up with something better than that.

In the meantime, I kept reading, kept priming my father's memory with recollections of birthdays and vacations and the full-moon dinner debates: "That reminds me of the time Dr. Carver pounded his palm against the rim of his plate and the veal scallopine went flying. Do you remember that? Or the time Mrs. Lansky sent Ted over with a crepe pan and a bowl of batter, and none of us could get the hang of that damn thing."

Do you remember? I asked. *Remember,* I insisted. *Remember,* I begged.

Then one afternoon, somewhere near the end of Harper Lee's *Mockingbird,* Dad gasped as I described how Jem and Scout were attacked in the dark schoolyard, and then he nodded his head when Boo Radley came to the rescue. I told a nurse, who found the doctor, who reacted with a consoling smile.

These days, Dad is able to follow a story for a little while before drifting, so I read to him the same way my mother used to read to me. I gesture and emote, acting out the role of each character as broadly as I can. He seems to enjoy the show, and we have most recently begun to tackle *Gone with the Wind.*

The medical wing of the Rose Tree Assisted Living Center functions more like a hospital than an apartment building. Busy nurses in rubber-soled shoes march past the rooms' always-open doors. Occasionally, poignant parades of frail men and women dependent on four-legged walkers inch their way through the corridors. I hear the nurses' singsong instructions to them: "Out for a stroll, Lester? Do you know where you are today? If you're headed to the terrace it's not this way. It's behind you." Their voices pitch and dive, as if they're speaking to a litter of stray kittens.

At first, I refused to believe Dad would not fully recover. But as the months have passed, I've adjusted my expectations. All I ask for now is that he gets well enough to move out of the medical ward and into one of the center's fully staffed apartments. But there are days when even that seems too much to hope for.

I hear Beth outside the room, making her way back from delivering my father to the physical therapist. "Nice scarf you have on today, Esther," she says to one of the stray cats. "Oh, and you have your handbag, too. Going shopping, are you? Umm-hmmm. No, honey, it's not Saturday. Let's get back to your room, okay?"

A telephone rings at the nurses' station and I watch an aide push a cart filled with bedpans past the door. This is the section of the Rose Tree that the residents fear most, and I understand why. Death lingers too close here, and there never seems to be enough air. I hate that my father is trapped in this place, with people whose minds and bodies are crumbling like brittle plaster. Where even the healthy residents clutch on to scraps of normality with heartbreaking urgency, as if bending down to touch their toes every morning with all the gusto they can muster might keep them from floating away. I straighten Dad's bed-spread and tell myself that the worst has passed, and soon both our lives will be back on track.

The only client I see on Thursdays is Patrick Capparella, a teenager who is having so much trouble fitting in that he tried to kill himself eight months ago. He has a standing four o'clock appointment, which means I have most of the day to myself. Usually I use the time to needlepoint or do laundry, but I don't feel like going back to the house. If Mrs. Stevens used an overnight courier to mail the things she found, they'll be on my doorstep by three o'clock. It is still early, so I head to the gym for a swim.

The package is waiting when I return.

The address book is the size of a man's hand, much smaller and much slimmer than I expected. Mrs. Stevens wrapped it inside a plas-tic bag before sticking it inside the mailing envelope. Its stair-stepped tabs, which descend from A to Z, are tattered and curled, and this par-ticular alphabet includes the letters Ñ, CH and LL, proving that my mother brought the book with her from Guatemala. I remember that she once told me she and Dad had to leave the country in such a rush that they only took what they could carry and the documents they needed to cross the border. I think of the mountain of clutter that has already accumulated in my life: the flower vases and the metal wind chimes; the desk lamps and the silver-plated napkin rings; the walking shoes and running shoes and tennis shoes that I feel I can't live with-out. I try to imagine my parents winnowing down their choices, figur-ing out what were their bare essentials, and deciding that this tiny book would make the cut. Was it their way of bringing their old friends on the journey with them? Or did the collection of addresses just happen to somehow land in the pile of papers they needed to start their new lives?

Inside the book's cover, I see my mother's maiden name—Regina Acosta—written in faded blue ink. I recognize the pretty slant of the capital R and the diagonal slash she used to cross her t's. In my head, I see her signing my yellow cardboard report cards with her strong artist's hands. I run my finger along the little tabs and open the book to M for no reason in particular. Every line is filled, beginning with Maldonado, Andres, and four different people named Martinez. My mother listed names, addresses and, in most cases, telephone numbers. These, I think, must be the names of the people in the wedding pictures—Sylvia Medina, Roberto Moreno, Norma Monzon. Every page I look at provides me with a peek into her past, dozens of names in blue and black, recorded in both a rolling cursive and a squat, pudgy print. I look under A for other Acostas but she did not list any. And under DeLeon she included my grandmother Olympia, but not Pancha.

I flip to the back of the book, where Mrs. Stevens carefully secured the mysterious letter with a plastic clip. The single sheet of onionskin stationery rustles as I unfold it. Using my palm, I carefully smooth the paper against the kitchen table and immediately see 2 JULIO 1976 written in clear block letters. I feel a ripple slither down my spine and take a closer look at the rest of the note. Pancha's handwriting scuttles across the paper in a tangled snarl. It's no wonder Mrs. Stevens couldn't decipher it; even in English it would be a chore to decode.

I try to find a word or two that look familiar, but my Spanish is worse than her penmanship, and the only terms I can make out are *yo, la, el* and *tú,* which will never get me to the heart of the matter. I follow Pancha's uneven script to the end, where she signs off with only her first name, printed boldly at an angle and underlined with not one but two strong strokes of her pen.

Slowly folding the top and bottom of the letter back toward its middle, I try to consider what this means to Dad, and to me. How could my father have been mistaken about something as monumental as his own sister's death? It's impossible. The letter must have been written by a different woman named Pancha. The name can't be that uncommon in that part of the world. I look at every name in the address book to find another Pancha, but there isn't one.

I open the letter again and search for any resemblance the strings of undiscernible script might have to Dad's longhand. I look for any hint the puckered e's and flattened s's might offer about the author's age. I tell myself the note can't be important if Mom shoved it in the back of the linen closet, folded inside a long-forgotten address book. But something about Pancha's handwriting gnaws at my logic. Her sentences look blunt and relentless, like loud, insistent yells. And the more I look at them, the more I need to know what they say. The offer Lauren made last night comes rushing back to me, and I leave a message at her house asking if she really thinks the Hispanic reporter would translate Pancha's letter for me.

Even though I've lived in Philadelphia for almost a decade, Lauren is probably the only person I could honestly call a close friend. Aaron was the one who socialized, for work and for fun. As a political reporter for the newspaper, he was paid to schmooze, not only with city and state officials and their public relations people but with protesters and activists and all the other attention-hungry folks swirling around that orbit. My role was to listen.

Lauren began working at the *Monitor* on the same day Aaron did, and because she was from out of town like him, they became instant office buddies. I met her about a week later at a party one of the veteran writers threw for the newcomers, which I thought was going to be great fun but which turned out to be an endless night of loudmouthed journalists talking about their stories and themselves while their spouses stood in an uncomfortable clump in the kitchen, waiting to go home.

Lauren was the only staffer who bothered to spend any time with us, and before we knew it she and Aaron and I were eating weeknight dinners together and teaming up to see Sunday matinees. We showed her what married life was like, and she introduced us to one boyfriend after another as her search for the perfect man stretched from her late twenties into her mid-thirties.

For almost a decade, Lauren knew us as a happily coupled twosome, the kind of people who ordered return address labels that said THE NILES, like we'd merged into one human being. Of course, that was before Aaron started seeing another woman behind my back.

Lauren caught them in the act, not me. When he first began taking long lunches with a young new coworker, Lauren said she tried to ignore it. But at the same time, she was listening to me complain that something between Aaron and me felt seriously wrong. When she confronted him, Aaron promised her things would shake out, so she let the matter drop. But late one Sunday afternoon, when the newsroom was almost empty, she walked into the darkroom and found Aaron and the assistant unbuttoned and unzipped. She told him that he had to tell me what was going on or else she would.

At first Lauren tried to be friends with both of us. But there is no such thing as a neutral party in divorce and she was forced to pick a side. Now she's my best friend and things are awkward for her and Aaron at work.

I sit myself down in front of the address book again and pick up the telephone.

"It's me again," I say to Lauren's machine. "How about dinner here? Say, seven? We can have pasta. I have a bottle of Merlot. I want to show you what Mrs. Stevens sent."

I hang up and pat the leather cover of the address book with my palm. I thought I'd seen everything my mother left behind. Twenty-one jars of ceramic glaze, eight pounds of unused clay, one damp sea sponge the size of a silver dollar and four dry ones. Six unread Agatha Christie novels. A blue jar of Noxzema face cream. Sixteen just-finished pieces of pottery that she had placed in the trunk of her car that morning. And now comes this, delivered to my doorstep like a telegram from the past. I have to find out what the letter says. I need to know if Dad recalls anything about it. Or whether Mom folded it into the middle of the Christmas tablecloth to keep it secret, even from him.

Carefully, I tuck Pancha's letter back between the final pages and slip the address book inside the plastic bag. I wonder if I should take the letter to the Rose Tree and let my father see it. Maybe he'd recognize the address book, or his sister's handwriting, if he took a long enough look. I check my watch. He'd be eating or napping now, and a visit in the middle of the day will do nothing but confuse him. It will have to wait.

I throw the mailing envelope into the wastebasket under the sink and slide the address book to the middle of the table. I go to change clothes before Patrick arrives for his session, and when I finish I walk into the kitchen and look at the book again. I try to picture my mother as a very young woman, even younger than she was on her wedding day. What, I wonder, did she think her life was going to be like when she first opened that green cover and began to make a list of her closest friends? Whose name did she write first? Which one meant the most?

When I was little, she told me there was no use in dwelling on the past. She said that if you spent too much time looking back, all you'd ever see is what could have been. Even as a kid, I knew that when she spoke like that she was talking about Guatemala, and of course I believed her. Partly because neither she nor my father had ever offered more than the barest details about their lives before coming to America, and partly because whatever happened to them there didn't seem to matter much anymore. Not to them, and certainly not to me.

But maybe I was wrong, maybe they had cared about their past more than they admitted, or at least about this one small piece of it.

CHAPTER 4

My mind drifts back to Patrick's session as Lauren drives us to the newspaper. I always look forward to my fifty minutes with him. Unlike most sixteen-year-old boys, he speaks in full sentences instead of grunts and mutters. He likes old movies and told me once that I reminded him of a young Natalie Wood.

"In *West Side Story*?" I asked, picturing wide-eyed Maria singing "I Feel Pretty" and feeling truly flattered.

"No," Patrick said with a frown, "the goody-goody in *Rebel Without a Cause*."

Not many kids his age know who Natalie Wood or James Dean are anymore. But Patrick takes refuge in the overblown legends of the Hollywood greats. He holds on to the quixotic tales of anonymous young men and women who started out as bumbling, small-town misfits and somehow found their place beneath the lights. He wants to believe their success stories are true, because if they're not, what hope is there for a square peg like him?

"This is a bad idea," I say when Lauren pulls her car into the newspaper's parking lot. Now that the Merlot is beginning to wear off, I'm questioning her plan. I haven't stepped inside this building since Aaron and I split, but somehow during dinner I let her talk me into coming to the *Monitor* to show Pancha's letter to the bilingual reporter.

"Nah, this is good," she says as she lifts my mother's address book from my lap and pulls her keys out of the ignition. She is already several steps away from the Honda when she realizes that I am still sitting in the car with my seat belt fastened.

"He's an investigative reporter from Miami," Lauren says, as if his journalism credentials will lower my resistance. "They've got him on night rewrite until he gets to know the city."

I get out of the car and hold out my hand, indicating that I'd like her to give the address book back.

"You said you wanted to figure this out," she argues, standing between me and the *Monitor*'s front door.

"It doesn't have to be tonight."

"Don't worry, Aaron isn't working, and neither is she. I checked the schedule."

I used to love visiting Aaron at the newspaper because inside it's like a college dorm. Every desk is littered with papers and cold cups of coffee. Battered television sets are perched on top of dented file cabinets and unsteady bookcases, and are always tuned to twenty-four-hour news or sports networks. There is never a moment when a telephone isn't ringing. The reporters and editors bang away on their computers while the photographers and graphic designers figure out where the pictures and stories will go. To them it's routine, but to me it's amazing that every morning they start with nothing and by nightfall have collected enough information to fill the dozens of pages that will land on my doorstep at dawn.

The pace is relentless and everyone has a deadline to meet, so they're always curt and in a rush. Except when it comes to gossip. For that they make time. That's why I'm sure every single one of them knows how Aaron fell in love with Patty Jen while he was trying to have a baby with me, and that is why I don't want to go in there.

"Maybe I should wait," I say, "and try my dad tomorrow."

Lauren walks toward me, takes my elbow and tugs. As far as she's concerned this is a Nancy Drew mystery begging to be solved, and when she's like this nothing will stop her. The truth is I admire her determination, envy it. I could not do what she does on a daily basis. Train wrecks, shootings, protests, she walks right up to them with nothing but her camera for protection. When the World Trade Center was attacked, she took a train to Manhattan and marched straight into the choking smoke and ash to see the destruction for herself. Once she spent half a year hanging out with the scum of the Ku Klux Klan so she could chronicle them firsthand. When she decides to do something, she does it, so I know my wavering emotions on this subject will carry no weight.

The security guard stationed at the lobby entrance says he hasn't seen me in a while. Where have I been?

"Fine," I say, dodging the question.

It is almost ten o'clock, four hours past early deadline, and if I'm lucky most of the reporters will be gone. The elevator opens onto the third floor and in front of me I see a reception desk with a nameplate that says: P. JEN. Half a dozen weary tulips droop over the edge of a dark blue vase beside her telephone. There's a crisp florist's bow around the neck of the vessel. A stab of anger cuts through my ribs. Tulips were our winter tradition.

Lauren breezes past the desk, but I stop and take a long look. A book-size calendar sits precisely in the middle of the dove-gray surface, its cover closed and a silver ballpoint pen positioned diagonally across it. Two tidy stacks of mail and a pile of faxes await her attention in the morning, and on top of her computer I see snapshots, proudly displayed in polished silver frames. The first is of them together. He, nearing forty, standing behind her with his arms around her waist; she, not yet thirty, beaming up at him. The second is of her pregnant. She looks astoundingly young, like a college girl with a face that is round and soft and dreamy. Her body, pictured in profile, curves like a mountain stream, and the bliss in her eyes says this baby is just the start. I think how easy it must have been for her. No doctors. No shots. No disappointments. Just a touch. A kiss. And then life.

I punch the elevator button to go back down.

"Nita . . ." Lauren is calling me from the City Desk, where she is standing next to a man with dark hair and round, rimless glasses. She has already handed him the address book and he is looking inside of it.

"Come on," she says.

The man sets the book on top of his computer keyboard as I walk over.

"Juno," he says, extending his hand.

The sleeves of his light blue Oxford shirt are rolled up to the middle of his forearms, and his lemon-yellow necktie hangs askew. When I meet his grip, I notice a patch of gray at his temples and lines that will soon become creases at the corners of his dark brown eyes. I can see why Lauren likes him; he looks shrewd and just this side of dangerous. I know he likes her. All men do. She is textbook pretty, with ash-blond hair cut in a sexy layered style, wide blue eyes, and a tight athletic build.

"If you're too busy . . ." I begin.

"Twenty years in the business and they've got me chasing fires and watching the eleven o'clock news." He checks his watch.

"Not for long, though," Lauren says as she rolls two office chairs our way.

"Three more months, but who's counting? Anyway, if City Hall doesn't explode and we don't get hit by an earthquake, I've got about an hour to talk."

I take a quick look around the room and see that only the metro and foreign editors, the page designers and a half dozen copy editors are at their desks. If I were to turn my head one degree farther to the right I'd see Aaron's desk, decorated with the plaster bust of John F. Kennedy we bought for two dollars at a flea market in Dallas. But I keep my eyes from drifting that way. Lauren points to the address book and tells Juno about the letter while the insistent phones at three nearby desks go unanswered.

"Sure," he says, "no problem."

He reads Pancha's letter to himself twice, chewing on the cap of a ballpoint pen, while we wait.

"This is all you've got?"

I nod. "What's it say?"

"It's an answer, basically. But I can't figure out what they're discussing."

"Let's hear it," Lauren says.

Juno adjusts his eyeglasses and reads:

> My dear Regina: You are right. It is time. A family this small can-
> not afford a rift this wide. Now that we are all in a safe harbor, there
> is no reason for continued silence. It took me so much longer to see.
> But I hope you understand that it was idealism that kept me blind.
> I will wait to hear from you. Pancha.

The three of us look at one another without saying a word. Juno reads the message again, and again we are speechless.

"Can you write it down?" I finally ask.

Juno swivels his chair so he is facing the computer screen and, with his fingers flying over the keys, he taps out Pancha's words. When he's finished he hits PRINT and turns to speak to me.

"Lauren says this is from your aunt?"

"Well, that's who signed it. But I didn't even know she was alive."

Juno raises his eyebrows. Lauren mumbles, "Dead end," as she digs out a pack of Winstons from her coat pocket.

"Not necessarily," Juno answers. "What's her last name?"

"DeLeon."

Using the good side of his chewed pen, Juno begins writing D-A-L-

"No," I say. "It's D-E-L-E-O-N."

"Del-YONE?"

"We say Da-LEE-on."

He cocks his head.

"What ethnic origin?"

I shift my weight. I should have known he'd be one of those His-panics who feels the need to know which minority slot to put you in, as if the nation your family came from before you were even born makes a difference.

"Guatemala," I grumble.

He raises his eyebrows again and this time I notice a smirk cross his lips.

"Ah," he says. "Guess things have changed a bit down there."

I know Lauren thinks this guy is charming, but so far I'm not impressed.

"I can search for her on the Internet," he says, clicking into a Web site and typing in her name. While he waits for information to pop up, he tells me his last name is Hernandez, and then he adds sarcastically, "Which I pronounce Hernandez."

I hear Lauren chuckle and I give her a sharp stare that lets her know I don't think his joke is funny. I'm more than ready to go. I reach past Juno's elbow to retrieve my mother's address book, and the moment I do the telephone on his desk rings. His hand bumps into mine as he answers the call, and for a few seconds our elbows are intertwined.

"City Desk," he barks, shooting me a wink as we disentangle ourselves.

Who the hell does this guy think he is? I step around him and grab the address book and Pancha's letter.

"Just a minute," he says, lowering the receiver onto his right shoulder and clamping down on it with his ear. To Lauren he whispers, "Gotta take this." Then he turns his back to both of us, wipes out what is on his computer screen and begins typing notes as he resumes the telephone conversation. Lauren gives him a playful farewell punch on the shoulder as I begin to head back to the elevators.

"Just a sec," Lauren calls to me, and I stop and watch her walk to a bank of computer printers, where she picks up the translation Juno made for us. As she passes his desk again, he wraps his hand around the bottom of the telephone receiver and tells her good night.

"You too, Miss Da-LEE-on," he says to me, *"muy buenas noches."*

"Another winner," I tell Lauren as the elevator takes us to the lobby. "Juno? You'd love him."

Outside, Lauren lights her cigarette and we both step through the lazy trail of smoke that hangs in the cold night air. A few streets away police sirens blare and I wonder if that is what Juno's phone call is about. When we reach the car, I look up at the sky before climbing inside. In Dallas it would be studded with white winter stars. Here, I see only clouds and shadows.

"You know, Nita, it *is* kind of weird that you don't speak Spanish, isn't it?"

"Why? Do you speak it?"

"No, but my parents aren't from South America."

"Central," I say. "Central America."

"That's what I mean. It's their language."

"When they lived there I suppose it was. But after they moved to Texas they spoke English, nothing but."

"But that's what's weird. That they just dropped it."

"In Dallas? In the sixties? I'd call that smart."

I can't expect Lauren to fully understand. Her family's roots reach back to the colonies.

"They became American citizens as soon as the law allowed. I was in the third grade," I say. "It was such a big deal for them, you can't imagine."

I remember watching them study for the exam, reciting the names of the same people and places that I was learning in elementary school—Lexington, Concord, Jefferson, Grant. They quizzed one another over their dinner plates while I plowed through my meat and vegetables.

"Mom marked the day on our calendar with one of those toothpicks attached to a tiny American flag," I tell Lauren.

"Right, I know those."

"May twelfth, 1972."

"That made you . . . ?"

"Eight."

I recall how Mom took me out of school at lunchtime that day and brought me home to change clothes. I peeled off my plaid corduroy jumper, my yellow Keds and my anklet socks and traded them for the new navy blue dress that had been hanging in my closet for weeks and was now lying, freshly pressed, on top of my bed.

"She gave me a pair of new red shoes," I say, remembering the Mary Janes that were as shiny as wet nail polish, "and a little purse that matched."

"Patent leather?" Lauren asks with a smile.

I nod. I had never carried a purse before, and wasn't quite sure what I was supposed to put inside it. Mom suggested I put a comb and one of Dad's handkerchiefs inside. I can still hear the stiff brass clasp shutting with an adamant snap, and I remember how the sound of it together with the click and clack of my new shoes made me feel tall and poised and important.

I tell Lauren how Dad met us at the courthouse that afternoon and lifted me into his arms as we stepped through the wide revolving door. I expected the three of us to walk straight into a wood-paneled courtroom where we'd sit at a table before an old, white-haired judge. He'd be so impressed with my parents' answers to the citizenship quiz that he'd bang his gavel like an exclamation point and rule that they were perfect Americans. I imagined there would be a brass band on hand to play the "Star-Spangled Banner" as the three of us stood at attention with our hands over our hearts, gazing lovingly at a gently waving American flag. I expected someone like Dinah Shore to sing, her voice making a showy climb to "the rockets' red glare" before sliding smoothly back down to "the home of the brave."

Of course what really happened was something completely different. First, we went into a cavernous office on the ground floor of the big courthouse. The gold letters on the door told me it was the INS, but it looked like a bank to me. At one end of the room there were six rows of metal folding chairs set up like an audience in front of five ladies who worked at a counter behind glass. We weren't the only ones in there waiting. Half of the chairs were already taken by ladies in linen and silk and men with polished shoes. The white marble floor was scuffed with black lightning bolts made by the thousands of soles that shuffled over it every day. The walls were bare plaster and tossed everybody's voices into the center of the room, where words and sentences melted into a constant hum that was more like a feeling than a sound.

After we sat down a man approached us. Wide bodied and ruddy faced, he pointed at Dad and the three of us stood.

"Ma'am," he said.

My mother and I followed the man past the women behind glass, through a doorway and down a long hallway. I knew this man wasn't the judge. He wasn't old or white-haired or wearing a robe. He was bald and squinty-eyed like Festus on *Gunsmoke* and he wore a wrinkled white shirt with a leather shoestring tie that was held together just below his lumpy chin by a chunk of turquoise shaped like a lima bean. He stopped in front of an office near the middle of the corridor and cleared his throat. Then he pulled a white handkerchief out of the back pocket of his dark trousers and wiped his mouth before ushering us inside and leaving us there.

I slid into the wide bottom of a wooden office chair, letting my red shoes dangle over its edge. My mother took her place. The metal desk we were facing was piled with towers of manila folders overflowing with paper. I wondered what Dad was doing in the humming waiting room with no one left to talk to.

"Regina Flor DeLeon?" Another man walked into the office from a door behind the desk and startled both of us. He had brown hair that touched his collar and a thin mustache. He read my mother's name off a form and sat down without looking up at us before she answered.

Lauren lights another cigarette and cracks her window to funnel the smoke. "Did you take a test?"

"My parents did," I say, remembering how stiff Mom looked in that chair. She was so nervous that, while the man behind the desk spoke, she bit the dark red lipstick off her bottom lip.

"What were the questions like?"

"Easy. Like how many people are in the Senate, and which president freed the slaves. I remember thinking the guy was saving the hard questions for later, but he asked three or four and that was it."

When Mom was done, the man said I could stay in the room while he brought Dad in. While they were gone, I looked at the photographs hanging inside gold frames on the back wall. The White House, the

Capitol, President Nixon. I also discovered that if I slid to the edge of my seat, leaned back on my elbows, and pointed my toes, I could touch the floor with the tips of my new shoes.

The rest of the story comes rushing back into my head as clear as if it happened yesterday.

My father followed the man inside and sat.

"Diego Eduardo DeLeon?" the man asked.

My father nodded. Then the man asked about somebody I'd never heard of, somebody with a Spanish name.

"Yes, I'm familiar with his name," Dad said.

"Was he a friend of yours?"

"He was president of Guatemala."

"Uh-huh," the man responded, writing something down on a new sheet of paper.

I remember wondering why he was quizzing Dad on the history of Guatemala. Was this a part of the test? He continued asking about the Guatemalan president, and Dad's answers were short and direct. Dates, places, things like that. My mind began to wander, and I started counting the number of floor tiles between my chair and the far wall. I counted how many times I could swing my feet while the man asked his questions, and then how many times I could swing them during Dad's replies.

Then the man asked the one question I will never forget. "Mr. DeLeon," he said, "are you a Communist?"

At the time I had no idea what a Communist was, so I stopped swinging my legs to hear my father's answer. I looked at the man sitting behind the desk, his pen ready to write down whatever Dad said. He kept his eyes locked on my father's, and his face looked like he'd just issued a double dare. I watched Dad's shoulders inch back until his spine was stiff and I could see his neck turning dark red. Whatever a Communist was, my daddy didn't appreciate being called one, and I knew from the way he was clenching his jaw that the man behind the desk was in big trouble. I grabbed the arms of my chair and braced myself for the scolding Dad was about to give him.

"No," was all my father said, his tone as firm as iron.

The man behind the desk kept looking at him, waiting for more. Dad stared back. They stayed like that for a few long moments, and finally the man behind the desk looked down at his pen and moved on to the same dumb questions he'd asked Mom.

I remember thinking that whatever battle these two had just fought, my father had won. And before I knew it, they were both on their feet and the man was shaking my father's hand.

"Take these," he said, handing Dad two blue cards, "and proceed to courtroom eighteen on the fourth floor."

The instant we stepped out of the man's office, Dad scooped me into his arms and twirled me around like we were dancing.

"Let's get Mom," he said, "and get this show on the road!"

As the scene fades from my mind, I turn to Lauren. "The swearing-in ceremony was actually pretty moving."

"I've taken pictures of a couple," she answers.

"Anyway," I say, "that's the day my parents were done with Guatemala, and Spanish, and anything else that wasn't all-American."

When we reach my house, I tell Lauren I've changed my mind about the address book. What's the point of trying to figure it out?

"But what about Pancha?"

"What about her? She's out there, or she isn't. Either way she isn't part of my life."

"Your dad might want her to be."

"Laurie, he can't even spell his own name right now. I don't think he needs this on his plate."

She shrugs, and as I climb out of the car her cell phone begins to ring. My key is already in the front door lock when she cracks her window and shouts that the call is for me.

I wait for her to bound up to the front porch.

"It's Juno," a static-filled voice announces when I press the receiver to my ear. "I think I found her."

A chill slides down my back and Lauren can tell by my reaction that it's something big. She pulls the phone away from me before I can respond. "Call her inside—it's a better line." She gives Juno my number while I unlock the door. Without bothering to peel off our coats, we walk straight into the kitchen and stand in front of the telephone, waiting for it to ring.

"First I tried Guatemala City," Juno explains, clearly proud of his quick detective work.

Lauren is listening on the cordless that I keep in the bedroom.

"But I got nothing. Then I tried the bigger states. Texas, California, Florida. But no Pancha DeLeon."

I am sitting at the kitchen table, staring at the address book as he speaks.

"I was about to give up when I realized what I was doing wrong. Her real name isn't Pancha."

"What?" I hear Lauren say.

"I knew Nita would get a good laugh out of that. *Qué idiota!* I was searching the databases for a Pancha."

Juno is so pleased with himself that he doesn't seem to notice that I am not laughing. That, in fact, I have no idea what he is talking about.

"Hey, how about a clue for the gringa?" Lauren quips.

"For men, Pancho is a nickname for Francisco. So I figured her name must be *Francisca*. I tried birth records in Guatemala, but they aren't on-line. So I plugged her name into an e-mail directory and bam, there she was."

I heard someone gasp and realized it was me. "Where does she live?"

"Don't know, it's just her e-mail address. Do you want it?"

I take a moment to catch my breath, and then say, "Aaron took the computer."

"Her ex," Lauren explains. "You know him. Aaron Nile, the metro reporter?"

"Oh," Juno says, caught, for the first time, completely off guard.

I listen as their conversation briefly veers off track, and I know they are filling time until I speak.

Finally, Juno says, "I could e-mail her from here if you want."

Lauren tells him yes. "Say someone in her family is looking for her, but don't tell her who just yet. And get her address and phone number."

Inside my coat pocket I feel the folded translation of Pancha's letter. I pull it out and read it again. *You are right. It is time.* My mother had planned something with this woman, something that never got done. Did Pancha know how suddenly Mom had died? Or was she still waiting for an answer?

"Yes," I say.

"Are you sure? Because once I hit that button, it's out there."

I look at Lauren, who has walked into the kitchen with the cordless still up to her ear. She's so certain of my answer that she sets down the phone and opens the refrigerator door as if the conversation is done. In her mind I have no other choice. But I keep Juno on the line, waiting, while I run my fingers over the worn leather of my mother's address book and think of all the names inside. Do I really want to know about this part of her life? For more than twenty-five years I have wondered what she would have eventually revealed about herself to me, what stories about her life she was saving to tell me when I grew up. I have imagined what she might have looked like in late age, whether she would have approved of Aaron at first sight and if she could have eased me through the divorce. I have pictured us sitting in my dining room together, two grown women with their elbows on the table, lingering over bars of dark chocolate and mugs of black tea. In my mind I've attempted to age her, but her young oval face is the only image locked in my memory, her radiant smile and her loving eyes. For me she'll forever be the mother I knew as a child.

I open the address book and stare at the handwriting. Is this a gift Mom left me? A message delivered twenty-five years late? Or is it a piece of the past she intended to pack away forever?

"Nita?" Juno asks, sensing my hesitation.

"Yeah," I say. "Go ahead."

CHAPTER 5

The next night, Juno calls to say there is no word and I tell him it doesn't matter. But that's not the truth.

I had trouble sleeping, wondering what Pancha might look like, where she might be, what she might have to say. I've tried to build her face in my mind, using my father's cheeks and eyes and lips. But I can never bring her into full focus, not so I would recognize her on the street.

"She'll surface," Juno says. "It's just going to take a little more time."

"It's not important," I answer.

"Hey, don't give up so easily. The game has barely started."

That's exactly what this is to him, a game, and, as far as he's concerned, finding Pancha isn't what it's about. Juno wants to impress Lauren. I know how it will go. I'll get two calls from him, maybe three, however many he thinks it will take to prove to Lauren he's a generous guy. Then he'll tell me that he would love to be of more help but he's just too busy, and do I happen to know if Lauren is seeing anybody exclusively?

"Look," I say, "I've changed my mind. So you don't need to waste your time."

"Give it a few more days. I'll do some more digging."

I shrug, knowing the motion doesn't translate over the phone.

"You still there?"

"One week," I answer. "Then we're done."

"By the way," he adds just as I'm about to hang up, "I'm sorry I made that crack about your name last night."

The apology is so unexpected it catches me off guard.

"I was out of line," he says without a trace of swagger in his voice.

"Don't worry about it," I mumble.

"I've been to Guatemala a few times," he continues. "Beautiful place."

"Is it?" I ask, even though I meant to say that I've got to hang up now.

"Lake Atitlán is so amazing it's hard to imagine anything can top it, don't you think?"

"I don't know. I've never been there."

"Really?" Juno asks. "Never?"

"No."

"Well, I guess that means we have at least one thing in common. I've never been to Cuba."

I have no idea what brought on this change but his arrogance has completely vanished and, before I know it, Juno and I are in the middle of a long and pleasant conversation. I tell him that my parents did not talk about Guatemala around me or anybody else, and he tells me he's from a big Cuban family in Miami that can't stop talking about Cuba.

"So how come you've never been?"

"My parents would kill me with their bare hands if I set foot on the island before Fidel Castro is dead and gone," he answers with a slight chuckle.

What surprises me most is that Juno is a really good listener. I know what it takes to hone that skill. People don't speak directly. You've got to excavate meaning out of what they say, like an archeologist sweeping dirt off priceless relics. Once you've pulled enough bowls and spoons and combs out of the earth, you can start to piece together a person's life if you know which fragments to keep. Juno considers every word, examines every sentence, and weighs the importance of the messages that have been included against those that have been left out.

In my counseling sessions I use the tilt of my head or the slant of an eyebrow to let my clients know I'm still with them as they speak. But Juno doesn't even need eye contact to prove that he's absorbing everything you say. With nothing more than a few soft "hmms" and "uh-huhs," he kindles a remarkable sense of intimacy.

I fill him in on how Mrs. Stevens found Pancha's letter and the reason she was going through his papers. He tells me his uncle died from a stroke three years ago and then rushes to add that he didn't mean to imply Dad was going to face the same fate.

"It's okay," I say, really meaning it.

As we speak, I hear telephones pealing in the background and the muffled voices of people at work. I'd almost forgotten that he was calling from the newsroom. It's a quarter to seven, which means the metro reporters are ending their day. But Juno is just getting ready to sit up all night and wait for news to happen.

I hear someone call out his name, and although he cups his palm over the receiver as the man speaks, I can tell it is an editor barking orders.

"I'll get right on it," Juno says as he takes his hand away. "Listen . . ."

"I know the drill."

"Sorry." He sighs.

I'm glad he's after Lauren, I tell myself, because I don't want to get involved with a journalist again.

"Just let me know if anything happens with Pancha," I say.

"Right. Um, Nita?"

"Yeah?"

"Would you like to have coffee with me tomorrow? There's a little place Lauren told me about."

Every bone in my body tells me to say no. One friendly phone call does not make Juno a nice guy. Even after our long talk, his mind is right back on Lauren. He's using me to get to her.

"Or," Juno goes on, "if you'd like, we could do lunch."

Say no, I tell myself. Tell him you are busy.

"Sure," I hear myself answer, "lunch sounds fine."

"It's the Square Meal Cafe, on Nineteenth."

I don't bother to write it down, because I won't be going.

"Twelve thirty?" he asks.

"I don't know. . . ." I begin, only to hear the editor's booming voice approaching Juno again.

"Okay," Juno says in a rush, "see ya then."

The dial tone wails in my ear while I try to figure out what I've just done. I would know if Lauren liked him, wouldn't I? Of course I would. She would tell me. There's no time to call her, as I hear my next client arrive.

Joy Taggert shows up alone and leans into my shoulder the moment I open the office door. Already in tears, she stands perfectly still as I give her a firm embrace. Without a word she takes her place in the corner of the love seat and pulls the Bon Voyage pillow onto her lap. Trembling, she drags a ball of wet tissue across her ruddy cheeks and takes a long, jagged breath.

"Is it Frank?"

She nods, bites her bottom lip and clutches the pillow closer. She'd called me that afternoon to squeeze in an emergency session, telling me it was urgent, so I'd expected as much.

She shakes her head and looks up. Her eyes are raw and swollen, her lips pale. I wonder how she managed on the highway. I lower myself beside her on the love seat and cup the palm of my left hand so she can toss out the tissue that has absorbed all it's able. She is still not ready to speak and all I can do to help is smooth her hair.

"Money down . . ." she finally says in a convulsive whisper that immediately dissolves into another wave of tears. Pressing her eyes shut, she lets the sentence go and swallows hard before trying again.

"After the last session, Frank said this was nothing but money down the drain." Slowly, her voice regains its balance and her shallow breathing slows.

For a moment I consider moving back to my regular seat but it's clear that she'd rather continue her story looking at the windows at the other end of the office instead of at me.

"I asked if he wanted to see somebody else. Or if he wanted to stop for a couple of weeks, and he laughed like it was a joke. I mean he *laughed*, Nita, with his head tilted back and his eyes watering so much he had to wipe them. He laughed so hard it scared me."

Whether she's aware of it or not, Joy has described the exact instant her marriage shattered. It happens like that. Snap. It's unfixable. You may not recognize the final blow when it comes, but later, when you look back, you see that the signs were clear. After months of thorny silence and hundreds of belligerent wars over the smallest of things, after reaching out and recoiling so many times that you don't trust your own timing, after feeling like any room in any house is too tight for the both of you, the last thread of the frayed cord finally rips and you are left with two mangled halves of what used to be a whole. By the time one of you gets around to saying *I want a divorce* it sounds like a line from a bad movie, anticlimactic and delivered too late.

"His eyes were cold," Joy says, still visibly shaken. "Hard. Like I'd never seen them before."

I think back to the day Aaron left. I was sitting at the kitchen table in the pewter light of a dull winter morning, listening to boxes filled with his things thud against the house's thick walls as he tried to rush. It took two trips for him to haul away what he considered his essentials. We tossed words at one another like darts, and the rhythm of our conversation was so out of sync that our sentences stumbled over each other as if we were a couple of drunks.

"I'm just gonna take—"

"Yeah, it's—"

"What?"

"Sorry. Did you want . . . ?"

"No. My truck's over—"

"Right."

I told him he could have the turn-of-the-century photographs of Paris that we bought on the honeymoon, the free weights and all of the bluegrass CDs. I offered him the futon, too. But he left it. I should have expected as much. What did he need a lumpy mattress for? I may have known precious little about the woman he was leaving me for, but one thing I knew for certain: he was sleeping in her bed.

I sat at the table and pretended to read the newspaper while he and a guy I'd never met carried out the stereo cabinet, the computer and the pull-out sofa. I remember they showed up unannounced on a Sunday morning. I asked Aaron to give me half an hour to shower and leave, but he ignored me completely. I had just enough time to pull on a pair of pants and a sweatshirt before he led his pal into our bedroom. They scooped up one of the heavy nightstands, grunting and groaning the way that men do, and then they proceeded to lift and slide and turn the other pieces of furniture from other rooms in the house sideways to fit them through the door.

I think Aaron enjoyed trapping me in the kitchen, barefoot no less. The symbolism was so crude it was almost laughable, a perfect slice of dry humor that we both prized. When he passed by I automatically looked into his eyes because that's what we had always done, exchanged quick glances that said: "Get it?" But instead of responding with a wry smile, he shook off my look like it was mud.

Joy tells me that Frank used the egg timer exercise to tell her about his affair, holding her hands and staring straight into her eyes as he said he was tired of their life together.

"I knew it," she admits in a whisper, "but I wasn't ready for him to leave."

"Joy," I say softly, "you're more ready than you think."

For the next forty-five minutes we talk about loss and how to begin taking small steps toward a new future. The moment Joy's car pulls away, I telephone Lauren and tell her about Juno's invitation.

"Go," she says. "He's been asking me all sorts of questions about you at work."

"Like what?"

"You know. The regular things."

No, I tell her, I don't know. It's been thirteen years since my last first date.

"Trust me," Lauren says. "It's you he likes. Not me."

I feel the muscles in the back of my neck flutter, and when Lauren asks me what I intend to wear, the flutter turns into an icy chill.

The next afternoon, when I arrive at the café five minutes late, I see Juno reading a newspaper at a table near the front. He is wearing blue jeans and a thick black cable-knit sweater that makes his shoulders look boxy and broad. His acorn-colored tan stands out in the crowd. Engrossed in the story in front of him, he does not see me as I peel off my coat and set it on a row of pegs beside the cash register.

The narrow dining room is full of people whose noisy conversations bounce off the exposed-brick walls. The theme of the place is stripped-down chic. None of the wooden chairs matches and the tables are bulky, thrift-store antiques. Lightbulbs dangle from long dark wires that descend from exposed rafters. And in the middle of each table sits a mason jar filled with a modest bouquet of zinnias and marigolds.

Juno has just finished taking a sip of coffee when I step to the table. He presses his lips together when he sees me, forcing himself to swallow before he stands and says hello.

"I hope that didn't burn your throat," I say.

He shakes his head as he pulls out a chair for me. I set my handbag down on the floor and notice that Juno has tucked a gym bag beneath the table. As he settles back into his seat, I pick up the one-page menu that is in front of me and scan it while Juno takes a long, silent look at me. I know what he sees. My eyes are round and my nose is short. My mouth is small and my cheeks are wide. There are no sharp angles in my build, just smooth, meandering curves. I'd call myself attractive, but I know I'm not the woman men look at first. Not like Lauren, who always steals the show. I'm the one they have polite conversation with because I'm standing next to her. The one they'd settle for.

I'm glad I listened to Lauren and put on the coral-colored cashmere turtleneck and black jeans that she suggested. Anything else would have looked too fussy.

"Looks good," I say, even though the offerings are completely run-of-the-mill.

"I don't know too many places yet," Juno answers.

The ease with which we spoke last night feels impossible to recapture in the light of day. I spread my napkin over my lap. He takes another sip of coffee. Neither of us is certain how to begin.

Luckily, the waitress appears and asks if we are ready to order.

"What's the soup?" Juno asks, sounding grateful to have something else to focus his attention on.

"New England clam chowder," she says without taking her eyes off her order pad.

Juno looks across the table, inviting me to go first.

"Sounds perfect," I say.

"Bowl or cup?"

"Bowl."

The waitress, a thin, pale brunette in her early twenties, is dressed in a vintage beaded cardigan and a narrow wool skirt. She scribbles on her pad and then stops and stands perfectly still, waiting for Juno to speak.

"Cheeseburger," he says. "Well done. No onions."

She scoops up the paper menus and turns on her heel without saying another word.

Juno and I both begin to laugh.

"Welcome to Philadelphia," I say. "The land of cheerful and courteous help."

"If you want coffee you can have some of mine," he says, pushing his cup between us. "I don't think we're going to see her again for a while."

I like his sense of humor.

Juno pulls back his coffee cup and wraps both his hands around it. His fingers are long, with knuckles that bow out like knots tied in a rope.

"This winter is killing me," he groans.

Because it's still March, I spare him the fact that the worst of winter hits Philadelphia late in the season, with the heaviest snow sometimes falling as late as April.

"My first winter here," I say instead, "I drove home from work after a storm and saw a knee-high wall of snow at the foot of our driveway. It had been piled there by the snowplow. Our neighbors were all out shoveling their walks, and for some reason I thought my car would roll right over the mound if I gave it enough gas. So I backed up, squared the headlights, and careened into the bank."

Juno leans back in his chair and grins.

"The tires whined," I say, "big clumps of ice flew up against the windshield, and just after the front fender cleared the mound, the engine stalled. I tried to open my door, but it wouldn't budge. I pushed on the passenger-side door but it was wedged shut, too. So I popped open the hatchback and crawled out the back."

Juno's laugh is loud and throaty.

"I hadn't counted on the snow being so deep," I explain. "Actually, I'm not sure what I thought. But my neighbors stood and stared at me like I was a lunatic."

Our food arrives and before the waitress can rush off, Juno touches her arm and asks if we can order something to drink. She blinks.

"I'll have a Sprite," I say, even though she is not looking my way.

"And I'll have another cup of coffee with cream."

When I taste the chowder, I'm surprised that it's quite good.

"Where were we?" Juno asks between bites. "Oh, winter. Right. It's been hell. The week before Thanksgiving, Lauren took me shopping for a coat. I've never owned a pair of gloves or a scarf or anything heavier than a baseball jacket. So we walk into Boyds and she literally had to school me on the differences between duffel jackets, overcoats, split linings, zip linings, boiled wool, worsted wool and camel's hair. Even after I told the salesman I'd moved up from Florida, he spoke to me really slowly, like I had a mental disease."

I wonder if he mentions Lauren so often because she's the only person we have in common, or because he's more attracted to her than Lauren thinks. She's so used to men falling for her that she's generally sized them up and rejected them before they even notice.

". . . and my sisters," Juno is saying, "they've put me on a mailing list of a catalog that sells ice-climbing gear. It's a joke. I think. But maybe it's not."

Actually, I'm enjoying his company so much that I'm just going to let myself believe he's interested in me, at least through dessert.

"Has your family been up to visit?"

"You kidding? They won't come until summer."

"Sounds like they miss you, though."

"Oh, it was a madhouse when I went home for Christmas," he says. "Parents, uncles, aunts, everybody carrying on like I'd been away for three years instead of three months. Full-scale Cuban drama. *Lágrimas y abrazos.* You know how that goes!"

"Sure," I tell him. But, of course, I don't. After Mom died, my entire family consisted of two people.

The waitress does not ask if we want anything else before she tallies the check, but Juno hands it back to her and says he'd like dessert.

We both order cheesecake and coffee, and in protest the waitress slams the entire pot in the middle of our table and leaves it there.

I tell Juno about the fullmooners, and he says he'd love to meet my father one day.

"What does your dad do for a living?" I ask.

"Nothing now," he says, "but for thirty-five years he ran a print shop."

The conversation never slows, and before we know it, we are the only customers left in the place. I look around and find the waitress leaning against the cash register, glaring at us with her arms crossed.

Juno pays the bill and leaves a more than generous tip.

"I should run," I say when we step outside. The gusty air stings as I fumble with my gloves. Juno, who is ensconced in a knee-length shearling, throws his gym bag over his shoulder and squints into the wind. Out of our comfortable bubble of talk, we are awkward again.

"I had a nice time," I say, and then wonder if people even say that anymore.

"I'll call," he answers, holding out his hand.

CHAPTER *6*

*I*t's been three days since I first mentioned Pancha to Dad and he still has not shown any sign of recognizing her name. Each time I visit, I remind him about the letter and explain that Juno has launched an e-mail search to find her. But the pieces of the puzzle still have not come together.

I want to believe that if I say just the right thing to Dad, recollections of his sister will magically reappear. It's crazy, but I let myself think it's possible, especially since the leader of Dad's therapy team told me yesterday that he's begun to identify a few very small words. This long after the stroke, a stride like that has got to mean something. I'd like to think it means Dad has found a foothold and has started to climb. But the leader also told me there's been no progress in Dad's dexterity. He can take only a few steps with the help of a walker, his hand movements remain clumsy, and his ability to swallow is as bad as it was just after the attack. It could be, the therapist said, that Dad's come as far as he's able. But only time will tell.

Reports like that leave me more angry than assured. They only underscore how much of medicine is still guesswork. How much even the doctors can't know. Still, I feel so good today that the update barely fazes me. Juno is stopping by the Rose Tree on his way to work to meet Dad. And, on top of that, I have wonderful news that I know will make my father's day.

Since our lunch yesterday, Juno and I have spoken twice for hours at a time, both last night and this morning. We've covered everything from Bosnia to Bonnie Raitt, and no matter how long we stay on the line, our good-byes come too soon. When I meet him at the reception desk, we exchange quick pecks on the cheek. He is wearing an olive green sweater that's been knit to look fashionably rugged. If his haircut were better, he would look like a high-priced lawyer working for a worthy cause.

It's five in the afternoon, the prime social hour for the more active men and women at Rose Tree. The air is heavy with the onion smell of institutional food, and in the lounge, adjacent to the dining room, at least twenty women wearing boxy knit pantsuits are playing cards at the six square tables in the back. Three or four men are sitting or standing at the other end of the big room watching a pretty, dark-haired anchorwoman deliver the news from the center of an extra-wide TV screen. Nobody seems to notice that the volume is set so high that the floor vibrates when she speaks. Everyone I see is older than my father by at least ten or fifteen years. I wonder what Juno thinks.

Linda, the listless front desk regular, has already packed her things and is waiting impatiently for her night-shift replacement to arrive. She drums her fingers on her vinyl lunch box as Juno signs in.

"Keep this visible, Mr. Hernández," she says flatly as she hands him a guest badge. Then, to my utter surprise, she shoots me a conspiratorial wink.

Juno and I walk down the main hall to the medical ward, passing white-haired men and women leaning on canes and pushing four-legged walkers. Juno says good afternoon and smiles. It feels as if I've known him forever, as if we grew up next door to one another, or were best friends in elementary school. As if being with him is just right.

"Remember," I say when we reach the entrance to Dad's ward, "he understands most of what you say, but he can't answer very well."

Juno nods and reaches above my head to swing open the door. When we reach Dad's room, Juno agrees to remain in the hallway until I introduce him.

"Dad?"

"Nee!"

"I brought somebody to meet you today."

My father is in his wheelchair, which someone has parked next to the window. Not that there's much of a view. Just one skinny sapling, which, at this time of year, looks like a broomstick stuck in the dirt. I walk over to him and move the chair so it's next to the bed.

"You look good today." I plant a kiss on his forehead and smooth his hair back after I do. His left hand takes hold of mine and gives it a weak squeeze.

"Dad," I say, taking a step back, "I'd like you to meet my friend Juno. I've told you about him. Remember?"

Juno steps into the room and stands by my side.

"Professor DeLeon," Juno says in a strong, deep voice, "it's truly a pleasure."

Dad tilts his head and tries to shift in his chair. Juno steps forward, clasps my father's good hand between both of his, and delivers a firm and formal handshake.

"He's helping me look for Pancha," I say.

Juno perches on the side of the bed where Dad can see him without having to lift his head. Beside Juno, Dad looks small in his chair. Thin and slope-shouldered. But his eyes are as vivid and intense as ever, and I can only imagine what is racing through his head.

"Nita tells me you teach Latin American literature." I notice Juno is using the present tense. "We'll have to discuss Neruda someday. I never got through the *Obras Completas*, but I've read my share."

Dad moves his jaw, but his lips don't form any words.

"Whenever you're ready," Juno answers without a beat of hesitation. "I'll need some time to go back and brush up a bit."

If I wasn't sure before, I'm certain of it now. Juno is a good man.

"Dad," I ask, "do you know what this is?" From my handbag I produce a slip of paper with dates, times and the words "American Airlines" printed on it. I set it on Dad's wheelchair tray and he bends at the waist to take a closer look. I wait a few moments to see if he can make sense of what he's looking at, but it's clear he can't. Randy has been planning the trip for weeks, but I didn't mention it because to Dad that is an eternity.

"The fullmooners are coming," I say to help him out. "Tomorrow!"

First Dad shows no emotion and then, slowly, he manages a wide, wobbly smile. For an instant we are both transported back to how things used to be. I can see him puffing on a fat cigar while one of the other professors pontificates, his mind so finely tuned that he is already three steps ahead of the argument. Looking at him now, I realize that for the past months I've been so focused on getting him here, getting him settled and getting him started on his recovery, that I haven't stopped to think about how cut off he must feel. How incredibly lonely. Suddenly, the image of a new needlepoint pillow flashes in my mind—a red valentine heart trapped behind a row of black iron bars.

"That's great!" Juno exclaims. "Nita told me about the professors."

"Aww?" Dad asks.

"No," I answer, "not all of them can make it. But it's the best of the bunch. Professor Stevens, Dr. Carver and crazy Ted Lansky."

"Carr?"

"Mrs. Stevens says she'll come next time. This visit is just for the boys. So I guess I'm going to have to keep you knuckleheads in line all by my lonesome."

Dad's expression shifts, which means that somewhere in his head he is forming words. I can tell by the glint in his eye that he's thought of a snappy comeback. With his chin held high, he begins to deliver his punch line. But when he hears his voice corrupt one syllable and then another, he squeezes his lips tight and stops speaking.

"Want to try that again, Johnny Carson?" I say, straining to keep my voice upbeat so he won't feel disheartened. But inside, my own heart is breaking. To shake it off, I get right back to the fullmooners, explaining that I offered to lodge them at my place, but they insisted on staying at the hotel halfway between my house and the Rose Tree Center.

"I'm going to have to check their luggage for ropes and crowbars to make sure they aren't planning to crawl through the hedges at midnight and bust you out of here."

Dad grins. Maybe he really is doing better.

Candide, Dad's night attendant and my favorite of all his caregivers, pokes her head into the room. I like everything about Candide. Her thick Jamaican accent makes her words sound like music, and her tender smile has the power to heal. She is, I think, somewhere in her mid-forties, but it's hard to tell. I have yet to spot a single sign of aging on her smooth dark skin, although more than a few of the close-cropped curls on her head are wiry and gray.

I introduce her to Juno and tell her about the fullmooners. "You're going to love them," I say with a crack of sarcasm in my voice. "They're the uncles nobody wants at the wedding. Too loud. Too opinionated. Too pushy."

"You want to use the art room for a night? It's got a sink and a good table. And it's far enough down the hall that they can stay up late and be as loud as they want."

"You can do that?"

"Darling, I'm in charge of your daddy at night, and he deserves a little party. Don't you think?"

"It's okay?"

She nods her head and playfully warns, "As long as he doesn't womanize."

When Candide leaves, Juno says he should be going, too.

"I'll walk you out," I say. "Okay, Dad?"

This time, my father stretches out the fingers of his left hand as straight and steady as he is able. Juno takes them in his grasp and gives Dad another shake.

"Thank you," I say when Juno and I reach the reception desk.

"For what?"

I feel the hot sting of tears pooling in my eyes. I don't want to cry. But if I try to speak, I know I will.

"Hey," Juno says, gently placing his hand on my shoulder. "He's a fighter. And so are you."

Here it is again, that feeling of knowing Juno as well as I know myself. I want to kiss him, wrap my arms around his neck and let my tears soak into his sweater. But this is the wrong place for that. The evening receptionist is watching our every move, and more than a few of the old people in the lobby are staring at us, too.

We hug and say good-bye.

When I get back to Dad's room, he gives me his version of the thumbs-up sign.

"Juno?" I ask. "He's a good friend."

My father cocks his head and then points to the television to let me know he hasn't forgotten our plans to watch *Casablanca* tonight. I push in the videotape and it begins to play. The familiar music swells and I turn out the overhead light so the picture will intensify. As I settle on Dad's bed, a map of Africa appears on the screen and the narrator tells us that Casablanca is where people, desperate to start new lives, wait and wait and wait.

CHAPTER 7

When I get home, I find Juno on my doorstep.

"Lauren gave me your address," he says, as if anticipating my question. He is wearing his thick shearling coat and a green plaid neck scarf. His hands are shoved deep inside his pockets and the tip of his nose is red.

"How long have you been here?"

"Just got here. I'm on my dinner break. I thought I'd leave this in the mailbox."

"Come in."

I ask for his coat but instead of handing it to me he takes a folded piece of paper out of its pocket. "She answered," he says.

It must be bad news if he came all this way to tell me. If it was good news he would have called.

"Do I want to read this?" I ask, suddenly unsure exactly what bad news would be. That he didn't find Pancha? Or that he did?

"Yeah," he says. "I think you do."

"Give me your coat," I say, keeping my eyes away from his hand. "Would you like some coffee?"

Juno slides his arms out of his sleeves without letting go of the paper. After I hang the heavy coat in the closet, I pivot and head toward the kitchen. Without a word, Juno follows.

"I'll get it," he says, spotting the coffeemaker on the counter. "You should read this."

Pancha has written her e-mail like a business letter:

> *Dear Madam or Sir,*
> *I have hesitated to reply. To call your message regarding my family unsettling would be an understatement, and the fact that it has come through a third party raises my concern. I am eager to communicate with Regina or Diego DeLeon, my brother and sister-in-law, but I am not going to give my address or telephone number over the computer to somebody I do not know.*
> *You must tell me who you represent before we proceed.*
> *I await your reply,*
> *Francisca DeLeon*

"She's a shrewd one," Juno says when I look up.

It's only then that I notice he has not only found the coffee inside my disorganized cabinets but has also dug around to locate the coffee filters, and now he is about to toss two scoops of the chicory blend into the machine. I expect his quick familiarity to irritate me, but it doesn't. I actually like that he feels at home enough in my house to help himself. I only wish I felt comfortable, too.

"She sounds angry," I say, hoping Juno might help me pick an appropriate reaction.

"She's just being careful."

The coffee machine gurgles and I wonder if any of the food in my refrigerator is presentable.

"I brought a laptop if you want to answer right now."

Do I? My emotions are tugging in opposite directions. Of course I want to meet the person my mother reached out to twenty-five years ago. Of course I want to look into the face of my father's only sister. But why didn't my parents ever speak of her? They must have had their reasons. Do I really want to know what they were? I've been through so much over the last year and a half—Dad, the divorce, the painful, hard work of getting my own life pieced back together.

"Cream?" Juno has filled two cups and is liberally spooning sugar into one of them.

"I'm sorry," I stammer as I open the icebox and lay my hand on a carton of skim milk. "This is all I've got."

Juno sits himself down at the kitchen table while I quickly put together a couple of tuna sandwiches.

"You don't have to give her your phone number or your address," he says, sensing my hesitation. "Just tell her your dad is sick and let the next move be hers."

"Is that what you'd do?"

"Me?" He laughs. "If I found a long-lost aunt, I'd run and hide."

I bring our sandwiches to the table and Juno sets his hand on top of mine. Still standing, I lean my hip against his shoulder and feel the knot in my chest begin to uncoil.

"How's your dad?" he asks as I take the seat across from him. He knows I want to postpone making a decision about Pancha, and he's going to help me out.

"Well, I could tell he liked you."

"Mmm," Juno murmurs as he chews, leaving me to guess whether he's commenting on the sandwich or Dad's opinion of him.

"I think seeing the fullmooners is going to do him a lot of good," I continue.

"They sound like quite a bunch."

"You want to meet them?"

"Thought you'd never ask," he says, putting the remainder of the sandwich down and reaching for his cup.

"Really?" I wonder if he's just teasing.

Juno nods.

"We're going to have dinner at the Rose Tree when they're here," I say. "You're welcome to come, if you don't mind spending your Tuesday night in a nursing home with a crazy crew of cranky old men."

"You going to be there?"

"Sure."

"Well then," he says, tipping the rim of his coffee cup as if he were making a toast, "I can't think of anyplace else I'd rather be. I'll ask for the night off."

I try to pretend the words he's tossed across the table are no different than any others, but I feel my face begin to blush. I reach for his plate and quickly take it to the sink.

"Listen," he says, "I've got to get back, but I'll leave the laptop."

"I don't know how to use the Internet."

"It's easy." Juno stands, walks to my side and places his cup in the sink. "All you need is a phone line."

With his coat on but not fully buttoned, he goes out to his car and gets the computer, which I tell him to bring to my office. I make room on the desk by moving a short stack of books to the side, and when I'm done I notice that Juno is looking directly at a pillow I forgot to remove from the love seat after my last session.

"One of my sisters crochets, too," he says before turning his attention back to the laptop.

I don't bother to correct him because the moment passes quickly, but I am pleased that my work caught his eye.

In no time, Juno is tapping the computer keyboard with quick and practiced strokes. From somewhere inside the machine comes a ding and a whir and, finally, a choppy voice announcing that he's got mail. Shoulder to shoulder we lean over the little screen and he shows me how to address a message and send it on its way. His upper arm presses gently against my sleeve, and a smooth spot just behind his ear smells faintly of sandalwood soap.

"See how easy it is?" Juno asks, his eyes so close to mine that I can see how gracefully his dark eyelashes curl.

I nod. "Piece of cake."

Cupping my chin in his hand, Juno tilts my head back and presses his lips against mine. I lean into the kiss, inviting him to make it last. When our tongues meet, my hands glide over his shoulders and around his neck. We separate for a moment to catch our breath and then, wrapping his arms around the small of my back, Juno pulls me toward him again.

"God," he says, resting his forehead on mine. "I've really got to go."

"Okay." I plant another kiss on his flushed lips. I feel Juno's hand slide over the curve of my hip, and the sensation makes my pulse start to race. I wrap my fingers around his and stop him from going any farther.

"Right," he says, after taking a deep breath. "You're right."

He logs off the computer and asks if I understand how to log back on. Holding his hand, I say yes and lead him to the front door, where we fall into one another again.

"Go," I finally whisper.

I watch him walk to his car, every nerve in my body wildly charged. When I close the door, all I can think of is how much I want to touch him again. I let the feeling sink in and then pick up the phone and dial Lauren's number.

"We kissed," I say, hoping she's there.

I hear a click and then, "I knew something was brewing. Tell me everything!"

I don't repeat every detail, but I do say that Juno's grace around Dad is what ultimately won me over.

Lauren clears her throat, to let me know she's waiting for better stuff.

"Okay," I surrender. "That, and his incredible eyes."

"Uh-huh," she croons. "It's that intense reporter's glint you like."

Her words hit me like cold water. Am I falling for another man like Aaron? Someone who lets the newspaper rule his life? No, I tell myself, Juno's a family man. As soon as that thought pops into my head, another wave of disappointment washes over me. He's certain to want children.

"You there?" Lauren asks.

"I shouldn't have." I sigh. "I can't see it going anywhere."

"Jesus, Nita, you don't have to marry the guy. Just have a little fun with him. You deserve it."

I smile. But I'm not like Lauren. I don't know how to play the field.

I dated one guy in college before I met Aaron and got married at twenty-six. Eleven years and one divorce later, I'm back in the singles world, having slept with only two men.

"Just let it play out," Lauren tells me, "and enjoy the trip."

I close my eyes and recall the feel of Juno's hands against my skin. Despite my doubts, I can't wait to see him again.

I tell Lauren about Pancha's e-mail and the fullmooners' visit. She asks if she can come to the dinner at the Rose Tree to meet the professors when they are here.

"I'm counting on it," I say. "I'm not sure how long Dad can hold out socially, and I'll need some help smoothing over the rough spots."

"Do you think they'll let me take their pictures?"

"Oh, Laurie, they'd love it."

Finally I tell her that I don't know if I want to write back to Pancha. "Maybe I should just leave well enough alone."

"It's up to you," she replies haltingly.

"What? There's something you aren't saying."

"You need to at least tell her about your dad. She has a right to know."

Following Juno's instructions, I bring the laptop back to life after I hang up the phone. I stare at the screen with my fingers resting on the keys. Lauren is right. I have to answer for Dad's sake, if not for my own. Slowly, I begin to type, but I end up rejecting each of my answers before the thought is even finished.

> *Dear Pancha:*
> *You don't know me but . . .*

> *Dear Pancha:*
> *I am your niece . . .*

> *Pancha:*
> *This is Juanita, Diego and Regina's only daughter . . .*

The problem is that I'm not sure where to start. Juno said to keep it simple, to let her know Dad is sick and to leave it at that. Nothing too emotional, nothing but the facts. I exhale and begin again.

> *Pancha:*
> *I was pleased to receive your reply. Our communication is going through a third party because I do not have a computer of my own. The address you are writing to belongs to a newspaper reporter, who is also a friend. I asked him to help me locate you because I thought you should know that Dad is recovering from a stroke here in Philadelphia, where I live.*

I give her my telephone number and a brief update on what Dad can and cannot do, careful to leave out the fact that he has yet to respond to her name. After reading over what I've written at least five times, I decide it's how I want it—straightforward and clear. Underneath the final line I write, *Your niece, Juanita,* and then I press the key that casts it into thin air.

My stomach is filled with the prickly uneasiness you feel when you're waiting for the answer to a question you might be sorry you asked. There's no way to know how Pancha will respond to the e-mail, how many times she may read and reread the words that I've written, or how cautiously she will consider her reply. All I know is that I've launched a message in a bottle to someone who knows my parents' history but is nothing but a vapor cloud to me. On the computer screen I see a tiny envelope with wings suspended over the words *your message has been sent,* but there is no way of knowing where in the world it has flown.

Normally, at this time of night, I would get ready for bed, but I'm too wound up to sleep. I pour myself a glass of wine and sit underneath the strong reading lamp in the living room. Reaching into the wicker basket where I keep my needlepoint supplies, I pull out the profile-and-goblet canvas. It's nothing but two simple faces looking at one another eye-to-eye, but the message behind the illusion is that things are not always what they seem. When you look closer, the entire picture changes.

That is what I love about needlepoint. Not just this particular project, but every canvas I've ever stitched. No matter how closely you stick to the pattern you've picked, the piece takes on a life of its own. You might choose to leave out a tree originally drawn into the background, or decide that the sky could use more sun. Before you know it, the scene you thought you were making has changed and a very different picture has emerged.

By the time Juno calls, I've lost track of time.

"You still awake?"

"Just heading for bed," I lie.

"I wanted to say good night."

We stay on the line and let our silence speak for us.

"I'll call tomorrow," he promises, before we reluctantly say good-bye.

CHAPTER 8

I went into family counseling because I believed the people I'd meet would have distinct problems that I could fix. But the books I read in my classes and the studies I memorized for my thesis taught me that most problems fall into a few very broad categories. There are introverts and extroverts, open aggressors and passive ones. There are people who strive to dominate others, and folks who unhappily submit. Eventually I learned to recognize them all. But tonight, as the fullmooners walk off the airplane that brought them from Dallas, I see three old men who fit into no other category except the sweet and strange one reserved for true eccentrics.

Dr. Carver, whose eyesight is so feeble he can't see past the reach of his own arm, is the first to emerge. Round shouldered, bald and bearded, he walks out of the shadow of the passenger ramp and into the fluorescent light of the airport terminal looking considerably confused and suspicious of where he is headed. His khaki trench coat is rumpled at the waist, as if he kept it cinched throughout the entire flight. The handle to his beat-up leather briefcase is clenched in his left hand, and every time he moves the satchel swings like a pendulum across his knee.

Immediately behind him is Randy Stevens, dressed in a baby-blue windbreaker, a pistachio-colored golf shirt and a pair of crisp cotton golf pants that are relentlessly plaid. He carries himself like he is the most self-assured of the bunch, trim and tall and glowing with an amber tan that he feeds with a round of golf each and every day. For years he has tried to persuade the others to join him on the greens, but the invitation has never been accepted.

Dad used to tell me that Randy's penchant for the outdoors came from the fact that he grew up in East Texas, hunting deer and fowl and playing football for his small town's high school team. He was the only kid at that school who listened to Bach and Beethoven on the radio on Saturday afternoons, who memorized Shakespeare's sonnets so he could recite them to the girls, and who mapped out chess moves just for fun. Randy knew the only way he wasn't going to get pummeled for being that different was to be better than the rest of the boys at their regular games. I don't know how much of that is true, but the steady exercise Randy has gotten over the years has obviously done him good.

Placing his hand on the small of Dr. Carver's back, Randy gently pushes him out of the path of the other passengers who are impatiently streaming around them. Together, they step to the side and wait for Ted Lansky. Randy has a handsome wine-colored portfolio tucked under his arm, and I wonder what manner of books or papers the professors felt compelled to bring.

The plane seems to have been filled with businesspeople toting black computer cases over one shoulder and navy blue suit bags over the other. It is a Monday night and as they rush down the terminal's wide corridor, I watch them press their palm-size telephones against their ears.

Luckily, the plane has arrived at gate A-1, which means I can see the fullmooners from my spot behind the security rail, near the X-ray machine. I know Dr. Carver can't see anything that far away, so I won't bother to wave until Randy or Ted looks my way. Meeting people at the airport is no longer a warm or personal experience. Fathers aren't allowed to scoop their children into their arms the instant they get back from a business trip. Girlfriends can't rush to the gate and kiss their lovers. Uniformed guards and stiff metal fences keep people apart until there is enough distance between them and the airplanes to risk saying hello.

Dr. Lansky is the last of the fullmooners to walk out and, as usual, everything about him is white. His skin is as pale as talcum powder and the clear plastic rims of his glasses blend right in. His dress shirt is white, and so is the small patch of undershirt visible underneath its unbuttoned collar. His pants and shoes and belt are white and the hair on his head swirls like a dollop of whipped cream from his sideburns straight up. He has dressed this way for as long as I can remember, surrendering sometime in his early forties to the double punch of divorce and severe color blindness. If he's not wearing white, he's wearing black. But never the two together. Over his shoulder he has slung a large canvas tote bag that, to my surprise, is unabashedly red. With all three of them accounted for, they turn toward the main corridor and begin walking toward me. I wave my arms over my head, although it's hardly necessary because everybody else has gone and I am the only person left waiting.

I'm tempted to drive them straight to the Rose Tree to see Dad, but I know it's too late to get him worked up. And I wouldn't do that to Candide, especially since she is being nice enough to let us break about a dozen rules tomorrow. I suggest we eat dinner someplace downtown, since their visit is going to be short and they won't have time to officially take in the sights. Before I start the car, I give the professors the choice of Vietnamese or Indian or Thai, and they say any one of those would do fine. I turn the heat on high and head toward the city's sawtoothed skyline as I try to think which restaurant they might like. Soon we are in the tangle of downtown traffic and I point out a few of Philadelphia's more interesting landmarks.

"The statue on top of City Hall is of William Penn," I say. "The Oldenburg clothespin sculpture is on that corner over there, and in a minute we'll drive by Independence Hall." The streets are clogged with office workers in a hurry to drive home. City buses trudge along the right-hand lane, oblivious to the gridlock building up behind them.

Dr. Carver asks if I happen to know the spot where the nation's early abolitionists met and if I could drive past the home where W. E. B. Du Bois lived when he wrote his most famous works. I should have known better than to think a quick cruise by the Liberty Bell and Betsy Ross's house would be enough for this crew. I tell him I'm sorry but I have no idea where either of those places might be, and as the car inches closer to South Philadelphia I suddenly know where I want to take them for supper.

"How about a place where the waiters sing opera and the tables are crawling with mobsters?" Immediately, the fullmooners agree.

Over a huge pasta dinner with authentic red gravy and two bottles of imported Chianti, I fill them in on Dad's slow recuperation. Silenced now and then by a young waiter or waitress performing a Mozart or Puccini aria, I also tell them how my new career as a counselor has helped steady the shifting sand under my own feet. Doting on me in a way I can't help but love, the professors say I look good and, during a natural lull in the conversation, Ted Lansky pats my hand and declares in a soft voice that divorce is hard for everyone who goes through it.

To keep the night upbeat, Dr. Stevens pulls out a stack of snapshots from a golf trip he and Mrs. Stevens took to Myrtle Beach in January. After we pass them around, Professor Lansky informs me that he's become a regular contributor to an Internet chat room about railroad history.

"The world's largest manufacturer of steam engines was right here in Philadelphia," he says in a tone that insinuates he is telling me a bit of history I should have already known. "Baldwin Locomotive Works."

"Really?" I ask between bites.

Bewildered by the hole in my education, Dr. Lansky slides into an impromptu lecture about the once grand and mighty Baldwin company and its slow, painful demise. He tells the story well, dramatically boiling it down to its essence, the way a good professor would.

When our waitress arrives with the dessert tray on her arm, she leans in and announces in a loud whisper that if we look over her shoulder we'll see Little Carlo Cappuzi standing at the door, next to his tall, fashion-model wife. With the subtlety of a pack of Elvis fans, we whip our heads in that direction and spot a short, dark-haired man in his mid-twenties dressed in a dark expensive suit, chatting with the maître d'.

Finally, a slice of local lore I know plenty about. Before the divorce, Aaron worked on a series of stories explaining the two major mafia families and their power struggles. He and a photographer secretly followed the major players around town, snapping candid shots of them through long zoom lenses. For weeks, he stayed out all night chronicling the back-stabbing and violent tug-of-war between the factions' leaders. Or at least that's what he told me.

"Little Carlo," I inform the fullmooners, "is the crown prince of the Cappuzi family, which was run by his father, Big Vic, until he was sent to prison two years ago." I have got the professors' full attention and, for the first time in my life, I am lecturing them.

Over the years I have kept up with each of the professors through Christmas cards and regular telephone updates provided by Mrs. Stevens. But it has been a solid twenty years since we've all shared a table. As much as I delighted in the group's fiery give-and-take when I was a little girl, it held absolutely no appeal to me by the time I was seventeen. With the close-minded sanctimony that only a teenager can muster, I declared the gatherings a tedious waste of my time and made sure I had someplace else to be whenever the professors came over. Back then I considered myself lucky to escape, but tonight I can't help but wish that I'd stayed at my father's table longer, because the truth of the matter is the crazy dinner debates were lavish feasts of love.

We order three desserts and pass the plates to one another between long sips of decaf. When the check comes, I have to slap their hands to convince them that I intend to pay.

It is almost midnight by the time I finally get the professors to their hotel. Before saying good night, I ask if they'd like to sleep late the next morning, thinking that while they rest I will pick up the spiral-cut ham that I ordered and the other groceries I'll need to cook dinner.

"Don't know about them, but I'll be up at eight," Randy says as he lifts his suitcase, and the two others, from the trunk of my car. Professor Lansky and Dr. Carver, who are standing one pace behind the red taillights, exchange a quick glance.

"How about eleven?" Dr. Carver says dryly, taking his battered brief-case from Randy's hand.

"Eleven sounds good," Professor Lansky echoes.

Randy responds by closing the trunk with a firm shove.

"Will you be bored to death?" I ask.

"I'll find something to do."

The problem is he won't. The only thing close to this hotel is a pan-cake house, and beyond that a noisy six-lane road that leads to down-town Philly going east and the suburbs going west. There's no place to walk, no place to shop and not a drop of charm for miles. He'll be a prisoner.

"My friend Lauren and I are heading to the farmers' market first thing," I say. "Would you like to come along?" He agrees to meet us in the lobby at a quarter to nine.

I'd hoped to dash straight in and straight out of the farmers' market, but if Randy is coming along that is going to be out of the question. Every time someone sees the Reading Terminal Market for the first time they can't help but linger, and you can't blame them. First they are seduced by the sumptuous smell of melted sugar and cinnamon bub-bling on freshly baked sticky buns that sell as quickly as they're made at a stand just inside the front door. Then they're stunned at the sheer size of the place. Tucked inside the belly of an old arched-ceiling build-ing that was once a train terminal, the market takes up two entire city blocks and every inch of it vibrates with the din and motion of butch-ers, bakers, poultry sellers, fishmongers, vegetable farmers, cheese mak-ers, ice cream purveyors, candy salesmen, flower merchants, fruit dealers, sausage makers and exotic spice importers doing brisk business. The stalls, more than eighty of them, are manned by Amish farmers, Asian fishermen, and German butchers. Italians and African-Americans and Russians and Poles, even New Age vegetarians greet their regular customers by name and refer to the people they don't know as "Pal."

There are a few stands where tourists can buy a plug of fresh saltwa-ter taffy, a warm cookie or a thick corned beef special on rye for break-fast or lunch, but most of the market is reserved for serious shoppers who show up with wicker baskets or well-worn canvas bags nestled in the crooks of their arms.

When we arrive the next morning, Lauren agrees to show Randy around while I get my errands done.

Maggie, the produce lady, says hello when I walk up to admire her pyramid of pink grapefruits and tilted baskets of bright yellow lemons. She has displayed the fresh-picked organic greens that she sells by creating a mosaic out of the red leaf, Bibb and romaine lettuce and arugula. It is accented by colorful islands of radishes, cucumbers, artichokes, carrots and tomatoes. To one side of that arrangement there is a rainbow of green and red and yellow bell peppers, and to the other side she has bundles of pale white asparagus neatly tied together with pretty blue ribbon.

"A dozen in each bouquet," she says.

I take two bundles, and she carefully wraps them in sheets of silver tissue paper, as if they were priceless pieces of crystal. Making my way to other booths, I buy two pounds of tiny new potatoes and some small onions that I intend to glaze with maple syrup. I add a fistful of fresh parsley and a couple of loaves of freshly baked olive bread to my take and, at Mr. Papadakis's booth, I scoop three ladles of marinated Greek olives into a plastic container and give in to the lure of a half-pound block of moist feta cheese. Now my basket is full, and I can feel the muscles in my upper arm strain as I try to keep it steady. I'll have to put this stuff in the car and come back for the ham and the dessert.

When I find Lauren and Randy they are standing in front of the Penn Dutch Pretzels stand eating honey-colored twists capped with dark mustard. They look like father and daughter, laughing and nodding in enthusiastic agreement over one another's observations.

After Mom died, Mrs. Stevens became so much like a mother to me that I never stopped to wonder why she and Randy never had children of their own. It wasn't until Aaron and I began to have problems getting pregnant that Mrs. Stevens told me about her three miscarriages. She said watching me grow up helped her fill the emptiness. But as I look at Randy, standing shoulder to shoulder with a woman who shares his lean build and concise athletic moves, I wish he'd been given a chance at full-time fatherhood.

When the fullmooners stride into Dad's room at the Rose Tree, the expression on his face shifts from confusion to recollection to utter joy as each one of them leans down and lands a kiss on his cheek and a pat on his shoulder. When I step forward, Dad points toward the folded aluminum walker leaning against the far wall and, using his left hand, he motions for me to set it up for him. The room fills with a nervous quiet as I snap the contraption open and plant it at the foot of his wheelchair. Slowly, he leans forward and sets his hands on the top rail. We all hold our breath as he lets his feet drop to the floor and begins to unsteadily lift himself up. I have to fight the urge to tell him to stop. I see him giving the task his full concentration and, when he has just about straightened his back, the fullmooners cheerfully rush to his side to help the rest of the way. Standing, Dad holds his head high and looks all three men straight in the eyes.

"It's damn good to see you, Diego," Randy says.

Dad moves his lips, but from where I am standing I can't hear his answer. The men help Dad back into his chair and put the walker back against the wall.

"Wasss no?" Dad asks.

I worry that the professors won't understand Dad's speech, and I know it will break my father's heart if his friends are unable to decipher his jumbled English.

"Things are awful, Diego," Ted Lansky answers in a low, serious tone. "Really bad. Randy still hasn't kicked his golf habit. And since you left it's only gotten worse."

My father smiles.

"And, as you can see," Randy shoots back, "Ted is still dressing like the Good Humor man."

Dr. Carver joins in and playfully asks about the food in this place, and Dad answers by making a sign to indicate it's just so-so.

There's no reason for me to stay; they certainly aren't going to need any help keeping the conversation going.

"I'm going to head back and start getting things ready for dinner," I announce to nobody in particular. "I'll come back and get you at one, so Dad can get a little rest."

The four men look my way and nod.

At home, I set a small tower of plates and bowls inside a sturdy cardboard box and then place a dark blue tablecloth, a cluster of silverware and a stack of white napkins on top of the dishes. In another box, I pack the four tall silver candlesticks that Aaron's parents gave us on our wedding day even though, as decorations go, they are probably going to be way over the top. But, I tell myself, it doesn't matter. I don't care if I tilt toward excess because I want everything about this dinner tonight—the guests, the food, the table—to whip up enough alchemy to lift Dad out of the confines of the Rose Tree for a few glorious hours. Familiar music will help spin the web, so I set aside a few CDs the full-mooners might like. I have no Herb Alpert in my collection, but I figure Edith Piaf, Wynton Marsalis and Tony Bennett should do the trick.

Because the ham I bought is already cooked, I only have to heat it up for an hour before Lauren and I head over to the Rose Tree. In the meantime, I'll wash the asparagus, peel the onions and mince the parsley. I have the knife moving at a nice pace when the telephone rings. I don't want to stop to answer it but, after three more rings, I give in. My mind is still on my cooking when I pick up the receiver and say hello.

"Regina?" the caller asks.

Hearing my mother's name sends an electric shock down my spine. For a moment I cannot breathe.

"Is that you?" asks a voice I don't recognize.

"No," I stammer. "There's no . . . who is this, please?"

"Juanita?"

I try to swallow but there is no saliva in my mouth.

"Pancha?" I answer.

"*Ay, mijita,* I forget you are a grown woman now. I thought you were Regina."

Every word she speaks, every consonant and wide-mouthed vowel she delivers, travels over the line in the same rich accent my mother had. My body and mind are numb. She must not know. She can't know, if she's asking for Mom.

"Hello?"

"Mom isn't here," I finally manage.

"Oh, this is your house, then? This number?"

"Yes."

My thoughts are balled up in a knot. She's called to ask about Dad. But I have no idea where I am supposed to make this conversation go. Should I tell Pancha right now that Mom is dead? That she's been gone for decades and, for some reason that I don't know, Dad never bothered to inform her? Do I say that until a week ago I didn't even know she existed? Do I ask if I'm as much of a surprise to her as she is to me?

Instead of saying any of those things, I say absolutely nothing, and the persistent hiss of the long-distance connection thickens the tension.

Realizing that I am not going to hold up my end of the conversation, Pancha begins filling the void with rapid Spanish: *"Mira, mi vida. Tantos años han pasado y, bueno, yo no sé que—"*

"Pancha?"

"Sí?" Her voice wavers and now I can hear that she's nervous, too.

"I go by Nita, and, I'm sorry, but I don't speak Spanish."

I hear her take a deep breath and, silently, we agree to start over.

"Tell me about Diego," she begins.

I'm grateful she's asked about Dad first. Explaining his situation at least gives me a little solid ground to stand on. I tell her about the attack, and how I brought Dad to the Rose Tree. She asks me what the doctors have said, and I spend the next ten minutes filling her in.

"So that's where your mother is now?" she asks. "At the nursing home?"

I switch the receiver to my other ear. She's backed me into a corner and there's no graceful way out.

"She's dead," I say, just like that, letting the words drop like heavy stones.

I hear Pancha gasp.

"It happened on July fourteenth, 1976." My voice is flat and feeble.

I hate telling the story as much as I hate hearing it. "Mom stayed late at the gallery that night, to change the front window display. Her friend, Mrs. Stevens, who owned the shop, had talked her into finally showcasing her own work and Mom wanted everything to be perfect.

"I was at swim camp. She would call me every night. That week, she talked a lot about the display. For other people's work, she draped yards of fabric over overturned buckets, sawhorses and pedestals to create a museum-like effect. She'd choose satin or burlap or whatever sort of material would play off the color and the texture of the artist's work."

"She was alone?" Pancha asks.

"Mom's work was stoneware," I continue. I'd heard Pancha's question, but I have my way of telling the story and, once I start, I try not to stop because, if I do, my mind wanders to places too painful to explore.

"She decided her work would look best perched on bales of hay and so Mrs. Stevens bought eight from a horse stable near the lake. She'd stacked the bales next to the back door and left for home at five. Mom had the strongest hands I've ever seen on either a man or a woman, and handling the bales wouldn't be a problem for her. She'd already lifted three of them onto a dolly and was almost at the front of the store when it happened."

Pancha is silent.

"The police said the robber ran in behind her . . . the bullet hit the back of her neck."

I remember Dad telling me the barest of these facts when we got home from swim camp that night, his voice choking on the words, his face buried in his hands when he couldn't go on. It would be on the news, he warned me, and in the papers the next day. We kept the television off for a week and somebody, probably Mrs. Stevens, took the *Morning News* from our front step every morning.

"Why didn't I know?" Pancha asks.

"I was twelve," I answer. "I don't know."

I tell Pancha about the address book, and how Mrs. Stevens found the letter she mailed to Mom a lifetime ago.

Catching a glimpse of the microwave clock, I realize I have to go. I promised Candide I'd come get the fullmooners around one o'clock so Dad could take a nap before the party. It's twelve forty-five. I begin to suggest to Pancha that we speak again soon, but she interrupts.

"I'm coming," she says abruptly.

"Excuse me?"

"This weekend," she says. "I've already got my ticket."

CHAPTER 9

I ask Lauren if she will come over and get the potatoes started while I fetch the professors. My voice is steady, but my heart is racing.

"You sound out of breath."

I tell her about the phone call, about Pancha announcing that she is coming to see Dad and how that sounded like a fine idea, until I put the telephone down.

"You don't want her to come?"

"She sounded like my mother."

"That's why you don't want her to come?"

"No. I mean, her accent sounded just like my mother's." I say this knowing there is no way to explain the hold Pancha's voice had on me, how I closed my eyes to let its melody flow down to my feet. How the uphill climb of her questions and the pitch of her replies transported me right back into Mom's arms. When she spoke, I saw myself sitting, curled up like a cat, next to my mother on the sofa with my head in her lap, drifting in and out of sleep while she combed my hair. Each word Pancha said sharpened the memory of Mom's palm gliding over my forehead, my temples and the tips of my ears, and the sensation seemed so real that I imagined if I lifted my hand I might actually be able to touch her again. I got so lost in the voice that a good deal of what Pancha said disappeared into the haze.

"It didn't really hit me until after she hung up," I say.

"You stay there. I'll go get the fullmooners."

I think of the professors and how long they've been a part of my life. Randy and Carla Stevens stood in my living room the night I went to the senior prom, snapping pictures alongside Dad. On my wedding day, the men and their wives sat in the pew reserved for family, and each professor took his turn giving Aaron fatherly advice. If they knew anything about Pancha, they would have told me by now. Wouldn't they?

I look at the calendar tacked to the kitchen wall. The black-and-white photograph above the dates is an Ansel Adams landscape of the Grand Canyon, an abstract portrait of soft light and bottomless evening shadows. I mark a P in the box for this Friday, and before snapping the cap back onto the pen I draw a fat exclamation point that fills the square.

Meeting Pancha will be good, I tell myself. It's what Mom wanted and, I think, what Dad wants as well. She will be able to tell me what Mom's letter was all about and maybe even explain what kept the family split for so long.

When I walk inside the art room at the Rose Tree, a small galaxy of cardboard moons and glittery gold stars is dangling from the ceiling. I smile at Candide.

"I didn't put them up. He did." She juts her chin toward Juno as he steps through the doorway with string and tape and scissors in his hands.

"You did this?"

He sets the tools in the middle of a counter that runs the entire length of the back wall. "They're half-moons," he answers with a shrug, "but you catch the drift."

"They look terrific," I say, offering him an appreciative kiss.

In the art room there are four well-worn wooden tables that are big enough to accommodate eight. Paintbrushes sprout out of dented Folgers and Maxwell House coffee cans that sit in the center of each tabletop. And next to the cans are square baking pans filled with a jumble of colored pencils, crayons and felt-tip markers. At least two dozen pairs of scissors have been stored on individual cup hooks underneath a long wall of cabinets, which are also stocked with supplies. About forty pinch pots and painted pieces of ceramics perch on a wide wire shelf rack next to a kiln that looks like a silver spaceship. And the room's cinder-block walls are decorated with smudged pencil drawings and cheerful mosaics of roosters made from dried beans and lentils.

The sweet warm smells of the fresh bread, the creamed potatoes and the baked ham slowly begin to mingle with the starchy scent of dried paste and construction paper as Juno brings the food in from my car.

"This one's ours," Candide says, pointing to the table farthest from the door.

I unfurl the cloth that I brought from home, but it isn't long enough to cover the surface.

"Wait." Candide steps to the far end of the counter, where a roll of white butcher paper hangs from a sturdy metal brace. "It's not Martha Stewart," she quips, "but it works for us."

Together we wrap a long strip over the tabletop, neatly folding and taping the edges under each of the four corners to make the edges smooth. I drape the tablecloth in a diagonal and set the candlesticks on top of it.

"Fancy," Juno comments from the doorway, carrying my portable CD player and the disks I selected.

Candide checks her watch.

"Lauren said she'd have them here by eight."

"Good," Candide answers. "I'll go get your dad ready."

Juno turns the lights out when she leaves and, although a fluorescent glare from the corridor seeps underneath the door, the room is dim. The cardboard moons begin to glow a muted yellow green, and when I light the candles, the stars over our heads sparkle. He slides the cork out of a bottle of wine and hands me a long-stemmed glass of white.

"I don't think I should."

"Just one," he says, "before everybody else gets here."

"I wish you'd known Dad before," I say, taking the Chablis and leaning against the counter next to him. "Back when the fullmooners were at their best."

Juno is shuffling through the stack of CDs as I speak. When he finds one he likes, he slips it into the player. The music begins and, after a soft, seductive introduction, Edith Piaf's throaty French fills the room. Juno clinks his wineglass against mine.

"From what I see," he says, "this evening could rank right up there."

When Lauren arrives with the professors, it's clear Randy isn't the only one enchanted by my best friend. Ted Lansky, dressed completely in black, swings open the art room door for her, and it occurs to me that the three of them have probably been scrambling to beat one another to every latch and knob and door handle they've happened across during their short trip from the hotel to the nursing home. Lauren, of course, is loving it.

The decorations catch their eyes immediately. Dr. Carver, who is carrying Lauren's three Nikons as well as her lumpy equipment bag over his shoulders, takes a moment to allow his eyes to adjust to the soft light. Dr. Lansky, his red tote bag in hand, looks up, twirls, and smiles. Randy, carrying a small box in his hands, plants a peck on my cheek to say hello and then heads directly to the table, where he lays five fat cigars across the plates he has assumed belong to the men.

"Hey, what about the girls?" Lauren teases, picking up one of the expensive imports and rolling it between her fingertips. I glance over at Juno, who has already begun pouring wine for the fullmooners, and draw his attention to Lauren with my eyes. She is flirting, actually flirting, with my father's retired friends. I take another sip of wine and tell myself it's nothing. This is how Lauren is with men, why they adore her. It's a generous gesture, really. She could be out on a real date instead of spending her night with us.

"You can't smoke those here," I say more harshly than I mean to.

"I know," Randy replies. "I thought we'd just hold them, for old times' sake. Here," he says, taking one more cigar out of the box and handing it to Lauren with a dramatic bow. She accepts it with a coy smile and steps to my side.

"They're adorable," she whispers. "I see why you love them."

I open a second bottle of wine and, behind me, I hear Juno introducing himself to someone, saying, ". . . yes, like the city in Alaska."

Nobody wants to sit at the table before Dad arrives, so we all stand beside it, sipping wine and making small talk for what seems like a long while. I begin to worry that maybe something has gone wrong, that any moment now Candide will summon me into the hallway to say Dad isn't up to this and we need to call the whole thing off. Nervously, I step into the center of the circle, holding a tray filled with marinated olives, feta cheese and slices of olive bread. They're not the sort of appetizers you expect to eat standing up, but everyone makes a polite effort to help themselves.

Finally, Candide opens the door.

"Ladies and gentlemen," she announces in her rich island clip, "the guest of honor."

Candide rolls Dad into the room. He is dressed in a dark suit, a starched white shirt and a silk paisley tie, the one set of good clothes that has been hanging in his closet since he moved here. In the background, Edith Piaf insists, *"Je ne regrette rien,"* and, as I watch my father approach, I wonder how anyone who has lived life can honestly say they have no regrets.

Juno pulls a wooden chair aside to make a space for Dad next to me, and Candide uses her foot to set the wheelchair's brakes. While the fullmooners and the others take their seats, I set the side dishes on the table. We invite Candide to join us, pointing her to one of the two place settings not yet taken. But she holds up her hand and says, "I'm supposed to be working." She agrees to stop in every now and then, and maybe sit down for dessert. Before heading back to the nurses' station, she stops at my side and slips a plastic plate with a raised back rim in front of me. She also hands me a fork and a spoon with fat rubber handles and hand straps. As I take them, I nod.

Suddenly the menu I picked because it would be easy for me to prepare seems all wrong for Dad. The ham, the asparagus, the glazed onions, they all need to be cut into pieces he can scoop up and swallow easily, and I don't want to humiliate him by dicing his food in front of everyone. Candide pats me on the back and says, "Fix his plate over here." I cut a slice of ham off the bone before Candide delivers the rest of it to the table. With Lauren's help, she brings the side dishes back to the counter so I can place portions onto Dad's plate and render them fork-ready. By the time we get back to our seats, the other men have served themselves and are waiting to begin. I slide Dad's plate in front of him and Dr. Carver stands to propose a toast.

"It may be a long road, Diego, but we're here to help you walk it."

"That's right," Randy says, and Dr. Lansky nods.

Dr. Carver sits back down and everyone takes a sip, including Dad, who leans down to reach the straw sticking out of his special water glass.

Lauren grabs one of her cameras and starts clicking away, and then Juno stands.

"Nita has told me about your dinner debates, and I'm honored to have been invited," he says to the group. "She's warned me that you can get pretty rough. But I come from a big Cuban family, so you are going to have to just about carry someone out on a stretcher before it seems like anything more than regular dinner conversation to me."

The professors answer with a hearty laugh, and then, as if nothing had ever changed, they begin.

First they gripe about the terrible way standards have slipped at the university since they've retired. Ten minutes later they've moved on to whether the scruffy young people they've seen on television smashing windows and marching in protest of globalization have any idea what they're fighting against. Dr. Lansky insists they do. He says the kids have credible points and, to the accompaniment of loud and playful groans, he supports his argument with a string of statistics meant to show how corporate takeovers and international mergers have battered free commerce all over the world. Juno, immediately captured by the spirit of the game, jumps in to say that while Ted's numbers may be true, the young demonstrators he's interviewed seem more interested in sailing bricks through sheets of plate glass at Starbucks than restructuring the world market.

The exchange is fast and heated, and for an instant I worry that Dad won't be able to keep up. But I watch his expression as the fullmooners' words swirl around him. Their voices are medicine, unlocking the tension in his neck, relaxing the muscles around his left eye. Instead of straining to understand each volley of the give-and-take, he lets its rhythm wash over him and joyfully savors the sound. What was I thinking when I told Mrs. Stevens to put his house up for sale? How selfish was it of me to believe it would be better for him to live in Philadelphia? It's more convenient for me, that's all. What I should have done is move back to Dallas. Never mind my counseling practice—it's not exactly flourishing. Never mind this thing with Juno, whatever it is trying to be. I'll go back. After Pancha's visit, I'll talk to the doctors about transferring Dad. And after dinner, I'll call Mrs. Stevens and tell her to fire the real estate agent.

As the night moves on, the table conversation bounces from politics to books to a tirade against bias in the press, which, of course, puts both Juno and Lauren on the defensive. Sometimes Dad nods his head like he understands, and other times his concentration falters. There's no way of telling how much he is taking in, but it doesn't matter. The sheer energy of the fullmooners has invigorated him.

With perfect timing, Candide returns just as Lauren and I begin to serve dessert. She takes the seat next to mine and, after two sips of coffee and half a piece of cake, she tells us it's time to start wrapping things up.

Dr. Carver reaches into his red canvas bag and pulls out what looks like a scrapbook. "We made this for you, Diego," he says, passing the leather-bound album to the head of the table.

I move closer to my father's side and slide his plate out of the way to make room. He lifts the book's cover with his good hand and finds a black-and-white picture of himself that must have been taken when he first arrived at the university. His sideburns are long and his wavy black hair skims the top of his shirt collar. He is in a double-breasted jacket and a neatly knotted tie. He dressed that way all the years that he worked at the university, long after the official dress code was abandoned and the younger professors began standing before their classes in the same blue jeans and sweaters their students wore. He had never been the sort of teacher who pretended to be his students' peer. He believed there was supposed to be a difference in their stations, and his wardrobe was one of the symbols of that divide.

On the next page, Dad finds a letter from the university president printed on a sheet of orchid-white stationery adorned with a gold-foiled stamp of the school seal. Following that are snapshots of the campus, with the name of each building printed in block letters beneath its image. And then, in the middle of the book, there are messages from former students. Dozens of them, typewritten so they'll be easier for Dad to read.

It is late and, even at his best, Dad wouldn't be able to make out the words. So I read a few of the comments aloud.

People say college is where you learn how to learn. But, Dr. D, it's you who taught me how to think. Get better soon, Greg Mission.

I can count the professors who made a difference on one hand, and your name takes up four fingers. Dianne O'Donnell.

I'm a high school teacher now, trudging through Cervantes and Márquez with seventeen-year-olds. Thanks to you, I can sometimes even get them to follow. Mike Eldred.

Lauren points her lens at my father's face as he runs the palm of his left hand over the notes in front of him.

"One hundred and fifty-seven," Randy informs us proudly.

Dad looks at him for a long, tender moment and then dips his eyes when his chin begins to quiver.

"I'll read every single one of them to you, Dad."

"No," my father answers in a surprisingly deliberate voice. "I wwwill."

By now our coffee cups are empty and we toss our napkins on the table and rise to say good night. I follow as Candide directs Dad back to his bedroom, where she ducks so he can wrap his arm over her broad shoulders and then swoops him into his bed with a smooth, practiced pivot.

"Nee?" Dad murmurs as I start to take off his shoes.

"It was nice, wasn't it, Dad?"

He nods and leans back on the two stiff pillows behind his head.

I want to tell him how sorry I am that I made him move here. How I'd acted out of panic and fear. I wanted him close to me after the stroke because the telephone call I got from Mrs. Stevens shook me to the core. I needed to be in control. I needed to see him get better in front of me. But by the time I pull off his second sock he is asleep. Silently Candide lifts her finger to her lips to let me know she'll do the rest.

Back in the art room, Lauren, Juno and the professors have already cleared the table and stacked the dishes next to the deep stainless steel sink. Randy and Ted Lansky have opened the cabinets in search of dish soap and Dr. Carver is wrapping the leftover ham using the same piece of aluminum foil that it arrived in.

"We'll take care of this," Randy says over his shoulder as he peels off his navy blue golf sweater and removes his gold wristwatch.

"Want to help bring down the Milky Way?" Lauren asks as she and Juno step onto the seats of two chairs and reach up. Soon the sounds of the running water, the professors talking and our chairs sliding across the floor drown out Tony Bennett's greatest hits. It doesn't take long for Lauren to abandon her post so she can take more pictures, and when Juno and I both have our arms full of moons and stars we meet at the wastepaper basket next to the sink, where I finally tell him that Pancha called.

"What did she say?"

All three professors stop washing and drying when I mention Pancha, and Lauren gets a good shot of them holding a sudsy wineglass, a carving knife and a pink-checkered dish towel.

"She's coming to see Dad," I say. "This weekend." The professors shut off the faucet, wipe their hands dry and exchange furtive glances that make me think they have something to say. But they stay quiet.

"Where does she live?" Juno asks. "What does she do? Has she been looking for you too?"

If she mentioned her address I didn't hear it, I tell him. If she described her work, I've already forgotten. I explain how Pancha didn't know Mom had died, and from the corner of my eye I see the professors looking at one another again.

"What?" I blurt out. "What do you know?"

All three of them avert their eyes, fiddling with the dish towels or rewrapping the leftovers instead of answering.

"Listen, I hate to break up a good party, but it's time for you people to go home!" We all turn to see Candide in the doorway, playfully crossing her arms and tapping her foot.

"Yes, ma'am," Dr. Carver chimes, plunging his wrist into the soapy water to pull the plug. Juno and Lauren begin taking the boxes back to my car, and the fullmooners hurriedly follow them out to the parking lot. I thank Candide for allowing us to have the supper, and she suggests giving Dad a break from any visitors tomorrow.

By the time I get to the parking lot, Juno and Lauren have reached their cars and are waving good-bye. The professors have already climbed inside my sedan. Our doors shut like a chain reaction, and when we back out of our parking spots the only light strong enough to cut through the night fog comes from our headlights.

I tell the fullmooners that Dad can't have visitors tomorrow and suggest that they might want to come to my house for brunch before they head back to the airport. I give them a few moments, hoping they will start talking about Pancha again, but none of them takes the initiative.

"That was very nice," Ted Lansky says from the backseat.

"Mmm," the other two murmur. "Nice."

My shoulders tighten.

"Are you going to tell me or not?" My question hangs in the air as the car tires rustle over the damp asphalt, threatening to drift off course if my attention slips. Dr. Carver, who is in the passenger seat, clears his throat.

"We do know a little about Pancha," he finally says.

"Not a whole lot," Randy rushes to add.

I feel my jaw clench, and the grip I have on the steering wheel tightens. The hotel appears on our left, and I pull into the circular drive and leave the car idling steps from the front door. I hear the professors' seat belts unlatch and, as quick as a reflex, I push the electronic button to lock them in.

"Tell me."

"This is the sort of thing Diego would have told you himself, when the time was right," Randy begins, pressing his back into the seat and focusing his eyes out the side window. "But when Carla told me you couldn't get him to remember . . ."

"Mrs. Stevens knows, too?" There is a shrill edge to my voice I cannot control, a tone of strained composure.

"No," Randy says, shaking his head. "Believe me, she was as surprised to find that letter as anyone."

"Listen." Dr. Carver sighs. "This is neither the time nor the place." I press my hand against the dashboard.

"Nita," Randy says, "one of the reasons we came here was to tell you, but it's a complicated story and you need to understand the context of the—"

"Look," I snap, "I don't care about the goddamned context. Just tell me what you came here to say." I turn off the engine and cup the car keys in my hand.

"Pancha fought for the right wing," Randy says just above a whisper. "In the attempted revolution."

I'm hearing his words, but I have no idea what he is talking about, and the expression on my face lets him know it.

"Your dad was connected to the government," he continues, "that was overthrown in the coup."

"What government? What coup?" I look at Randy like he's lost his mind. Dad has never been anything but a literature professor, that I happen to know for sure.

"It's too late to get into this now," Ted Lansky protests.

"Why don't we leave the rest of it for the morning?" Randy pleads. "When we can explain it to you properly."

I look into the other fullmooners' eyes to gauge whether Randy is talking nonsense. But their expressions are somber.

"All right," I say, too tired to try to make sense of what I've just heard. "I'll pick you up at ten."

CHAPTER *10*

~~~~~~

*W*hen I get home, I see Juno's car parked at the curb.

"This is becoming a bad habit," I say playfully when he meets me at the front door.

"You took so long, I was about to leave."

I slide my key into the lock and tell him the crazy thing the full-mooners said about Pancha and Dad.

"Well, there *was* a revolution in Guatemala," Juno says as we step inside. "In the fifties, you know."

I'm sure the professors' historical facts are right, but they must have somehow misconnected the dots. If there was a revolution, what would my father have to do with it? I explain that the fullmooners have promised to tell me what they know about Pancha at brunch tomorrow.

"Why don't you come and hear for yourself?" I step into the foyer, but Juno doesn't follow.

"I loved what you did for your father tonight," he says, leaning against the door frame with his hands in his coat pockets.

"Me? You're the one who made the room look so nice." I extend my arm and invite him in.

"I'd better not." He glances at the floor. "I'll want to stay." He lifts his eyes to see my response, and I answer with a subtle smile.

What should I tell him? Technically, this is our third date, if you count our visit to the Rose Tree. Inviting him to stay is acceptable after three dates, isn't it? Who cares if it's appropriate or not? There is something special about this man and I want him with me tonight.

"I just wanted to tell you that I think your father is a marvelous man, and you . . ." he says, stepping into the house, "you are an unforgettable woman." He closes the door and a gust of cold air swirls around us. He leans toward me, and when I feel the smooth leather of his glove against my cheek, I close my eyes. His lips are warm and certain as they glide from my mouth to my neck to the rise of my chest. I stroke his thick hair and pull him closer.

"How about taking this off?" I suggest, tugging at the shoulders of his bulky coat. His hands fly over the buttons and, with one quick shrug, the heavy shearling tumbles to his feet.

"This way," I say, removing his gloves and kissing his fingers as we walk down the hall.

At the foot of the bed, he pulls off his sweater and shirt and slowly lifts my top over my head. With one of his fingers, he slips the straps of my bra from my shoulders and kisses the marks they've left behind. I undo the hooks and Juno stops to watch as the lace falls away. I remove his glasses and set them on the nightstand and, when he slips his hand under my skirt, I feel my heart pound. We lower ourselves onto the bed and finish undressing one another.

"*Eres tan hermosa,*" he whispers in my ear, pressing his skin against mine.

Sometime before dawn, Juno says he should go.

"Mmm," I answer, running the tip of my finger along the stubble on his cheek.

As we made love, he spoke to me in Spanish, whispering words that sounded beautiful in the dark.

In the morning light, I look around the bedroom. When Aaron lived here, it looked like a hunter's lodge. There wasn't a ruffle or flower in sight. The dressers were stained a deep walnut, and the comforter and pillows on the double bed were dark shades of brown and green. I decorated it that way because I believed that if a man liked where he slept, he'd grow happily rooted to that bed.

It was the first room I redecorated after the divorce.

With Lauren's help, I stripped the brown off the dressers and painted them a clean, uncompromising white. I replaced the burnished brass drawer pulls with antique cut-glass knobs that glimmer in the morning light. I bought a queen-size mattress, covered it with expensive sheets and gave the comforter a new life inside an ultrafeminine cover made out of floral fabric. Now the decor hovers somewhere between French country chic and a Vermont bed-and-breakfast. I like it and, at the moment, Juno doesn't seem to mind.

He brushes my hair off the back of my neck. "You are a classic Latina beauty."

"I am?"

"You don't see it?"

"No," I say, kissing his chin. "I don't think of myself as very Hispanic."

"What do you mean you're not Hispanic?" He looks at me straight on. "Juanita is not exactly a British name."

Last night I loved hearing Juno speak Spanish as his passion built. I swam in the seductive sound of my own name when his body peaked. But that was a private pleasure. A moment in time. I've never been called Juanita in the real world, and I don't intend to start now.

"It's Nita," I say, nestling myself back into his chest. "Everywhere except here."

Juno rolls on his back, his eyes pointed toward the ceiling. I don't know what he's thinking, and I don't want to ask. Please don't let him be one of those minorities who waves his cultural credentials around like a battle flag. I had enough of those types in college, always pestering me to join the Latino association of this and the Latin American council of that. I never understood their rush to join groups that separated them from the mainstream, when they'd be the first to cry discrimination if other people did the separating for them. I rest my head on top of Juno's chest and let that thought fade. The only thing I want to focus on right now is the sound of him breathing in tandem with me. I close my eyes again, and when I awake I see him dressing.

"Should I make eggs or French toast?" I watch his shoulder blades chisel the plane of his broad back.

"Shhh," he says as he buttons his shirt. "I'll come back and help you with brunch."

"What time is it?"

"Early. Go back to sleep."

I move my legs to the spot of warmth he's left behind.

"Milk," I say before he steps out the bedroom door.

"Hmm?"

"We could use some milk. If you want French toast."

After Juno has gone, I drag his pillow over my head and greedily inhale his scent.

Three hours later, the fullmooners have spread a tricolored map of Guatemala between the coffeepot and a leaf-shaped bottle of Vermont maple syrup. They've come prepared, with a small mountain of books that have pages already earmarked with colored paper clips. At the airport I'd wondered why they were carrying briefcases. Now, I realize, they've been anticipating this moment since they packed for the trip.

"First," Randy begins, "you need to remember that this happened during the height of the Cold War."

I look at the map as if I'm eager to become absorbed in the story, but underneath the table I am running my bare foot along Juno's shin. It's been two years since I've been made love to and I am enjoying feeling as light as a bubble. All I want the fullmooners to tell me is what they know about Pancha and how long they've known it.

"Are you familiar with the United Fruit Company?"

Juno shifts in his chair and pensively nods to let me know that he thinks I should at least try to pay attention. Reluctantly I slide my shoe back onto my foot and answer Randy with a soft "No." I've already lost patience with the conversation.

On the table, Randy has set up a small spiral-bound notebook so it stands like a pup tent. He flips to the first page and I see UNITED FRUIT COMPANY written in black. This is Dr. Carver's cue, and he rises from his chair ready to speak. Oh, for God's sake, I think to myself, they have an entire song and dance ready. Why didn't Mrs. Stevens tell me?

"What the hell does this have to do with Pancha?" I huff. "Just tell me what Dad told you."

Calmly, Dr. Carver continues. "The United Fruit Company made its fortune selling bananas. . . ." The pitch of his voice is a full step lower than normal. It's his lecturing tone. Just as I am about to lash out, Juno reaches under the table and takes my hand in a firm grip, silently imploring me to give the fullmooners a chance.

I exhale and try to listen, but Dr. Carver's delivery is dry and tortuously plodding.

". . . by this time the company had become the single largest landowner in Guatemala, as well as the owner of the only railroad line to the coast."

How, I thought to myself, can any of this arcane history be linked to me? I'll be the first to admit I don't know much about my father's childhood, but I do know that his mother worked as a teacher when he was a kid, and his father—who died of a heart attack before he was forty—had been the manager of a small radio station. What bananas and railroads and international commerce have to do with him is beyond understanding.

". . . The plantations were run in a paternal fashion, providing the workers with housing and medical care. But the overseers were quick to snuff out any attempts made by the workers to unionize or to improve their working conditions."

Juno clicks his tongue when Dr. Carver says this, and once again I tell myself to pay attention.

Over the next half hour, Dr. Carver, Ted Lansky and Randy Stevens lay out a historical path that leads Guatemala from one corrupt dictator to another, and they make it abundantly clear that the United Fruit Company routinely lined pockets to make sure laws and tax breaks went the company's way.

"We've got forty-five minutes before we have to leave for the airport," I say impatiently. "So, how about getting to the point?"

"Let's skip to Arbenz," Randy advises, sifting through the pages of his spiral notebook until he gets to one that reads: JACOBO ARBENZ, PRESIDENT 1950–1954.

"Ah," Juno says, raising his eyebrows.

"What?" I ask.

"I think what they're getting at is that Pancha and your dad were involved in the 1954 coup, the one that was backed by the CIA, and—"

"The CIA?" I aim a cold stare directly at Randy.

He rubs the bridge of his nose and glances down for a long moment before meeting my gaze.

"Arbenz was elected on the promise that he'd break the back of the United Fruit Company," he says. "He said he'd make the Americans pay their fair share of taxes, that he'd raise workers' salaries and stop allowing foreigners to get rich off the backs of Guatemalans." Randy's voice is harnessed, as if by controlling its volume he might also be able to control the impact its message might have. "Your father was one of Arbenz's most ardent supporters."

I'm not sure what reaction Randy sees on my face, but inside I feel a wave of bile rise to my chest. I have no idea what this information means, but something tells me it isn't good.

Randy explains that this particular president of Guatemala was loved by liberals and intellectuals like Dad. Inspired by Roosevelt's New Deal, Arbenz backed progressive new laws that focused on improving life for the lower classes instead of appeasing the rich.

Yes, I think, that sounds like something Dad would support. My stomach relaxes a bit. But, when I glance around the table, I see the professors peering cautiously at me, wondering how I'll react when the rest of the story unfolds.

"The problem was that when Arbenz decided to take on the United Fruit Company," Randy continues, "he, essentially, provoked the United States. He passed a land reform act that called for the Guatemalan government to take back a huge chunk of the company's land. He built a railroad so the company's rail line would not be the only way to transport goods to the coast, and he established electric companies so the fruit company would not have a monopoly on power."

Juno puffs air out of his cheeks. "He didn't just step on America's toes, he trampled on them, didn't he?"

Together, the fullmooners nod.

"I'm leaving out a lot," Randy says, "but after a couple of years the American government and the CIA decided they had to get rid of Arbenz. So they accused him of being a Communist."

Instantly, I think back to the day Dad became a citizen and the staring match he had with the man at the INS. *Are you a Communist?* That's what the officer had asked. And I can still see the outrage on Dad's face. Anybody who knows him knows Dad is the sort of Rotary Club citizen who never lets a Fourth of July or Memorial Day pass without hanging a flag over the front door. Both my parents were always left wing, but they were unabashedly patriotic.

Quickly subtracting decades in my head, I figure Pancha couldn't have been older than twenty at the time this coup in Guatemala was going on, and Dad would have been about twenty-two. They were too young to have played any significant role in the political shenanigans the professors are talking about. Coups. Communists. It's just ridiculous.

"The CIA built a case against Arbenz," Randy says, "claiming he was under the thumb of the Soviets, and even Chairman Mao. They invited journalists down to Guatemala to see how anti-American he was."

"Well, wait a minute," Juno responds. "Arbenz *was* anti-American, and he *did* have Communists in his government."

Ted Lansky rolls his eyes, as if Juno's statement is hopelessly naive.

"Read this," Ted says, pulling a thick paperback out of the stack and sliding it across the map.

"Look," Juno says, stiffening his back. "I'm not an expert, but you're painting this with awfully broad strokes. Nothing about this was so black and white—it was a huge tangle of grays."

"All right!" I interrupt. "Can we get back to the point? What does this have to do with Pancha?"

"Lots of families were torn apart during the coup," Dr. Carver says. "Some of Arbenz's supporters even turned against him, leaving the entire nation hopelessly divided."

I nod.

"Your father stood by Arbenz until the bitter end, and continued to fight for his ideals for many years afterward. But Pancha felt Arbenz had let Guatemala down, that he had been bought off by the Communists."

"So she stopped talking to Dad?"

"She left the family to join the right-wing forces that helped the CIA overthrow the Arbenz government, and then she continued to back the anti-Communist dictators after the coup. She fought against your father and everything he believed in."

"Wait a minute," I say, trying to sift the story through my mind. "You're telling me *Dad* supported Communists?"

Randy leans his elbows on the table. "It's not really clear just how much sway the Communists actually—"

"Hold on," I say again. "Just . . . hold . . . on."

The picture they've painted is impossible for me to believe. Mom and Dad loved being Americans. They reveled in anything that had to do with the red, white and blue. At Thanksgiving my parents would practically weep when they said grace, honestly moved by the idea that an entire nation reserved a day to count its blessings. I can even remember how proud they felt the day the astronauts walked on the moon. Dad bought a new television set for the occasion, and the three of us watched Neil Armstrong step onto the dusty lunar surface, cheering like crazy in front of the screen when he declared it a giant leap for mankind. And, on my eighteenth birthday, Dad not only gave me Mom's pearls as a present, but also an application to register to vote. If my mind weren't so jumbled I'd have a good laugh at the professors' theory, but I'm too angry to do anything but stand and turn my back.

"So what?" I finally say with a shrug. "They took different sides?

What could Pancha have done that was so bad when she was only a kid?"

Randy sighs. "We're not talking about peaceful protesters, Nita. Pancha joined up with honest-to-God guerrillas. People who kidnapped and tortured and assassinated hundreds of people. Your dad's friends, his colleagues, she turned them in. And, we're not certain, but we think she tried to turn your father in as well."

Could that be true? Could that be why Dad never talked about her? If it is, then why would Mom want to ever see her again? My head feels like it's full of cotton and I can't think clearly. Staring through the slit in the curtains, I see a narrow sliver of the street in front of my house, the bare old oak and the black mailbox standing sentry next to the curb. The afternoon clouds are heavy and low and it is impossible for me to tell where the horizon ends and the sky begins. Easter is around the corner but, from where I'm standing, there is absolutely no sign of spring.

CHAPTER 11

When the professors finish their presentation, I take them to the airport with every intention of coming straight home and telling Pancha to cancel her trip.

Juno stays behind to use the computer and find out more about Arbenz and the coup from the Internet. When I get home, I find him paging through the names and addresses inside my mother's address book. He takes out Pancha's letter and reads the words aloud: *A family this small can't afford a rift this wide.*

"You'll never know if you don't ask," he says, reading my thoughts.

I try to argue. "I can ask Pancha without having her come here."

"Sure," Juno replies. "But your mother wanted to settle things with her face-to-face. You have to decide if that's what you want, too."

"What about Dad?"

Without saying a word, Juno folds the letter and slides it back into the heart of the address book. He kisses me on the nose and holds me against his shoulder. *"Lágrimas y abrazos, mi amor,"* he says. "It's tears and embraces that make a family."

His words make me think about how hard Dad and I struggled to get through the worst that could have happened to us.

We weren't always comfortable together. After Mom died, it took Dad and me a while to learn how to be just two.

Neither of us knew how to run the house. Mom had always done the laundry, stocked the refrigerator and taken me to swim practice. She organized the details of our lives, made her pottery and, in between all that, worked part-time at the little craft gallery owned by Mrs. Stevens. Dad went to the university.

I was twelve that summer, and on the verge of entering the stage of life that is filled with blood and thunder. My poor father was completely unprepared. He thought women were supposed to take care of those things for one another. The same way they paid attention to which birthday party themes were spoken for and what color shirts their kids wore for last year's class photo. It was the women who were supposed to work out the telephone chains that would trip into action if, for some unexpected reason, school let out early or the car pool schedule changed because some mother had the flu.

I'm sure he had no idea it was that very chain that went to work the day Mom died.

I was away at swim camp when it happened. My friend Annette and I had just finished supper and were walking back to our rooms across the wide lawn near the diving pool. Damp towels and wet suits were draped over every balcony rail, bicycle rack and Adirondack chair in sight. Everything from our skin to our hair to the thick July heat carried the acidic smell of chlorine. Annette, a blue-ribbon backstroker from Waxahachie, was my assigned roommate and my newest best friend.

The counselors were all college students with topaz tans who went by crazy nicknames like Weasel or Queenie or Tick. The girl in charge of our floor was called China because she drank sun tea that she brewed in big jars on the front steps of Dexter Hall. That's where she was standing when she called out my name, on the very top concrete step of the dorm, holding a one-gallon jar of tea in her arms. The strong evening sun setting behind her was a blood orange–red and the thin clouds around it glowed purple and pink. The temperature had stalled somewhere in the high nineties, and the relentless humidity made even the night air feel stale. Annette and I were both slow eaters and were almost always the last two to get back to our room after our meals. When China beckoned again, we picked up our pace.

That night the high schoolers were playing their final water polo scrimmage and our dorm was going to watch. Annette and I both had a crush on a fourteen-year-old named Mike who mumbled hello to us the one and only time we dared to approach him, and the only thing on our minds was whether we'd have enough courage to speak to him again.

When we reached the steps, China handed the jar of tea to Annette and asked if she'd do her a favor and carry it inside. "Just set it on the reception desk, and then go straight to Sarah's room, okay?"

China's white T-shirt sparkled against her dark skin and some of her blond hair had turned a pale shade of green. Her blue denim shorts were cut to show off a good deal of her thighs and, like all the other counselors, she only wore shoes when absolutely necessary. Maybe that was why I sensed that something was wrong. There was a brand-new pair of Adidas on her feet.

"Something's happened," she said.

The first thing I thought was fire. My house had burned down and my parents were picking through the singed timbers with limp woolen blankets draped over their shoulders and gray flaky ashes smoldering under their feet. I thought how the posters on my bedroom walls—Mark Spitz with his chest full of gold medals, Elton John, and the sunny yellow happy face—must have fed the wild flames. I pictured my Carpenters and Stevie Wonder records oozing like lava all over the floor, and my strawberry- and watermelon-flavored lip gloss melting into puddles of pink goo on top of my dresser.

China took my hand and spoke to me like I was five.

"We're going to go to your room and wait for your father to get here, okay?"

I nodded and followed her into the lobby. A group of eight girls in the middle school group were huddled next to the wall of mailboxes, ripping into a care package mailed by some mom whose house was still standing.

When we got to my room, China sat herself on the edge of Annette's bed. It took me a minute to notice that someone had already packed my belongings. The dark blue duffel bag that I'd lugged up the front steps a week earlier was zipped and perched at the foot of my bed, and someone had filled my brass-buckled footlocker with all of my gear. Fins and goggles. Snorkel and kickboard. A big bottle of baby oil mixed with iodine that I kept inside an old plastic bread bag in case it spilled. I heard the Mickey Mouse alarm clock on Annette's side of the room tick every second away.

China got up and stepped into the hallway, looking, I suppose, to see if anyone was coming to help her.

I wasn't afraid, or worried, or fighting back tears. I wanted my father to hurry so I could get home and help Mom save whatever we could. My mind was floating in the thick smoke that I imagined had hovered over the roof of our house.

Then I heard China arguing with Annette in a loud whisper.

"I don't think it's a good idea," China said.

"Just for a minute?"

"Her father's on his way."

"What happened?"

"I can't say."

"Please? I swear I won't tell."

China stepped back into the room and closed the door. I could tell by the look on her face that she had no idea what she was supposed to say. So she said nothing, and that's when I started to tremble. Through the rusty window screen I could hear the rest of the elementary school campers assembling on the front steps, getting themselves ready to go as a group to the polo match. I heard a girl's high-pitched scream and it sounded as if someone had hurt her, not like she was just playing a game.

Somebody knocked on the door and I flinched.

"Can we be alone?" Dad asked the instant he stepped in.

When I saw the shock on my father's pale face, the fierce, unguarded panic in his eyes, I knew it wasn't a fire. It was something so awful that he was falling apart right in front of me.

"There was an accident," he whispered as he dropped to his knees and took my hands in his. "At the shop."

Dad's lips quivered and he pushed my long hair away from my forehead with an unsteady finger before he went on.

"Mom is dead."

I heard somebody scream, over and over. I collapsed onto the floor and began punching and kicking the side of my footlocker before I realized it was me. The pain that swept over me was so intense it turned into an emotion all its own, deeper than grief, darker than fright.

When I finally climbed into Dad's car that night, I slid into the front seat instead of the back, and I would never be able to do that again without missing her.

Our house felt more than empty—it felt foreign. The light from the windows hit the furniture at a different angle. The air-conditioning was too loud. Everything, from the coffee table, to the silverware, to the linen guest towels hanging in the front hall's powder room, seemed like scenery for a play missing its main character.

After the funeral, Mrs. Stevens told me I could call her Carla if I wanted, and that she'd like it if I would consider her a friend instead of just another adult. No grown-up had ever spoken to me like that before, and I was too young and too emotionally withdrawn to graciously accept the promotion. What I ended up saying was if it was all the same to her, I'd rather keep calling her Mrs. Stevens because what I needed wasn't another friend but a woman I could count on.

She closed the craft gallery for good, and from that day until I left for college she came over once a week to help Dad and me clean. She had to show us how to do the simplest things. How to replace the vacuum cleaner bag. How to add softener during the rinse cycle. How to sew on shirt buttons. She taught Dad how to braid my hair, and instructed me on how to use dabs of vinegar to erase spots from Dad's ties. Eventually we learned to manage. But every morning and every night we'd run across something that underscored Mom's absence. Vitamin tablets, a misplaced paintbrush, a wayward pen. I knew how much had been taken from me, but I was too young to understand how deep the wound could go.

We spent years figuring out how to take care of ourselves and one another. For so long after Mom's death we measured our moves by what we thought she would have done. Until, finally, we felt comfortable enough with our own judgment to stop questioning. Now I'm right back where I started, wondering what my mother would say.

I repeat the fullmooners' report to Lauren as we stride into the convention center, where she's been sent to take pictures of crews setting up the Philadelphia Flower Show. It is the nation's biggest garden display, and the newspaper always runs stories about the lengths to which the participants go to transform the cavernous meeting hall into an urban Eden.

Lauren flashes her press pass and we sail past the security guards. I follow as she speed-walks down the long, red-carpeted walkway that leads to the main exhibit hall. Before we get to the door, before we see the towering mountains of mulch or hear the growling engines of dozens of mini earthmovers and forklifts, we can smell the strong perfume of the tens of thousands of magnolias, roses, lilies and other, more exotic blossoms that have been trucked in at their floral peak.

Inside, stern-faced workers in overalls, dusty blue jeans and wet, grimy gloves buzz around us as they check and double-check the blueprints of the ponds, pebble paths, grottoes, gazebos and estate gardens they are creating.

This year the theme of the show is "Once Upon a Time," and the landscapers have gone all out. In a raised flower bed that will greet visitors the moment they arrive, three women are on their knees painstakingly placing individual chrysanthemum heads into a huge bed of moss. The flowers will become the crisp pages of an open book proclaiming the theme of the show in letters made out of twisted grapevines stretching a full six feet in height. The outer skirt of the storybook is already complete. It shows a ten-foot-long fire-breathing dragon with a scaly body made out of the iridescent green leaves of a plant I can't begin to identify, and mean-looking claws made out of thorny cacti. The flames shooting out of its mouth are a swirling inferno of bird-of-paradise stalks and other red and yellow feathery plants. The beast is attempting to scorch the book while, on the other side, a knight wearing a suit of armor made out of birch tree bark is coming to the rescue. It is an amazing sight, and by the time I take it in, Lauren has already shot a dozen frames.

"This shouldn't take long," Lauren says as she kneels to achieve a better angle.

"If it's true," I say to Lauren, "I don't blame Dad for not wanting to see her, and I don't want to be the one to bring her back into his life."

Lauren fishes another roll of film out of her bulky brown camera bag and scans the incredible scene before us. "So you're just going to ignore your mom's note?"

"I don't know." I sigh.

Lauren snaps a few more shots and then swings her camera over her shoulder, satisfied that she's seen enough.

"Let's get an early dinner," she suggests.

We walk to a place in Chinatown that serves dim sum twenty-four hours a day. I don't get downtown much anymore, and I am taken by how many people are rushing around in overcoats and dark suits with their minds on where they are headed or where they've just come from. Back when I worked at an ad agency, Aaron and I used to meet at a falafel truck for lunch. We would take our hummus sandwiches to a bench in a park next to one of the expensive hotels and throw the rims of our pitas to the pigeons.

"She's not just coming to see your dad," Lauren continues after we've ordered tea. "She's coming to set things straight with you."

"I suppose."

"If I were you, I'd e-mail her and say you'll decide if she can see your father after she gets here."

The first dim sum cart stops at our table.

"Shrimp toast. Sticky rice. Steamed vegetable dumplings," the waiter says as he lifts the lids off an array of bamboo containers.

"Yes, yes and yes," Lauren answers.

Using wooden tongs, the young man sets three dishes on our table and then takes the paper ticket the hostess left next to my plate and marks our selections. As he begins to push his cart away, Lauren taps him on the elbow.

"Any barbecued pork buns?"

He points to a waitress pushing a cart on the other side of the room.

I tell Lauren that I've started reading the book about Guatemala the professors left behind, and all it is doing is confusing me more. "I can't tell who the good guys are and who the bad guys are. Except for the CIA, they're always bad."

"That's why you need to meet her," Lauren says, pointing her chopsticks at me. "To get things cleared up."

I know she's right.

"You've got, what? Two days before she arrives? I'd start getting your dad ready. Maybe take the book in for him to see. Something."

The lady with the barbecued pork buns arrives and we take two.

"Of course, Juno's all into it," I say. "He's been searching the Web like he's investigating Watergate."

Lauren raises her eyebrows. "How's it going with him?"

I can't help but smile.

"You two were pretty cozy at the Rose Tree."

"Yeah," I say. "He's amazing, but I don't know if it's the right thing. He's so into his family, and I'm thinking about taking Dad back to Dallas—"

"Nita," Lauren interrupts, "just let it be what it's going to be."

I dunk a dumpling into the puddle of soy sauce in the middle of my plate and decide not to tell her that I'm also scared Juno will call it quits when he finds out I can't have children.

Another waitress with a cart pulls up to our table, but before she can tell us what she has to offer Lauren's cell phone begins to trill. I smile to let the server know she can move on. Lauren mumbles something into her phone and glances at her wristwatch.

"Ten minutes," she says.

Setting her unfolded napkin beside her plate, Lauren takes a piece of shrimp toast, wraps it up and sticks it into her coat pocket. She finds a ten-dollar bill in her camera bag and places it on the table. "Some sort of protest at City Hall," she tells me. "I've got to go."

Lauren rushes out the door and I'm left sitting alone in front of enough food for two. I love her, but this is why she's never been able to find the right person. Her job is her true love. She and Aaron are the same in that way: they like living large lives. That's why it didn't work with Aaron and me. I'm happy with a small life, quiet and uneventful. I pay the check and, on my way to my car, I can't help but wonder how the hell I ended up dating another reporter.

Joy Taggert tells me she's going away, to visit her best friend in Washington, D.C., a woman she traveled to Europe with when they were both in college.

"She never got married and I used to feel sorry for her," Joy says, the sting of resentment still fresh in her voice.

Frank has moved out, but he keeps coming back unannounced to collect one thing or another.

"Yesterday it was the fish poacher," Joy says. "Did he expect me to believe he was going to use it? He's never done a damn thing in the kitchen, except scramble eggs. It was for *her*. Can you believe that? Can you believe he would walk in and get it out of my kitchen for her!"

I've never seen Joy the way she looks this evening.

Without pencil liner or powder on her face, she looks beyond fatigued; she looks completely drained. Her fingernails, which have always been tastefully manicured, are unfiled and nude. She's wearing a brown, straight-falling corduroy jumper over a black turtleneck with charcoal-colored tights and ankle-high boots. The clothes look expensive, but they don't accentuate the figure I know she works hard to maintain. It is an outfit picked for protection, a dull cocoon.

She tells me more about the gut-wrenching week she has had, and as she speaks I begin to wonder what I am doing in this profession. Who am I to give her advice? A year ago I was cowering in the same cocoon.

I wrapped the final classes I needed to get my degree around myself tight, shutting out the world until I was ready to crawl out. And am I a better person now? No, just one who can point to my scars and tell her the tender skin will eventually harden.

"Frank needs to make a list of the things he wants to get and then he needs to make an appointment and collect those things on that one day. After that, Joy, you have to change the locks."

"My lawyer says he'll work it out so I won't have to go back to work," Joy says. "I haven't worked since the kids were born."

"How old are they again?"

"Ned is twenty-three and Caroline is twenty-five."

"How are they dealing with this?"

Joy manages a thin smile, but her voice stumbles when she answers. "Ned said Frank will come back. That I should just wait and he'll come back."

"And Caroline?"

Joy looks at me. "She's the one who suggested I visit Jean."

"Well, I think it's a great idea."

"She's an events planner for a company that builds shopping malls. Can you imagine that?"

"Hmm."

"She's going to take me to the spring trunk show at the Prada store in Atlanta."

"That should be fun."

Joy nods as if she agrees, but the expression on her face is asking *Will it?*

"It's been thirty-five years," she says. "Thirty-five years since Jean and I took that trip to Italy."

"What worries you most?"

"Maybe our lives are too different now. Maybe we've both changed so much we won't know how to act around one another."

"Are *you* that different?"

Joy looks down at her hands. She is still wearing her wedding ring. "I honestly don't know."

"I think you're going to find out that you're not. If Jean is the sort of friend I sense she is, you're going to feel like you're twenty again."

"I was the crazy one," Joy says. "Can you believe that? I was the one who had no fear."

"I believe it."

"That was what Frank said he loved about me."

For a moment we say nothing.

"Joy, see that pillow?" I ask, pointing to the needlepoint resting next to her arm. "I want you to have it."

She lifts the Bon Voyage pillow and looks at the suitcases stitched on its front like she's never seen them before.

"It's for you."

"It is?"

"Yes, it's been there all the time."

Joy smiles and starts to cry.

I set my hand on her forearm.

"I'll never forgive him," she sobs.

"Some things," I say, "can't ever be made right. All you can do is let time pass."

CHAPTER 12

"*I* know you understand what I'm saying." I roll Dad's chair to the picture window at the far end of the card room.

From this spot we can see the Rose Tree's garden, which has been forced to look outlandishly Victorian, with a white gazebo planted in the center of the lawn and a kidney-bean-shaped pond spanned by an arched wooden bridge that nobody with a walking cane would dare to cross. In the summer, I've been told, a family of wild geese walks the grounds freely, but they have not yet returned for the season.

Once again, I try to bring up the subject of Pancha.

"Is it that you don't remember, or that you just don't want to talk about it?"

Dad stares out the window and then casts his eyes toward the big-screen television at the other end of the room. Three women wearing sweatshirts and stretch pants have turned it on so they can watch a soap opera. It is early in the afternoon, when Dad usually is napping, but because it's Thursday and I have a session with Patrick and his parents in a couple of hours, I want to try to tell him again that Pancha is arriving tomorrow.

"The fullmooners told me about Arbenz," I say, tapping his thigh to direct his attention back to me. "And if you don't want to see her, that's okay."

Speaking slowly, I remind him how Mrs. Stevens discovered the letter to Mom in the linen closet. "Remember, I told you about it, Dad? Do you remember?"

I say there is no other conclusion to draw from the letter except that Pancha and Mom wanted to hash out the past. "Did Mom ever say anything to you about it?" I ask. "Did she ever show you the letter?"

Dad watches me pose the questions, keeping his eyes squarely on my face. But his expression doesn't waver, and when I stop to wait for an answer, he waits too.

Suddenly, on the television show something ominous occurs, causing a wave of suspenseful music to swell. The volume is so loud that it hooks Dad's attention again, and he looks over to see the camera lingering on the face of a handsome young man brooding over a troubling thought.

"She's going to want to see you, Dad. And I don't want to bring her here if it's going to upset you."

It is no use. His memory of Pancha is either completely blank or too clouded for him to form an opinion.

"You want to watch this show?" I ask.

He shakes his head and mumbles something.

"I'm sorry. I didn't catch that."

"Shew-no?"

"Juno?"

He nods. "Goo man."

"Yeah," I say as I point his wheelchair back toward the medical ward, "I'm afraid I like him a lot."

To finish the profile-and-goblet pillow I have to stitch the background, which will give the piece a sense of contrast and depth. Some stitchers fill it in as they go, working the entire canvas like a wave rolling to shore. But I can't resist the temptation of diving straight into the main design. For me, the background is a chore.

I'd hoped to have this pillow finished before Patrick's session, but with the professors' visit and all of the rigmarole concerning Pancha, I haven't had a chance to sit and stitch. Normally I like to keep my needlework simple and use stitches that cover no more than one or two holes of the mesh. But if I'm going to finish this piece quickly, I'm going to have to go out on a limb and try a horizontal brick stitch that gobbles up four holes with every pass. I thread my tapestry needle and push it through the canvas with the help of my favorite silver thimble. There's nothing but manic talk and annoying music on the radio, so I listen to the stillness of the afternoon instead. It's been a while since I've spent time alone without feeling lonely, but today the solitude feels good.

Juno spent last night with me, silently slipping into bed beside me at two in the morning. I love waking up next to him, but his presence has changed the entire rhythm of my day. I probably should have taken things more slowly, since he is the first since the divorce. But I get the feeling that with Juno it's all or nothing. And right now, I want the all.

I hold out the needlepoint canvas and take a look. Yes, the brick stitch design will highlight the profiles and the goblet nicely. I continue stitching and think about Dad and Mom and Pancha. I may never know what my father was really like when he lived in Guatemala, no matter what the professors, or my aunt, or books about the coup, tell me. Until Dad is able to speak for himself, I have nothing but other people's perceptions to depend on, and absolutely no way to know if I'm looking at the profile or the goblet.

"Pretend it's a news story," Juno says when he calls. "Every fact from every source you get is slanted, but when you piece them together, the picture becomes clear. You'll feel better when you know."

"Will I?"

"People need to know their history to know who they really are."

I'm not surprised by Juno's answer. But, I tell him, the history my parents wrote for me is the American story of newcomers wanting their child to fit in.

"Why does it have to go further back than that?" I ask. "If my mom and dad came here to start new lives, isn't that where my story begins?" It's hardly a foreign notion; America was built on discarded pasts.

"Well, that's a pretty shallow cultural pool to drink from," Juno says. "Wal-Mart and Bruce Springsteen, you want those to be your ethnic pegs?"

I don't like the sarcasm in his voice.

"Look," I reply, "I know assimilation is a bad word these days. I know we're all supposed to think of America as a quilt instead of a melting pot. But I can still remember sitting at my friends' dinner tables waiting for their parents to ask me the question they always got around to. *Where is your family from?*"

Juno keeps quiet as I continue.

"The first few times I said Lakeside Heights, thinking they wanted to know what part of the neighborhood we lived in. But that was never the answer they were looking for. 'No,' they'd repeat, 'where are you *from?*' It didn't matter that I'd been born in Dallas, or that I sat in the exact same classroom as their own child. It didn't matter that Mom dropped me off at the same Girl Scout meetings and swim meets that they took their kids to. It didn't matter that Dad taught their older sons and daughters at the university. In their eyes we couldn't possibly be as American as they were because we looked different. To them we had to be a *something*-American."

"Everyone's something-American," Juno argues.

"Yeah, I know, and maybe I would have felt differently about that if I'd grown up in a city where there were enough middle-class Guatemalans to build a nice neighborhood of their own. But I've never heard of a thriving Guatemalan enclave anywhere, have you?"

Juno sighs.

"In Dallas if you are brown, you are Mexican. End of story. It doesn't matter what your history is, because being brown means that if you didn't come here illegally, your parents probably did."

"So what?" Juno sniffs. "That's Texas prejudice, and you haven't lived there for a while."

"Fine," I answer. "If you are brown in Philadelphia, you are Puerto Rican."

"And that's bad?"

"You know what I'm saying."

"You're saying you wish that you were white."

Juno has set the easiest of traps, and I refuse to take the bait.

"Juanita," he says pointedly, "you can't be proud of your history until you know it."

"My name is Nita," I snap, "and don't patronize me with oversimplified clichés. How is knowing what happened in Guatemala fifty years ago going to change how people see me, or, for that matter, how I see myself?"

Before Juno has a chance to answer, I launch into a story about the summer between my sophomore and junior years in college. I worked as a hostess for an expensive steak house and one of the cooks asked me out. Even though we didn't have a single thing in common, I accepted. He was good-looking and popular and arrogant and I felt lucky to have been noticed by him. When he came to collect me, he shook my father's hand, and during dinner at a drive-in hamburger joint he told me he'd learned how to cook at the Vo-Tech. He drove me to the lake and asked me to describe what college was like. The more we talked, the more I liked him. And then, after we kissed for a while, he wanted to know what it felt like to be smuggled across the Rio Grande.

"So he was stupid," Juno says. "What did you expect? And, by the way, if you'd known your parents' story, you could have told it."

"You know what?" I answer. "I've got to go. Patrick will be here soon and I've got to get ready."

"Don't be mad."

"I'm not mad, I'm just tired of being told that I don't know who I am."

Since the goblet pillow isn't finished, I bring out my newest needlepoint pillow for Patrick's session. It shows an elaborate scene of a painter's easel in front of a window with a view of rolling hills and pale blue sky. Next to the window there is a table with a wide array of bright-colored paints and a collection of black-bristled brushes, and resting on the easel is an empty canvas, waiting for a stroke of inspiration.

It is one of the most ambitious canvases I have ever stitched. Not only because I drew the design myself, using a picture out of *Home & Garden* magazine as a guide, but also because each time I threaded my needle, I had to calculate the perfect number of black and brown strands of yarn I needed to mix together to create a realistic-looking wood grain. I did the same thing with the blues and the reds and the greens I picked to portray the sheen of the artist's paints and the mottled grass on the hillside. It is as close to making real art as I've ever come, and whenever I look at the stitching I wonder what Mom would say. She wanted me to be an artist and had patiently waited for the magic to occur.

When I was eight, she enrolled me in a drawing class, where I spent hours drawing cylinders and balls and cones that the teacher set in various patterns. She pretended to be impressed with the results, but even after months of practice everything I drew was still coming out looking flat and off-kilter.

She introduced me to pottery, but I hated the slimy feel of the wet clay oozing between my fingers. She took me to ballet and tap and piano and voice, and after two years of stops and starts, she finally asked me what in the world I wanted to do.

I told her I wanted to swim. I loved gliding through the water, feeling my hands slap the surface in clockwork rhythm as I sailed from one end of the pool to the other. So, poor Mom sat by the pool for hours while I learned how to do the breaststroke, the backstroke and the butterfly. She sat through a million practices and cheered alongside Dad during dozens of swim meets. She watched me get better and faster and stronger and always told me that she was proud. But she never got a chance to see me at my best, when I made it all the way to the state finals my sophomore year of high school. And she didn't live long enough to see how, once I started doing needlepoint, everything I'd learned in drawing class finally paid off.

I set the pillow on the left side of the love seat, where Patrick always sits. In his mind he doesn't fit in with other kids his age, which is why eight months ago his parents found him lying on the basement floor, still alive only because the beam he chose to wrap the noose around wasn't strong enough.

Mr. and Mrs. Capparella cannot afford private counseling so, before Patrick was discharged from the hospital, a doctor handed them a list of therapists subsidized by the county and told them to pick one. They chose me because DeLeon sounded Italian. They've stayed with me because Patrick is getting better.

When the therapy began, Mr. and Mrs. Capparella were pleased to hear that the suicide attempt had nothing to do with drugs or alcohol. Their boy, I told them, is a smart kid who is having a tough time figuring himself out. At his age, being different in any way gets translated into being abnormal, and that gets twisted into being someone to ridicule or shun, which understandably left Patrick feeling isolated and hopelessly alone on the afternoon he tried to kill himself.

Therapy, I told them, can help rebuild a sense of security as well as self-esteem, and every month we've seen progress. What I haven't told them is that what I expect Patrick to ultimately discover about himself is something neither he, nor they, are fully prepared to tackle. That is why I am leading the entire family down the road slowly, giving each of them plenty of time to steady their steps.

The problem we are facing at the moment is that George and Bonita Capparella are less than thrilled with the refuge their son has found in making elaborate home movies. Patrick started making the short films after I suggested he find a hobby to fill his time after school and on the weekends. When he first said he wanted a video camera, his parents raced out to buy him the best secondhand equipment they could afford, thinking he'd record the lives of the people in his working-class neighborhood, his high school's events and some family gatherings. But it turns out that Patrick had something entirely different in mind.

Using money that he saved from his summer job as an usher at the eight-screen cineplex, he rented a Clara Barton costume and bought piles of old clothes from Goodwill. He stuffed rags and crumpled newspaper into the pants and shirts and stacked the scarecrows into a pile in his bedroom.

One cloudy afternoon, he took the three dozen bodies that he'd made, laid them on the backyard lawn and rolled what looked like a small cannon into the center of the scene. Bonita phoned me in a panic. No, I told her. I had no idea what was going on, but if it didn't look as if Patrick was going to hurt himself, or anybody else, she should go along with it for the time being.

So, in the spirit of helping her son heal, Mrs. Capparella agreed when Patrick asked her to put on the Clara Barton costume. She held her tongue when he recruited his younger sister to fog up the backyard by dragging a metal tub filled with smoldering charcoal briquettes back and forth with the help of a long-handled garden hoe. What he'd created was a battle scene. Patrick positioned his new camera on its tripod and prepared to capture his homemade war on film.

With the sound of Saturday-morning suburban traffic in the background, he directed Mrs. Capparella to carefully step over the dying and injured soldiers strewn across the lawn. He looked through the camera lens and then walked into the scene to pull a leg this way and turn a torso that way. He instructed his sister, Gina, to make another sweep around the perimeter with the briquettes. When everything was exactly as he wanted it, when every dead man's arm and leg was in place and clouds of smoke were billowing through the scene at a steady clip, Patrick told his mother to fall onto her knees and raise her eyes toward heaven like a silent movie star praying for mercy.

Sensing that things were getting out of hand, Bonita removed her cape and told Patrick they were done. She had errands to finish. And, she added, stepping out of the battlefield, she expected all signs of war to be cleared from the backyard by dinnertime.

Since then, Patrick has been spending all his free time making costumes, scouring flea markets for props, staging other scenes and shooting them with the help of two friends from school. So far he's recreated Washington crossing the Delaware using a canoe and a nearby brook; Carrie Nation smashing cases of bootleg rum, which were actually Styrofoam ice chests filled with bottles of iced tea; and Custer's last stand, without horses.

I believe setting up and directing the films are helping Patrick develop a sense of control, but Mr. and Mrs. Capparella worry that his escape into the past and his costume making have turned into a strange obsession.

I invite Patrick's parents to sit in on our sessions every fourth week, and unfortunately it's the same grim scene month after month. I ask a question and there is a long awkward silence before anyone dares to speak. Patrick's father grinds his teeth, his mother crosses her legs or straightens her skirt, and Patrick sends me distress signals with his eyes. We drag through the uneasiness for fifty-five minutes, and when the time is up all three of the Capparellas pop out of their seats like pieces of toast. I'm not sure I'm up to it tonight. My mind is stuck on Pancha's impending visit.

I hear them entering the reception room and I take a deep breath to refocus. A chilly draft has followed them inside and it rolls into my office as they remove their hats and gloves and heavy coats.

"Now his schoolwork isn't gettin' done," George grumbles after sitting himself down. His voice tells me that, in his opinion, this problem has dragged on for too long. Digging his elbows into his thighs, he leans as close to me as possible and punctuates his message with his large hands. I look at Patrick, who has taken a seat in the leather chair next to mine, and he glances back with a grimace.

"He needs to get involved with some normal kids, do normal things," Mr. Capparella continues.

Bonita, a redhead who works as a supermarket cashier, keeps her eyes on her husband as he speaks. I can't read her expression clearly, but I notice that she has already crossed her legs and her right foot has begun to wag. Normally she is anything but demure, yet this evening I get the feeling she's agreed to stay quiet while George has his say. He is a big man, at least six foot three, who left the police department a year ago and now heads the security force at the Philadelphia stock exchange. His anger is not a surprise. He's told me several times that the only reason he agreed to therapy is because the doctors at the hospital prescribed it. If it were up to him, Patrick would be enrolled in military school.

"I thought this was a phase," he says impatiently. "But it's not going away, and the damn thing is twisted. Making dresses and capes and wigs. I'm not having any more of it."

When he stops speaking, the room vibrates in unsettled silence.

Softly, Bonita adds, "The history teacher called Monday and said Patrick wants to make period costumes in place of a research paper." George nods as she speaks, and then he raises one eyebrow and crosses his arms across his chest, resting his case.

Patrick, who is almost as tall and as broad as his dad but not yet comfortable with the height or the heft, slumps farther down into his chair and swings one of his long legs over the armrest as he mumbles.

"No!" George snaps before I make out what Patrick said. "It's *not* okay."

"Dad," Patrick's voice cracks, "Mom told him I'd write a two-page report to go with them, and he said it was okay."

Once again there is a long, ragged pause.

"Sit up straight," George says as he reaches over and slaps Patrick's dangling foot.

I like this family. They care more about each other than they realize, and regardless of tonight's tension they've worked hard to make things better.

"George," I say, "is it the films you have a problem with, or is it the costumes?"

"Look, if he wants to use a video camera why doesn't he join the journalism club at school?" George replies. "What's he need with the crazy getups?"

"They're not getups." Patrick groans.

"Whatever the hell they are," Mr. Capparella says.

"Patrick knows we're proud of him," Bonita begins. "It's just that his father . . . well, we both think he needs to be a little better rounded."

When I look over to gauge Patrick's response, he keeps his eyes focused on the far wall.

"I've told him if he doesn't come up with something else to film, I'm going to lock up the camera equipment," George says matter-of-factly.

"I don't want to be an asshole about this, but I'm . . . it's . . . we're out of options here."

I nod my head to let him know I am listening. "What about some lessons in traditional stage design?" I ask. "To help Patrick move his talent in a different direction."

Nobody answers.

"I think a theater program might be a good idea," I continue, knowing full well that Patrick will hate the suggestion. "You could take a class over spring break to try it out."

Bonita smiles and places her hand on her husband's knee. Patrick's cheeks begin to flush red with anger, but he doesn't say a word. I know that he is feeling as if I've sold him out, and I want to put my arm around his shoulders to show that I'm still on his side. I want to tell him that this is the only way his parents will be persuaded to let him be; that, in fact, we've won. But instead I say, "How about you collect information on two or three possible programs and bring it in the next time we meet?"

Patrick glares.

"Flip through some magazines," I say, fixing my eyes directly on his, hoping he'll look deep enough to read the real message I'm trying to give. "Check the colleges and local theaters and see what you come up with."

The heavy coats go back on. The scarves. The hats. The gloves. Bonita opens the door and once again the cold rushes in. As Patrick's parents exit, I gently place my hand on his shoulder.

"Trust me," I whisper. He flips up his collar in reply, saying absolutely nothing as he zips his brown leather bomber jacket tight.

I close up the office. I have canceled my regular Friday appointments so I can go and get Pancha at the airport, and I've cleared the calendar for the forthcoming week because I've decided the office is where Pancha will sleep. It has its own bathroom, the love seat converts into a bed, and it won't take me long to make it look more like a guest room than a work space. If I slide the old steamer trunk to the foot of the bed there will be a place for her to set her luggage. A tall crystal vase filled with fresh flowers on the desktop will help, and I can set the needlepoint pillows at the head of the bed to make it look more homey.

Juno phones again at ten o'clock, and I tell him I'd rather be alone tonight.

"Did we have a fight?"

I smile. "No, I just want to try to get a full night's sleep."

"I'll be good."

"Then," I tease, "you might as well stay home."

"So, I'll stop by?"

"No," I say again, "you'd better not." I tell him I want to be at one hundred percent tomorrow, although I doubt my nerves will allow me to get any real sleep. They've already killed my appetite and turned my neck and shoulders into cement.

"I'll drive you to the airport," he says.

"That's all right. You don't have to."

"She comes in at three thirty, right?"

"Three twenty-five."

"I don't have to be at work until six. I'll take you, if you want."

"That'd be nice."

I feel like I have to keep moving in order to stay calm, so after I hang up the telephone I run the vacuum cleaner for a third time, then clean off my desk. I throw the bedsheets that fit the pullout into the washing machine, along with a complete set of matching towels. Then, in my own bedroom, I start hunting for an outfit to wear when I meet her. I try a pair of jeans, but they look too shabby. I need to look pulled together, but not fussy. I veto a blue dress and half a dozen skirts. Finally I settle on a pair of black wool slacks and a violet boat-neck sweater. I will also wear my mother's pearls.

Sometime after eleven, I bring a cup of tea to bed and try to page through a magazine, but I end up setting it aside and turning on the television instead. I breeze through channels offering late-night comedy, infomercials and sitcom reruns. The only program that holds my attention is the twenty-four-hour news report. I watch until I begin to doze and then, just as I begin to drop off, the telephone rings.

I expect it to be Juno wishing me a final good night, so I answer with a sultry hello.

"Nita?"

It is Candide. My eyes snap wide open in panic.

"What's wrong?"

"No, darling," she answers quickly. "Nothing's wrong."

I've already jumped to my feet.

"Your father wanted to call."

I look at the alarm clock next to the bed. Eleven fifty-seven. I must have heard her wrong.

"Nee."

Dad's voice is thin but the sound of it makes my knees weak. I lower myself onto the edge of the bed and stare at the nightstand. Before the stroke, Dad and I had a standing telephone appointment, every Sunday night at nine, which we kept all through my college years and into my life with Aaron. After the stroke, whenever the phone rang on that night, I expected to hear him on the other end. I had to teach myself to let go of the anticipation. And now, his voice startles me.

"Is everything all right?" I ask.

"Pan-shaa."

My hands are trembling and I hold the receiver tighter to try to stop the shaking. "You remember her, Dad?"

I hear movement, and then a sigh.

"Take your time. I'm right here, Dad. Did you want to tell me something about Pancha?"

"Esssokly."

I wait for him to try again, but he doesn't. "She's coming tomorrow, Dad. She's coming here to see you."

"Pan-shaa."

"Right. Do you want to see her?"

He does not answer and I suspect we have come to the end of the conversation. I wait for Candide to get back on the line. But instead I hear Dad exhale and, in an almost painful drawl, he tells me, "Ess okay."

CHAPTER 13

*T*iny spears of ice pelt the windshield of Juno's car as we make our way to the airport.

"You called?" he asks as the wipers sweep from left to right and back again.

"Twice. It's still scheduled to be on time."

Juno shakes his head to say he doesn't believe it, considering the slick roads. He's driving with the overcautious concentration of a newcomer to the Northeast, getting passed by trucks and cars that toss even more sleet into his line of vision. It would have made better sense for me to drive, but my attention span is in tatters.

When we finally arrive, we check the flight board and find our way to Terminal C, where we are told to wait at the bottom of an escalator on which the passengers will descend. There are about a dozen other people standing with us, including three uniformed chauffeurs holding cardboard signs on which they've scrawled their clients' last names, and a very young mother with two fussy toddlers who have silver balloons that say I LOVE GRANDMA tied to their wrists.

Like characters in an abstract foreign film, we all look up and silently watch the empty steps glide down. Garbled announcements that are impossible to understand echo through the terminal. The young mother's children begin to fidget, tugging at both her arms as she tries to rein them in. Juno checks his watch, and the chauffeurs roll back and forth on the thick black soles of their sensible shoes.

"Yiieee!" one of the kids squeals when the first person finally appears.

Startled, I bite the inside of my cheek and swab the cut with my tongue. Juno takes my hand thinking, I suppose, that my nerves might be getting the best of me. His fingers are warm. Mine are ice.

Following a silent protocol the three chauffeurs have created for themselves, they form a row at the base of the stairs with their hats on, their signs up and their faces welcoming. The toddlers bounce like rubber balls as their expectation builds. When the first passenger, a blank-faced businessman, reaches our level, he steps around us, keeping his eyes straight forward and heading for the sliding doors. I scan the other faces moving toward us but see no one who I think might be Pancha. There are far more men than women on the escalator, most of them in formal business suits or khaki pants and sports jackets. A pink-faced man speaking into a cell phone extends his hand toward one of the chauffeurs, who immediately takes his suit bag and briefcase and asks if he had a good flight.

There is a pudgy lady with a helmet of red curls and square-framed eyeglasses that are attached to a string of beads around her neck, and a painfully thin woman in a knee-length sweater, peg-leg tights and suede desert boots who is carrying a beat-up backpack over her shoulders.

The young mother spots her guest and leans down to show her children where their grandmother is standing. I look to where she is pointing and see an attractive old woman with gray hair that has been carefully combed back from her high forehead. She is wearing a beige coat with a furry collar and a slash of bright pink lipstick that is the wrong shade for her olive complexion. She is gripping the rail tightly with one hand while in her other she holds the handle of a black tapered walking cane. Behind the grandmother I see an angular, late-middle-aged woman with dark hair that reaches her waist and has been swept over her right shoulder by a silky purple scarf that she's tied behind her ear Gypsy-style. It is difficult to see the rest of her outfit because she is wearing a heavy pea coat. But the hem of her earth-toned skirt skims the tops of expensive-looking high-heeled boots.

The old lady steps off the escalator with a wobbly hop, and I expect the children to rush toward her, but they do not. Instead, she finds her footing with the help of her cane and moves aside as the toddlers stampede past her and the lady in the scarf into the arms of a fluffy-haired brunette riding two steps behind them. The kids stamp their feet and raise their arms, demanding that the brunette lift them. She can't be more than fifty years old, fifty-five tops.

For an instant, the old woman and I make eye contact and exchange amused smiles as the young family reunites. For that short moment, I wonder what the old woman is thinking, whether she is smiling because what we are watching is the sort of scene that has been played out a million times in her own life, or whether she might be like me and is smiling to hide a devouring regret. I hope it's not the latter. I hope that by the time I reach her age I will have stopped looking at children who belong to other women with naked envy. I hope I'll be able to look at their little faces without being bent on finding stains on their clothes, tangles in their hair, or other scraps of evidence to prove they would have been better off with me. I search the expression on the old lady's face. It's a quiet appreciation of the young mother's plight and, instantly, I know she's had children of her own. I'm alone with my resentment.

When I turn my attention back to the escalator, my stomach is fluttery and tense. I don't know why I didn't come equipped with a little sign like the chauffeurs. Two of them have already hooked their fish and escorted them out. Why did I expect to recognize Pancha? Why did I think she'd spot me?

"There?" Juno asks, pointing to the top of the stairs.

"Could be," I say, directing my attention to a short square woman with a dark blunt haircut and a fringe of bangs who is wrestling with a lumpy nylon carry-on bag that refuses to stay on her shoulder. I wave my hand and notice that she, too, is looking for someone. I feel goose bumps form on my arms. The woman smiles when she turns her head my way and lifts the bulging bag as if to say something important is inside it. She is shaped completely different from Dad. He has always been slender, and before the attack he paid close attention to his posture, which gave the illusion of height. This woman has rounded shoulders and no discernible waistline. As she gets closer, I focus on her face and search for a family resemblance. Her eyebrows are hidden by her bangs, but her coloring seems right. Still, I notice that her nose is not prominent, like Dad's. It is delicate and takes its time emerging from her face. And now that she is only a few yards away, I can also see that her lips are rather thin. When she finally reaches the landing, Juno and I step forward to greet her and she turns toward us grinning.

"I got it!" she exclaims as she sprints to the side of a woman standing only inches to our left. Juno and I watch as the round-shouldered woman drops the nylon bag to the floor and the other lady, who happens to have an identical haircut, unzips it and peers inside. We can't help but lean toward the bag, too, and that is when the two of them sense we are intruding. They stop their conversation abruptly, glower at us, and tote the bulging bag away in a huff.

The last remaining chauffeur meets his fare, a coat-and-tie man who plucks the sign out of the driver's hands and lands a playful punch on the driver's uniformed bicep. By the time we look back at the escalator, it has emptied and the people who filed past us moments ago have either left the building or are now making their way toward the baggage claim. Juno and I continue to wait, as if by standing perfectly still we might will Pancha to appear.

"She went to get her bag," I reason, thinking that maybe she didn't come.

We turn and, next to the sliding doors that lead to the taxi stand, I see the old woman with the cane standing beside the late-middle-aged woman wearing the scarf. They look lost, or a bit confused.

"Can I help you?" Juno asks as we pass.

"We're waiting for someone," the late-middle-aged woman replies.

Juno squeezes my hand and we stop. Suddenly I recognize every feature in the face that is in front of me: the perfectly oval eyes, the sharp, strong nose, the dramatic chin.

"I'm Nita," I say, expecting Pancha to react with a spark of recognition. But it is the old woman who responds first, opening her arms and pulling me inside of them. She seems fragile, so small and birdlike that the strength of her hands surprises me.

Locked in her grip, I notice that the top of her head barely reaches my shoulders, which means she must stand significantly less than five feet tall. Her shoulders begin to heave and I begin rubbing her back to try to comfort her. I turn to look at Juno, who is shaking hands with Pancha and saying something to her in Spanish. The old woman slowly releases me but keeps her hands locked on my shoulders. Her cane, which has an engraved silver grip, dangles from the crook of her skinny arm. Tears have made blotchy tracks in the coral powder on her cheeks and, still holding me at arm's length, she scrutinizes my face and mumbles something I cannot make out. I smile at her uncomfortably, not sure how to react.

Pancha and Juno chuckle.

"She says you're a little chubby, but you're pretty," Pancha translates. I nod to be polite but, honestly, the lady has no right. Then Pancha steps between the old woman and me and lightly kisses my cheek. I smell vanilla perfume when we touch, and hear the jangle of what must be a dozen silver bangles on her wrist.

Extending his hand to greet the old woman, Juno says, *"Con mucho gusto, Señora."*

Leaning on her cane, the woman holds out her tiny hand. "Olympia DeLeon."

Her name pulls all the air out of my lungs. I look into her face again, unable to swallow, unable to speak. She takes me into her arms for a second time and cradles my forehead against her neck. We both burst into tears and, instinctively, I hold her tighter.

"I didn't know you were alive," I whisper between a raft of sobs. She answers with a soothing stream of Spanish and ends up rocking me gently, repeating one word that I actually understand—*preciosa.* Hearing it makes me cry harder because it was the one bit of Spanish I can remember my mother speaking to me. Every night, leaning over my bed, she would kiss my nose and say, "Good night, *preciosa*," letting the syllables descend like delicate snowflakes. Now my grandmother—my *grandmother!*—is whispering it into my ear, running her fingers through my hair, wrapping me in my lost mother's love. I'm not sure how long we stand there clenched to one another, but when we finally let go, Pancha and Juno are standing beside four pieces of luggage, ready to leave.

Despite the heft of their winter coats, Pancha and Olympia shudder when a gust of icy wind assails us in the parking lot. I open the car door for Olympia and hold her hand as she steps inside. Juno tosses the suitcases into the trunk and Pancha buckles herself into the front passenger seat. I sit next to Olympia in the back, feeling the tingle and slight drowsiness that follows a good cry.

During the ride home, Olympia teaches me to say *abuelita,* which means grandmother, and *tía,* which means aunt. But the rest of the conversation is carried on, in Spanish, between Pancha and Juno, who makes a point to stop and translate the exchange for me.

"She's lived in Oakland for a while now," he says, leaning his head toward the backseat as he speaks.

"Eight years," Pancha adds in English.

"Olympia still lives in Guatemala," Juno continues, "in Antigua. Luckily, she was visiting when Pancha got the e-mail."

I look at my grandmother and smile. She pats my thigh and lifts my hand to kiss it. I think of the time Mom showed Guatemala to me on the globe. It was so small I never considered that it would have distinct regions that people would describe themselves as being from. But of course it does. Still, my mental picture of Guatemala has never gone beyond a vague impression of the Third World, so the name of the place where Olympia lives means nothing to me.

"You didn't tell me you'd be with someone," I say to Pancha, who is rubbing her hands to stay warm even though the heater is turned on high.

"You didn't tell me you'd be with someone, either," Pancha replies. "I didn't even know that you're married."

Juno keeps his eyes on the road. I wait for him to set Pancha straight with a wisecrack or a side look, or by lifting one of his hands from the steering wheel to say "well, actually . . ." But he does none of those things. Instead, he looks at me through the rearview mirror, his dark eyes searching mine for the right response.

"I'm not married," I say quickly. "Juno is my . . ."

I don't know what to call him; all I know is the glance we just exchanged was full of something deeper than simple friendship.

"We've been dating for a little while," Juno says, first in English and then in Spanish. Olympia nods her approval, and I feel unexpectedly pleased that she has given us her blessing.

The sleet slaps against the car windows and the wipers lick it clean. Pancha turns to look at her surroundings, but there is nothing to see on this portion of the highway except warehouses and an occasional workingman's bar. It's hard for me to link the story the fullmooners told me with the face in the front seat. Kidnappings and abductions? Guerrilla warfare and armed revolution? Pancha looks like someone who reads Tarot cards at parties, not a woman whose betrayal against Mom and Dad was so grievous that Dad could never forgive her.

Looking at her, I think about the documentaries I've seen in which old Nazis on the run are hunted down in obscure villages in South America decades after committing unspeakable war crimes. In those films, the camera almost always catches them ambling through the local market, thumping cantaloupes and bargaining for tomatoes like normal people. They look like harmless old men, anonymous citizens blending in with the pedestrian crowd, until the filmmaker confronts them and begins to ask questions. Then you watch the old men's faces turn to stone, and your backbone stiffens as phantoms appear in their cold eyes.

"I'm going to have to drop you off and head straight to work," Juno announces as Pancha pulls out the stem of her narrow-banded wristwatch and adjusts it to East Coast time.

"Four thirty-nine," I say, calculating that we will be pulling up to my house at about five fifteen.

Olympia asks a question in Spanish and Pancha answers with a shrug of her shoulders accompanying her words. I wait for Juno to translate but his attention has been diverted to the task of merging into the thickening turnpike traffic.

"We want to see Diego," Pancha says abruptly, like she's expecting to get an argument. I've noticed a tinge of judgment in her voice, a trace of blame for a wrong I have, apparently, already committed. Now her face looks drawn, her lips are tight. I think of the documentary filmmaker zooming in, filling his frame with her stern, defiant eyes.

"After dinner," I say, directing my words toward Olympia, who listens intently.

Juno, now in the general flow of traffic, repeats my answer in Spanish and takes the liberty of adding what I assume is a more detailed explanation of my plans.

"I told them it is dinnertime at the Rose Tree," he says, "and not a very good hour to visit."

The truth is I'm not sure anytime will be good. Not if Pancha is confrontational. For a few long moments nobody speaks and the silence is anything but a natural pause. It is brimming with apprehension, as if we all can see that an unsteady wall of bricks is ready to fall on top of us, and no one wants to cause the crash.

It's been hard enough for Dad to wrap his mind around the thought of Pancha walking back into his life, and I'll be damned if I'm going to allow her to upset him. Still, I wonder, what is going to happen when Dad sees Olympia? Or, worse yet, what is going to happen when she sees him?

$\mathcal{I}$ leave Pancha and Olympia standing in the foyer with instructions to make themselves at home while I walk Juno to his car.

Darkness has begun to fall, and if the sleet does not stop there will be ice on the streets within the hour.

"You going to be okay?" he asks, when really it's me who should be worried about him.

"I suppose."

He rubs my shoulders, pecks the base of my neck and, when I tilt my chin toward his, my lips. Bits of sleet slap our fingers and faces as we stand in the cold.

"Thank you for being here," I say as he climbs back behind the wheel. He wiggles his fingers to say good-bye and then he starts the engine. There is absolutely no reason for me to stay out here and watch his car pull away. In fact, anyone with sense would race back inside. But I keep perfectly still as he backs his Taurus out of the driveway and slowly swings its back end into the street. When I blink, cold drops fall from my eyelashes onto my cheeks and, when I raise my hand to wipe them, I see that the sleeve of my sweater is covered with quivering specks of frozen rain.

I hear the car's gears shift into DRIVE and see Juno turn his head to look my way. It feels as if he's leaving me at the mouth of a canyon, a dark hole I foolishly said I wanted to explore. Now I'm terrified to step inside it, afraid I'll lose my footing and tumble all the way down to the rock-hard bottom. Juno lowers his window and leans his forearm out expectantly, concerned that I have still not gone inside.

"No," I say, shaking my head in case he can't hear me. "It's nothing."

"I'll call," he mouths.

I nod, and when his window is almost closed, I turn back to the house.

Olympia meets me at the door with two bath towels in her arms. She tosses one over my shoulders and motions me to dry my hair with the other. I close my eyes and knead the thick terry cloth against my damp head until I hear the teakettle whistling.

"*Té?*" Olympia asks with a slight tilt of her head.

I can't help but laugh. Here she is playing the perfect hostess, in *my* house. I should probably feel guilty for having left her to her own devices, but I don't. There is a gleam in her eye that tells me she's enjoying her grandmother role, and given what is soon in store for all of us, I want her to be happy.

In the kitchen, I find Pancha sitting at the table in front of my mother's old address book.

"This is all you have?" she asks as Olympia lifts the kettle off the burner and the high-pitched whistle loses its steam.

"And the letter in the back," I answer flatly.

From the cabinet, I produce three mugs and three boxes of tea bags, which my grandmother would have had to stand on a stool to reach. Carefully she pours hot water into the mugs and then slowly places them on the table one by one. Her cane is hooked to the back of her chair. She does not need it for the few small steps it takes to cross my kitchen, but the movements clearly require her full concentration. I have no idea how young Olympia was when she became a mother, but Dad is sixty-nine, so she has to be in her late eighties today. She does not look her age. Her hair, held away from her face by two tortoiseshell combs and a handful of silver hairpins, is an attractive, tweedy gray. Her dark eyes glisten beneath heavy lids, almost invisible lashes and wispy snow-white eyebrows. Her neck is heavily wrinkled, her shoulders slightly rounded, but she does not need eyeglasses or the help of a hearing aid. This is how I thought my father would grow old, instead of in a wheelchair. How is this proud woman going to feel when she sees her son living with people in such advanced stages of decay? How many ways is it going to break her heart?

"Herbal?" Pancha asks when I bring the tea bags to the table.

"This one's oolong," I say, unsure of its caffeine content. "But the others are peppermint and rose hip." I slide the sugar bowl to the center of the table and Olympia helps herself to two scoops.

"I don't use refined sugar," Pancha declares. "Is there honey?"

It is not what she says—it's how she says it that chafes me. Her imperious tone makes me want to hate her. She should be grateful I welcomed her into my home. I take a good long look at her as I rise. The scarf wrapped around her head is made out of cut velvet and her outfit is Joni Mitchell chic—a black turtleneck, a coffee-colored Nehru jacket made of sueded cotton and a long, limp skirt of the same fabric. Her collection of silver bangles occupies a good four inches of her right forearm and an old-fashioned thin-strapped watch is clasped around her left wrist.

Up close, her late middle age is apparent. Deep lines fan out from the corners of her eyes and I can tell that the auburn highlights in her black hair are streaks of store-bought color meant to cover gray. Her knuckles are fleshy, but the skin at the base of her pale pink fingernails is slightly red and tight.

I find a plastic jar of honey stashed behind a round carton of Quaker oatmeal and a can of Pam. It is shaped like a bear and the honey inside has crystallized into a solid lump of amber. I set it in the microwave and zap it for thirty seconds, which does nothing but make the plastic bottle spongy.

"Hold it under hot water," Pancha advises, although she has not made a move to come over and help. I run the tap and stick the bear's rump into the stream of warm water.

At the table, Pancha has passed the address book to Olympia, who is now slowly turning the pages and reading every name written inside. The letter Pancha wrote to Mom is open in front of my stern-faced aunt.

"This is *really* all you have?" she asks.

I slam the bear against the side of the sink. *No!* I want to scream. It is not. I have my mother's decoupaged lunch box and her four work shirts in my closet. I have her last two tubes of Avon lipstick and a book of matches from 7-Eleven. I have memories of her beautiful smile beaming at me underneath the Christmas tree, and her strong fingers buttoning my winter coat. I have a father who may or may not ever speak again and a body that is willing, but not able, to produce children. And I have a family history that I never felt the need to know but has suddenly bubbled up like some kind of prehistoric tar. *That's* what I have.

Instead I nod and tell her that my best friend, Lauren, is going to be here in twenty minutes. She's volunteered to cook dinner for us tonight, using an amazing recipe for Southern fried chicken and garlic mashed potatoes that she wooed from a chef she dated for three weeks. She was expecting Pancha's arrival to be a happy affair and must still be thinking that we are going to have a party like we did with the full-mooners. I should call and warn her to stay away, but I don't because she's my rescue.

I ask Pancha to please translate what I've just said and to add that, after dinner, we'll go to the Rose Tree to see Dad. As Pancha speaks, I try to figure out when I can slip away to telephone Candide. I want to tell her about Olympia, to see if she has any advice on how to minimize the shock Dad is going to feel when he sees her.

With Pancha still translating, I explain once again how Mrs. Stevens came upon the address book, this time adding, for my grandmother's sake, that it was through the e-mail search for Pancha that Juno and I met.

Olympia crosses herself like a nun, and then kisses her fingers. *"Tu mamá. Dios la bendiga . . ."*

Pancha does not translate until I ask.

"She thinks it's your mother," Pancha says skeptically.

I look at Olympia, who nods. *"Sí. Ella te mandó Juno."*

"She says it's your mother who sent Juno to you."

Olympia rubs my fingers and I feel my face getting hot, a well of tears threatening to spill over. I don't want to cry because if I start I don't think I'll ever stop.

I ask if they'd like to rest or freshen up.

I take Olympia's suitcase and her shoulder bag into the office and Pancha follows carrying her own.

The pull-out love seat looks nice as a bed. The needlepoint pillows are arranged like a gallery at its head and the old steamer trunk anchors its foot. Olympia looks at it and sighs out loud. She must be exhausted. The flight itself was five hours long and she has to be beat.

I put Olympia's bags on top of the trunk. Pancha sets her luggage down near the door and takes a few steps around the office. She leans over the desk to study my diploma and then peers into the narrow waiting room.

"I'll take the futon," she says.

I hadn't expected to use it as a bed for them but, really, it is perfect. Together, Pancha and I slide the coffee table aside, pull the futon away from the wall and adjust its wooden frame.

"We could move it into the other room, next to the bed," I suggest, because the mattress has swallowed every inch of floor space between us.

"This is good," Pancha replies, stepping on top of the mattress to get across it.

"I'll take the coffee table out, and that will give you a few more inches."

She agrees and we lift the table and scoot it through the door. Inside the office, Olympia is already asleep on the bed, her head resting against the little mountain of pillows, her feet still inside her low-heeled pumps.

"We left the house at five thirty this morning," Pancha whispers.

"You must be tired, too."

"A little."

The doorbell rings.

"You rest," I say. "I'll get you a blanket and some sheets. Lauren and I will wake you up for dinner."

Lauren gets right to work, rummaging through the impressive collection of pots and pans that Aaron and I received as wedding gifts. She is a better cook than I will ever be, happily spellbound by the process. In the decade we've spent sharing meals, I have relied on six, maybe seven recipes to hold up my end. But Lauren has studiously increased her skills, and these days she can whip up anything from crepes to corn bread like a pro. For my birthday, she once gave me a refrigerator magnet that says IF WE ARE WHAT WE EAT, I'M FAST, CHEAP AND EASY, which pretty much sums it up.

Completely at home in my kitchen, Lauren buzzes about as I begin to tell her about Pancha, speaking low so my voice will not carry. Lauren winces when I describe the purple head scarf and the row of silver bangles, and she holds her hands against her heart when I tell her how much I already adore Olympia. This is why she is my dearest friend, because, no matter what, she'll take my side in love or war.

While Pancha and Olympia sleep, I rush to my bedroom and dial the Rose Tree. The receptionist transfers me to Dad's unit and the desk clerk says Candide is on the other line.

"I'll hold." I hear a click and then a bouncy instrumental version of "Tie a Yellow Ribbon." In the middle of the second chorus, the clerk comes back. "She hung up and then walked away before I could catch her. You want to hold some more?"

"No," I answer. "I'll call back."

Looking up, I catch a glimpse of myself in the full-length mirror, a shadowy reflection in the dull evening light. What missing pages of the DeLeon family history do Olympia and Pancha see when they look at me? Do they see traces of the lives Dad and Mom lived before our family was ripped apart? Or am I a living, breathing reminder of the ill will that's poisoned the ties between us for a generation?

"So, she's a hippie?" Lauren asks when I return. She is dipping the chicken pieces into a shallow wash of buttermilk and transferring them into a brown paper bag filled with flour and a mix of seasonings. She's already got two skillets filled with oil heating up over the stove's blue flames.

"With money," I quip.

"She's rich?"

"I don't know." I shrug as I wash the red-skinned potatoes. "I haven't asked what she does for a living, but her clothes look expensive."

Lauren rattles the chicken pieces inside the bag and then places them on a long sheet of wax paper. The telephone rings and I dash to answer it after the first ring so it won't wake my guests.

"How's it going?" Juno asks.

"They're asleep."

I consider telling him what Olympia said about Mom sending him to me, but I keep it to myself because if he were to scoff, the way Pancha did, it would hurt my feelings. And if he agreed too readily I'd suspect he was feeling pressured to answer that way.

"I called Candide," he reports hesitantly, unsure what my reaction will be.

I'm grateful, and surprised. "Just now?"

"Yeah."

"What did she say?"

"That there's no way of knowing."

"No way of knowing if Dad will recognize his mother, or no way of knowing if it's going to be too much for him to handle?"

"Both."

I hear a muffled voice in the background, and then, "Damn, I gotta go."

Is this how Juno has decided to let me know what I mean to him? Why else would he step knee-deep into my family's mire? Has he been digging into Pancha's past to impress me, or is he just so used to being part of an extended family that it's second nature for him to take on other people's problems? I think back to the fullmooners' table and how he lifted his glass and offered a toast to my father without an ounce of timidity in his voice. He loved the professors, thrived on their boisterous give-and-take. Whenever we're together, he jokes about his overbearing family and how much they meddle in his life, but it's obvious he can't live without that connection. Would he even consider a future with someone who can't give him children?

Back in the kitchen, Lauren tests the oil by flicking a ball of flour into the center of one of the pans. It pops and sizzles and quickly turns the flour golden brown.

"Perfect," she purrs as she steps from the counter to the stove, arranging the chicken pieces so the white meat is cooking in one pan and the dark meat in the other.

I fill a stockpot with water and set it on one of the back burners to boil for the potatoes, and in minutes the kitchen is filled with the irresistible smell of a simple supper cooked at home.

When I knock on the office door there is no answer.

Lauren is standing next to me holding two glasses of Merlot that she intends to offer as an appetizer. I knock again, a little louder, and because the lock is not latched, the door slowly glides open.

Inside, I see Pancha with her shoes off, sitting on the braided rug in the lotus position, her eyes closed and her back steel-rod straight. The swooshing sound of ocean waves is washing through the room and a thin trail of smoke is rising from the tip of a smoldering stick of incense. Lauren kicks my ankle, urging me to step over the threshold.

"Mija," Olympia murmurs softly when I enter. She is sitting up on the bed with one of the needlepoint pillows on her lap.

Pancha inhales, holds her breath for a moment, and then slowly lets it out, making a low-pitched hum. She stands, puts her hands in a prayer position and then turns and acknowledges us. Her eyes are a bit glazed and I can tell her thoughts are still hovering elsewhere. Her face looks softer than it did before and I can see now how striking she must have once been.

Lauren steps onto the rug and hands Pancha a glass of wine. "I'm Lauren," she says.

"Pancha," my aunt replies, blinking her thoughts back to the present and automatically extending her hand, "and this is my mother, Olympia."

Lauren walks farther into the room, carefully stepping over a tiny brass Buddha that is holding the incense. She presents Olympia with the second goblet of wine, and my grandmother accepts, cupping it in both hands.

"Where's that sound coming from?" I ask.

Pancha takes a sip before she answers.

"White noise," she says, tilting her head toward a small machine shaped like an open clamshell. "It makes the sound of a forest, the ocean, or a steady rain." She punches a series of black buttons to demonstrate and the room fills with the chirps of crickets, tweeting birds and the *ssshhhhh* of a virtual downpour.

"Yoga?" Lauren asks.

"And meditation. You?"

"I've been thinking about it," Lauren says.

Her answer astonishes me. Lauren has always hated the mere thought of exercise. She won't even go for a walk unless it provides her with an opportunity to smoke. Her job, she tells people, is exercise enough: carrying twenty pounds of camera equipment all day, squatting, twisting and stretching to find the best angle. I've always attributed her great figure to that, as well as good genes and plenty of nervous energy. It's hard to picture her sitting still long enough to attempt yoga.

"I'll show you some," Pancha offers. "You too, Juanita."

I start to correct her, but I tell myself at least she's making an effort to be cordial. "That'd be nice."

"It's much more physical than you think." Pancha snuffs out the spicy-smelling incense at the base of the little Buddha's feet and goes on to say something else, but the sound of a crashing wave drowns out most of the sentence.

". . . deeper connection," is all I hear when the noise recedes. "After a while you get hypnotized by the steadiness of your own breath and your muscles massage away tension with every move."

There is something about the mood of the room, the stillness of the deepening light, the swirling sound of the seashore, that keeps me from thinking she is feeding us pure bunk. Surprisingly, I know exactly what she is talking about, even though I've never sat on a mat and twisted myself into pretzel poses.

"It's just me and my body," Pancha adds, "and even if my mind is racing when I start, by the time I finish it's calm and clear." She bends down to turn off the sound machine, and when the noise stops the room suddenly feels bigger, hollow, the way the deck of the gym's pool feels when I come up from doing laps.

"It's like—"

"Swimming," I blurt out.

Pancha looks at me. "I suppose," she says, adjusting the knot in her scarf. "Although I've never heard anyone compare yoga to swimming."

"Well, that's what Nita does," Lauren explains, "swimming, and needlepoint."

It's no great revelation, no big secret that I want to keep, but for some reason I am bothered that Lauren has handed out those particular pieces of personal information about me so freely. I'm not sure I want Pancha to know that much about me, to know *anything* about me, until I know much, much more about her.

CHAPTER 15

Dinner is a disaster.

When Lauren brings the platter of chicken to the table, Pancha announces that she does not eat meat. She asks if the butter in the mashed potatoes is organic, and pointedly passes the bowl to Olympia when I tell her it's Land O'Lakes.

Reluctantly, she helps herself to the instant Caesar salad that I made by pouring it out of a plastic bag. She refuses the creamy dressing.

I'm inclined to let her get by with nothing but the greens, but it's clear that Lauren is flustered and Olympia is uncomfortable as well. So I invite Pancha to bring her plate into the kitchen, where I swing open the refrigerator and let her look inside. It's as forlorn as ever, a single woman's wasteland.

She frowns at the individually wrapped pieces of American cheese and the quarter pound of deli-sliced Canadian ham. She doesn't bother looking inside the Chinese take-out carton, which happens to hold a lunch-size portion of congealed curried shrimp and a clump of cold rice. When she reads the ingredients printed on an ancient container of mocha-cappucino-flavored yogurt, Pancha lets out an exasperated sigh. Having given up on the main compartment, she slides open the vegetable bin and discovers five bottles of Belgian wheat beer rattling around, and as a final resort, she turns her attention to the inside of the door. Peering over Pancha's shoulder, I see what she sees, a squirt bottle of French's mustard, a can of Reddi-wip and a half-empty package of cream cheese. I want to tell her that normally I eat better than this, but I doubt she'd consider Lean Cuisine much of an improvement.

"I've got eggs," I try.

Pancha shakes her head. "No eggs."

She ends up settling for a jar of Spanish olives and four midget gherkin pickles to round out the lettuce on her plate.

"Reading Terminal," Lauren suggests when we return to the table. "You'll love it."

Except, I think, for the Chinese butcher's booth, where freshly slaughtered ducks dangle from a rod by their tethered feet, and the Italian meat man's stand, where the center of the case is reserved for a plump pink pig with an apple in its mouth.

While we eat, the three of us are careful to keep the conversation centered on the harmless present. I haven't even hinted to Pancha that I know about the coup, and I don't want to crack that rotten egg during our first meal. So I make a point of showing polite interest when Pancha tells us that she is a lawyer who works for a social agency called D.A.M.E.S., which, she explains, stands for Domestic Abuse Medical and Educational Services.

"I shot a story on a women's shelter once," Lauren says between bites. "It was bleak."

Pancha nods solemnly and crunches another gherkin.

I look at Olympia, who is seated across from me, and it seems as if her mind is someplace else. She slowly slices a chicken thigh with her knife and fork. When she senses that I'm watching, she sets down her knife and looks up. Our brief and silent exchange probably seems like nothing more than a fleeting moment of coincidental eye contact to her, but for me, it's much more. Looking at her slender, aging face, I am able to read her thoughts. They flow into my head like a rush of water, liquid and unformed, but as clear in their meaning as if they were words I might speak myself. Just a few more minutes, she is thinking, maybe an hour, and she will finally be standing beside the man who, in her heart, is still her boy. She'll lean down and kiss his cheek and when skin meets skin, the years of separation, the miles that have divided their lives, the hurt, the anger and the distrust that rose into a thorn-covered wall will vanish. It will all just wash away in the flash flood of a mother's love.

Directing her attention back to her plate, Olympia slides a helping of mashed potato onto her fork. She will take this bite and then the next one. Patiently, she will sit through this dinner and the others that are sure to follow. She will make the best of this awkward introduction to a granddaughter she never got to watch grow, and she will endure every other twist and turn in the road that stretches before her if those steps will lead to her son's side.

I think back to the time Mom said we did not stay in touch with Olympia because Olympia wanted it that way. I can't imagine that sort of request coming from the woman seated across from me. Was Mom lying back then? Was she trying to protect me? Or was Olympia a different woman twenty-five years ago? And what about my mother's parents, the grandparents who died before I was born? I wish I knew the Spanish words to ask Olympia about them.

Turning my head, I look at Pancha, who is sitting across from Lauren. She is the reason we did not keep in touch. She is the one Dad wanted to erase from our lives, and I suppose Olympia got caught up in the clean sweep. What sort of torture must it be to know that your mother is alive and not be able to see or even speak to her? I would give anything to hear my mother's voice again, to hear her say one simple word, to listen to the waterfall of her distinctive laugh. But Pancha's betrayal pushed Dad away, and for some reason I still cannot fully understand, being cut off from his mother was the price Dad was willing to pay.

It's been difficult for Olympia to keep up with our table conversation because Pancha has not been as precise a translator as Juno was earlier. She's allowed entire exchanges to go by without informing Olympia what they've been about. When Lauren or I have stopped speaking to give Olympia a chance to get filled in, Pancha has summed up things by quickly muttering one or two words in Spanish. "Therapist" . . . "photographer" . . . "divorced". . . "farmers' market." That is all I think Olympia has heard.

Still, as I look at her now, I realize that what we say here doesn't matter. She's already seen half of what she came to see, and this banal chatter about my divorce and Lauren's workday and Pancha's quirky eating habits is nothing but one more stone she has to step over. Her calm resolve reminds me of a game my mother and I used to play when I was little. Mom would tell me that no matter how far away I moved when I grew up, she'd find a way to get there. *Anywhere?* I'd challenge. Anywhere, she'd insist. *Timbuktu?* I'd ask, and she'd nod her head and describe the tortuous route she'd take to get there. First she'd climb aboard a pirate ship, she'd say, and then she would make friends with a pride of lions, who would escort her across the perilous African plains and deliver her to the ruins where I was hiding. *What about Bora Bora?* I'd ask. Easy, she'd say and smile, sailboats and dolphins all the way.

I reach across the table and set my hand next to Olympia's plate.

"Tell her it won't be long now," I say, only partly aware that I am interrupting Pancha in the middle of a sentence.

"What?" Pancha asks.

"Tell her," I repeat. "Say we'll be there soon."

The lobby of the Rose Tree has been decorated with an Easter theme. Half a dozen white toy rabbits have been perched on top of the long reception desk in the lobby, each rabbit holding a little basket filled with chocolate eggs in its raised front paws. Cardboard cutouts of colored eggs and smiling ducklings clad in rain boots and bright yellow slickers march across the corridor's walls. The entire place looks like an elementary school or the children's section of the public library except, of course, for the bent and gray people mingling about.

I search Olympia's face as we pass the card room. As usual, the bigscreen television is blaring and clumps of old women are quietly playing bridge. Olympia looks at them blankly, as if they are actors in a movie she is not interested in watching. It can't be lost on her that she is older than many of the people in here and, at first glance, she could be mistaken for one of them. Maybe that is why she begins to plant the tapered end of her cane into the floor with fierce jabs as we make our way toward the medical ward and then picks up her pace until she is chugging down the main hallway like a locomotive.

Candide meets us at the nurses' station before we reach Dad's door. She shakes Pancha's hand and says "my pleasure" when she's introduced to Olympia. A concerned look on her face tells me she has stopped us for a reason. Over her shoulder I see a nurses' assistant rolling a medicine cart. The young woman's shoes squeak as she pushes it away.

"I need to borrow Nita for just a minute," Candide says to Pancha. "You can sit over there." She points to the four boxy chairs facing one another in a nearby waiting area. I shoot Candide a look that is loaded with questions, but her face offers no reply.

Olympia asks a question in a thin voice.

"She wants to know if Diego's all right," Pancha interprets.

"Oh, yes, ma'am," Candide answers using her most consoling tone. "I just need to go over a couple of things with Nita."

I guide my aunt and grandmother toward the waiting area and tell them I'll be right back. Whatever Candide has to say, it can't be good.

She waits for me in front of the art room where, just days ago, we'd watched Dad draw energy from the fullmooners.

"I tried to call, but I guess you'd already left home," she begins. "Juno told me about your grandmother showing up with Pancha."

"Is that a problem?" I ask, trying to act as if I haven't been worrying about the same thing.

The neurologist, Dr. Gorman, has told me before that a severe emotional shock can cause a stroke patient to emotionally withdraw, and Candide reminds me of the danger. It's a serious risk, she says, especially when a patient has trouble speaking. She says the image of a man clutching his heart after being confronted with bad news is, for the most part, made-for-television drama. But, Candide says, something as jarring as seeing his sister and mother could certainly lead to calamity.

"I'm thinking it might be too much," Candide warns.

"What should I do?"

She gives me a sympathetic smile. "Stall," she says.

"Stall?"

"Tell your dad about his mother, but give him a day or two before you bring them both by."

When she says this something heavy and dull clenches my ribs. What am I going to say to Olympia? And how the hell am I going to survive a long, tense night with Pancha?

Candide puts her arm around my shoulders and pulls me against her side.

"I'll help," she says.

"There's so much more to this than you can possibly know," I tell her, shaking my head.

"Darling," she replies, "with family, there always is."

I return to the waiting area and explain the situation. Pancha presses her lips together and takes a loud, impatient breath in through flared nostrils. She tells Olympia what is happening.

"I'm so sorry," I say to my grandmother.

"No," she answers softly. *"Entiendo."*

When I walk into Dad's room alone, he is glad to see me.

"Nee!"

He may have forgotten that I was supposed to arrive with Pancha at my side. His voice is too cheerful, his welcome too unguarded. He doesn't turn his head to look for a second person.

"Mooffee?"

He must have lost track of time. "No, Dad," I say, "no movie tonight. We need to talk about Pancha."

For the first time since I began mentioning her name, I see a ripple of recognition cross Dad's face. His smile fades and his eyes dart to the doorway. It's come back to him. His sister is supposed to be here, carrying almost fifty years of unresolved history with her.

"She got into town today," I say.

Dad shifts in his wheelchair, attempting, I think, to sit up straighter. "Pansha?"

"She's not with me right now."

He stops moving and listens intently.

"She brought somebody with her." I sit on his bed so we are eye-to-eye.

Dad blinks nervously.

"Somebody you haven't seen in a long time."

I set my hand on the wheelchair's tray table, and Dad covers it with his good hand. Does he know what I'm about to say? He closes his eyes and lets his head fall back so his mouth is slightly ajar.

"It's your mother," I say as gently as I know how. "Olympia."

Without opening his eyes, Dad takes one sharp breath. I watch his fingers clench into a fist, and then I see his nose and the tips of his ears begin to redden. He does not look at me when the tears begin to fall.

"She can't wait to see you," I say, my voice unstable.

Dad lowers his chin to his chest and then curls as far into himself as is possible in the wheelchair, pulling both of his arms in tight and pitching his forehead against the tray table. He cannot hold his tears. In an awkward embrace, I drape myself over his shoulders and feel his entire back convulse. His breaths are short and the base of his neck is hot against my cheek.

I don't want to be the confused child this time, standing stunned and speechless in front of the lifeless silver urn filled with my mother's ashes. I want to be strong. But it's no different now than it was then. Seeing my father weep terrifies me.

"It's good, Dad," I whisper. "This is good. "

Slowly, Dad's shoulders stop quivering and, after a few long moments, he is still. I stand and step to the front of his wheelchair, run my hand through his hair, gently coaxing him to look at me.

"It'll be okay," I say to console him. "I'm glad she's here. Do you want to see her? She's outside, waiting to come in."

He does not move his head.

"Dad, I love her already," I continue. "I really do."

He still does not respond.

"Dad?"

Something is wrong. I slide my hand underneath my father's chin and lift his head. His jaw is slack and there is a raspy gurgling coming from deep inside his throat. His eyes are open wide in alarm. I step behind him and, in a panic, push my fist underneath his ribs in case he's choking on a piece of food.

Nothing.

Rushing into the hallway, I scream for Candide, pounding the wall each time I call out her name. She and another nurse push past me as they run to Dad's side.

"Tell the desk nurse to get Dr. Gorman," Candide commands. "Go!"

I do as she says, and the next thing I know I'm standing outside the closed door of my father's room, flanked by Olympia and Pancha, the three of us holding hands as the doctor bursts through the double doors at the far end of the hallway. He is walking instead of running. Shouldn't he be running? He gives the three of us a serious look before he rushes past us, mumbling something I can't make out as he steps inside. Behind the door, I hear sharp voices and urgent rustling. Neither Pancha nor Olympia ask what has gone wrong. When Candide steps out a few endless moments later, her hair is disheveled and her face is flushed.

"He's fine," she says. "Lost his breath for a minute there. But he'll be okay."

Pancha tells Olympia, who immediately shuts her eyes and makes the sign of the cross, twice.

Now Dr. Gorman steps into the hallway with us.

"He had a little more trouble than usual swallowing all day today," Candide reports.

Dr. Gorman nods. "What we don't want is pneumonia."

I feel Olympia's grip tighten when she recognizes the word "pneumonia." Pancha releases my hand and I glance at her, silently requesting another round of translation.

Dr. Gorman looks directly at Olympia, nodding while Pancha speaks, as if he understands what she is saying. Does he speak Spanish? I never thought to ask.

"This is Diego's mother," Candide informs him. "And his sister."

Dr. Gorman gives them both a polite smile.

"Can I see him?" I ask, even though I know the answer will be no.

"Better let him rest," Candide replies.

"Tomorrow," Dr. Gorman says as he takes a step back toward the threshold. He leans his shoulder against Dad's door and is ready to push it open when he stops and looks directly at Olympia.

"Mañana," he says with a little bow. "You'll see your son *mañana.*"

CHAPTER *16*

*I*t is about eight thirty when we leave the Rose Tree.

I try to imagine what sour mix of emotions Olympia is feeling after having waited so long and traveling so far. Two steps, that was how close she was to her son after all this time, two immeasurable steps. Pancha and Olympia reach the door that leads out of the medical ward before I do and, as they exit, Candide pulls me aside.

"You told him?" she asks.

I nod.

She pats my arm. "Give him 'til tomorrow."

In the car, I ask Pancha if there's anyplace in particular she'd like to stop for groceries. She shakes her head and doesn't bother to translate for her mother. My hand reaches out for the radio knob, but I pull it back. Drowning out the silence with music would be rude, but to be honest, I'm not sure how the three of us are going to manage to get through the rest of the night. It is a quick drive home and the only sound to crack the quiet is the rattle of the cassette tapes I keep in a shoe box behind the driver's seat. The sleet, I notice, has stopped falling and, while the streets are still wet, they are no longer slippery.

At the house, the kitchen still smells like a summer picnic. I guess Pancha will eat salad and olives until we go shopping.

"Do you want to see what's on television?" I ask.

"I don't watch TV," Pancha says.

Of course not.

I lead them into the living room, where Olympia positions herself in front of my needlepointing chair and slowly leans against her cane to lower herself into it. The seat cushion is so deep it just about swallows her. Still gripping her cane, she shifts until her back touches the chair's tufted back, which makes her feet rise off the floor like a toddler's. Nonchalantly, she puts the cane by her side and wiggles her toes until her pumps drop to the carpet. I hurry to set them aside and push the ottoman beneath her free-floating ankles.

Looking over one of the armrests, Olympia sees the wicker basket in which I keep a few plastic boxes filled with embroidery floss, a slim wooden case made for holding needles and threaders, and a pair of small sharp scissors. On top of all of those things she finds the goblet canvas and, looking up at me, she sets her hand on the needlework.

I yank the chain on the reading lamp to give her more light. Gently she unrolls the canvas over her knees and takes a long look. Holding it at an angle under the strong light, she closely studies the brick stitch. Meanwhile, Pancha has settled herself into the far corner of the sofa, where she's paging through last week's issue of *Time* that Juno left on the coffee table.

"Muy, muy bonito," Olympia says before adding a comment I can't decipher. Pancha doesn't hear, and I don't feel like getting her involved. So I answer, *"Gracias,"* and seat myself on the floor at the base of the, reading lamp. Olympia smiles down on me, and I pull out one of the plastic boxes to keep our exchange alive. It's the sort of box you'd find in a hardware store, about the size of a clipboard and compartmentalized inside. A handyman would use it to organize little things like bolts and washers. A needleworker would use it to store thread. Inside mine, each section holds about a dozen different shades of embroidery floss wrapped around pieces of cardboard the size of a movie ticket, and each card is assigned a place next to a color that is in the same palette. The blue section begins with a slate tone that borders on gray and builds in

intensity. There is a shade that looks like a cloudless July sky, one that matches the blue of Paul Newman's eyes, and several that verge on purple or black. It's my own collection of pastels.

"*Sí*," Olympia says as she peers inside. "*Son muchos.*"

Again I smile, assuming by the cheerfulness in her eyes that she's complimenting me.

The needle I've been using to make the goblet project is stuck through one edge of the canvas, its tip woven through two strands of the tight mesh and its eye still tethered to a short tail.

"I use cotton more than wool," I say as I remove the needle and quickly thread it with a new strand of the floss I've been using to make the brick pattern. "It's probably not the best for things that get a lot of use, but it comes in so many more colors and I like how it reflects the light."

I'm aware Olympia can't follow what I'm saying, but it makes me feel better to fill the quiet room with conversation and, whether my words mean anything to her or not, she listens closely. She slides the canvas off her lap and hands it to me. I push the needle up from underneath and pull the strand until there is only an inch or two left on the underside. Holding that end of the floss down with two fingers on my left hand, I take the needle in my right and demonstrate the brick stitch for Olympia.

"It's a straight stitch, not diagonal," I say. "You count four threads and put the needle in. Then you bring the tip through the hole right next door and go up another four threads."

Olympia watches closely as I make three more stitches. Then I hand the needle to her. "You try."

She takes the canvas and leans back in the big chair to get more light. With the fingers of her left hand keeping the work taut, she glides the needle through the mesh in smooth and confident sweeps. Her stitches are even and neat, and working in steady rhythm she completes the row perfectly.

"Hey," I say and chuckle, "you already know how to do this."

"*Sí.*" She nods. "*Sé un poquito.*"

Sitting on the floor at her side, with both of our elbows resting on the wide arm of the easy chair, I feel as if I have always known her. As if, were we able to hold a true conversation, it would start somewhere in the middle of both our lives and continue until the end of time. I hand Olympia a pair of scissors that I've tied onto a long loop of ribbon and she snips a new strand of embroidery floss. When she's done, she instinctively pulls the ribbon over her head to wear the scissors like a necklace, the same way I do. Next I watch her rethread the needle. With her short brown fingers holding the wisp of thread without a single shake or jitter, Olympia moistens the tip by passing it between her pursed lips. Then she wraps the end of the strand around the needle's eye, making a tiny loop and pinching its base tight. Creasing her brow in concentration, she slowly slips the loop into the needle's oblong eye. And it's that tiny action, that gesture of unswerving determination that fuses her heart to mine. The move is as familiar to her as it is to me, and it makes me realize that between us language doesn't matter. Olympia DeLeon has been living in my soul since the day I was born, and there is no language that can make the connection more complete.

As she stitches another row, I glance across the room and see that Pancha has dozed off with the magazine in her lap. Her scarf has slipped from her head onto her shoulders, and the soft lamplight makes her long, wavy hair look like rippled silk. If she had arrived before the fullmooners filled me in on her history with Dad, would I have liked her?

"Un momento," Olympia says, setting down the needlepoint. She lifts her feet off the ottoman and begins shifting in her chair again.

"Do you want to stand?"

I slide the ottoman back a few inches, and Olympia sinks her cane into the carpet. I reach over to get her shoes, but she shakes her head to let me know she doesn't need them.

With both hands on top of the silver handle of her cane, she sets her narrow stocking feet on the floor and begins to lean forward. I position myself at her side and hold on to her elbow to help. She is so unsteady that, for an instant, I worry that if I push too hard she will topple. This is the first time I've seen her move like a woman her age, and I wonder if she's in pain.

I help her balance as she carefully takes a few steps away from the easy chair. Once we've made it to the living room's entrance, she taps my fingers to let me know it's all right to let her go.

"Sleep?" I ask, tilting my head and pressing my hands together underneath my cheek, like a bad mime.

"No," she answers as she motions for me to follow her into the hallway. I look over at Pancha, who is still asleep, and turn off the reading light as I leave the room. Olympia leads me into the office, where she walks straight to the steamer trunk on which her luggage is resting. She points to the smaller of the two bags she brought with her, a square-shaped duffel with so many side pockets that it looks like one of Lauren's old camera bags. I lift it, expecting heavy resistance, but it is surprisingly light. I hear a faint rattle come from something inside.

Olympia has perched herself on the edge of the foldout bed and the springs underneath the thin mattress squeal. I wonder if it is going to be too difficult for her to get in and out of this thing. I'll offer her my bedroom, where the bed is not only firmer but also sits a little higher, even though that will leave me here with Pancha during her entire stay.

Patting the comforter, Olympia invites me to set down the duffel and take a seat beside her. She unzips the bag and pulls out a long piece of fabric with blue and green stripes that make it look like a piece of ribbon candy. It appears to be the size of a bedsheet, but heftier than linen. Olympia unfurls it and I see that it is a tablecloth, decorated along its edges with intricate embroidery done in white, a perfect contrast to the textile's bold-colored weave. The needlework is geometric: zigzags and checkerboard diamond shapes alongside simple animal figures that look somewhat Southwestern. I've seen images like this before. It takes a moment or two for me to remember where. Then a shudder ripples through me. They are identical to the designs that were on the pieces of pottery my mother was putting on display the night she was killed.

All the vases, bowls and serving trays Mom had made that summer were still in the trunk of her car, safely cradled inside half a dozen cardboard boxes lined with shredded newspaper when Mrs. Stevens arrived. Dad asked the police to return all sixteen pieces to him and, months later, they did. Two had cracks down their middles, and one showed up chipped at its base. He gave the tallest and prettiest vase to the Stevenses, who still keep it in their den, and he put the rest of the set inside our china cabinet at home. We never used any of the pieces, never touched them, except to wipe off the dust that collected.

When school resumed that fall, Mrs. Stevens invited me to stay at her place until Dad got home from work. I didn't have anything to do after school until swim practice started, so I spent my afternoons with her. Sometimes she'd talk on the telephone or page through cooking magazines while I did my homework. But mostly she sat in one of the big boxy reading chairs in her living room and stitched.

One afternoon she informed me that her needlepoint club was going to meet and I was welcome to sit in. This, she said, was going to be a particularly exciting meeting because Diana Compton was bringing her aunt Pru's storage trunk, which was supposed to be filled with amazing canvases. I couldn't have cared less, and I asked if I could watch television in the master bedroom instead.

With an episode of *Hogan's Heroes* playing, I opened a bottle of pink nail polish that I found on Mrs. Stevens's dresser and began to paint my toenails. I heard the front door open and close as each member of the club stepped into Mrs. Stevens's house, and I tried to picture what the trunk would look like. If it was like the ones I'd seen in old movies, it would be bulky and stout and plastered with stickers from London and Paris and Istanbul. When Mrs. Compton arrived, I heard the heavy box thump into the foyer, and then I heard the women laughing as they slid it into the den. I decided I'd poke my head into the room and take a quick look.

Peering around the doorway that separated the dining room from the den, I saw the enormous box. Its dark leather shell was nicked and scarred and blotched with water stains. At least a dozen square and round and star-shaped stickers clung to its lid, but from my vantage point there was no way to read where they were from.

Mrs. Compton swung open the heavy lid.

"Wait until you see." She pulled out a cardboard box the size of a serving tray, and Mrs. Stevens asked her not to set it down on the wall-to-wall carpet until she could get a bedsheet for protection.

She smiled when she saw me and, despite my silent protests, grabbed my hand and pulled me into the den when she returned with the linen.

I eased myself onto the sofa between Mrs. Foster, whose son was on my swim team, and Mrs. Birmingham, who smelled like cigarettes and Shalimar. Mercifully, Mrs. Compton brought everyone's attention back to the trunk and I didn't have to hear them tell me how sorry they were about Mom.

Pulling out what ended up being nine cardboard boxes, Mrs. Compton explained that her aunt Prudence was married to the captain of a commercial ship and had accompanied him on several journeys around the world. Pru's own children inherited ivory carvings, strings of Tahitian pearls and delicate decanters made of Venetian glass.

"But Aunt Pru knew I was the one who should have this."

When she opened the first box, the women all leaned forward to get a closer look. Inside was a canvas, rolled up like a carpet, wrapped in yellowed tissue paper. As Mrs. Compton slowly revealed the needlepoint's design, the ladies abandoned their seats and wound up sitting or lying on the floor at the edge of the bedsheet like schoolgirls at a picnic.

I don't know if any of them had ever seen such intricate needlework before, but I certainly hadn't. I'd watched Mrs. Stevens make curly lettered monograms and stupid country baskets filled with kittens, and I thought every needlepointer's repertoire consisted of nothing but that and tired depictions of lighthouses standing on craggy cliffs. But when I saw Pru's work, I realized it could be beautiful.

The first piece, Mrs. Compton told us, was a portrait of Pru's husband, stern and proud in his dark blue uniform. The curls in his auburn beard tumbled to the middle of his broad chest, and Pru had somehow managed to capture the permanent sunburn in his cheeks, the wrinkles in his brow and the sea-green tinge in his hazel eyes. I wished my mother could have been there to see this painting made of wool.

Each canvas was more amazing than the one before it. One was the size of a pot holder and showed the side view of two tiny Chinese shoes, the kind worn by women with bound feet. Using stitches so small they would have fit inside the eye of a needle, Pru had copied perfectly the luxurious pattern woven into the red silk. Another piece showed a long row of sailboats docked in a foreign port. Pru had not only replicated the ships' complicated rigging, but had found a way to show how the sun played off the water below the vessels and the red tile rooftops above them. I had a hard time believing the intense portraits and rich still lifes were the result of a simple needle pulling yarn.

I couldn't help but think of Mom and all the classes and workshops she'd stuck me in, hoping an artistic spark would ignite. And now, there it was, burning like crazy inside of me. I marveled over every one of the incredible creations Mrs. Compton laid in front of me, and when the ladies left, I asked Mrs. Stevens to teach me how to stitch like Pru.

Once I learned the basics, I retreated into my own world of color and design. I'm certain that is what got me through that first, horrible year. I could feel Mom smiling every time I finished a piece, and knowing that I was making her proud allowed me to smile again.

Like Pru's designs, the zigzags, diamonds and hieroglyphics of Mom's pottery were scored into my memory. I'd always thought they were stock folk-art symbols that she had drawn on the stoneware to appeal to the health-food, macramé and Earth-shoe crowd. But now I take the Guatemalan tablecloth into my hands and examine the embroidery more closely.

"*Tela típica,*" Olympia says.

"Mmm," I murmur as I run my palm over the fabric. The thick, tight weave of the tablecloth delights me. It is surprisingly soft and as inviting as well-worn denim.

"*Maya,*" Olympia tries.

That, I understand.

According to the book I've been reading since the fullmooners' visit, Guatemala's Mayan Indians are the ethnic group that has suffered the most from the decades of political strife. Poor, uneducated and determined to live off the land the way their ancient ancestors did, they have been caught in the middle of the endless struggle. And still, in the face of cold-blooded murders, bold and brutal kidnappings and flagrant governmental abuse, the Mayans have continued to peacefully weave beautiful textiles that are prized around the world.

"Lovely," I tell her.

In the center of the tablecloth, only partly stitched, I see a faint sketch of a blanket of flowers outlined in fine blue lines. At least two feet long and about one foot wide, I can tell the sketch was drawn hastily, without any concern for detail. Most of the flowers consist of little more than four or five circles flanked by the suggestion of leaves. Straight-line stems, as well as ones that curve, have been penciled in with slashes here and there. And in a few instances, a crown of oval petals has been drawn around a center dot to show where daisies or zinnias or spiky thistles will emerge. At the base of the sketch I see a small wooden hoop that has been clasped to the fabric to stretch a fist-size portion of it tight.

"You did this embroidery?"

"*Sí.*"

Olympia's work is as incredible as Pru's. There is not a single stitch that is too long or too short, not one thread that has been pulled too tight or left slack. Somehow she's made each flower look unique. She's given each leaf a sense of texture distinguishing it from the one next to it. There are stitches that loop and swirl and skip and glide. The flower and vine motif grows from large to small as it travels across the entire tablecloth's hem in a perfectly straight four-inch-wide band. It is breathtaking.

From the tote bag, Olympia pulls out a box that is similar to the one in which I keep my needlepoint floss. Inside she has dozens of tiny spools of silk that glimmer like dragonflies' wings. She also has a pin-

cushion shaped like a tomato, impaled by half a dozen crewel and chenille needles, one of which is already threaded. She pulls that one out
of the cushion and hands it to me, along with the hooped fabric.

"I don't know how to make freehand stitches," I say apologetically,
my tone conveying my meaning.

Olympia makes a playful frown and takes the needle from my grasp.
When I try to hand the hoop back to her, she makes a gesture for me
to stop. Moving closer to my side, she slides the needle underneath the
fabric and then pulls it up so a strand of rose-colored thread becomes a
thin line between us.

She looks at me and I nod, ready to learn whatever she will teach me.

She loops the thread around and holds it down with her thumb.
Plunging the needle's tip back into the fabric, she quickly brings it up
again and repeats the loop.

"Chain stitch," I say.

She nods and, once again, hands the needle to me.

I make a loop the same way I saw her do it and press it down with
my thumb. I try to pierce the fabric gracefully, but the needle is much
thinner and more delicate than the ones I'm used to holding, and it
feels awkward in my hand. The fabric feels foreign, too, strong and a
little bumpy but with much more give than the stiff canvas grids on
which I needlepoint. The two chain stitches Olympia made are taut
and secure. My attempt is flabby. I scrunch my face in protest and
Olympia motions for me to try again. I attempt to follow the line of a
vine that she's drawn, but the wooden hoop bumps my wrist and my
second stitch veers off at an odd angle.

"This is why I stick to needlepoint." I sigh.

Olympia takes the fabric from me and slides the needle along the
strand of pink thread until it slips free. She uses the needle's sharp tip
to undo my messy stitches. Then, without uttering a word, she reaches
into her bag and pulls out a piece of scrap fabric the size of a dinner
napkin. She also takes out a piece of blue dressmaker's chalk. With fast,
sharp strokes she draws the outline of a winding stone walkway that
leads to a brick wall with an arched trellis. On the far side of the wall,

she sketches a tree trunk topped with puffy pom-poms of foliage. She fills the trellis with squiggles that I assume are flowers and a hailstorm of leaves. She flanks the stone pathway with diagonal slashes that will become shrubs and wild grasses.

Reaching over to the tomato pincushion, she selects a short, sharp needle with a small round eye and a spool of narrow silk cord the color of bronze. She cuts a strand that stretches from her knuckles to her elbow, and hands the needle and thread to me.

"Do you have a threader?" I ask and begin rummaging around in her box to find the little wire tool I depend on.

"Pfft," she scoffs, shaking her head. *"Mira."* Again she folds the thread around the needle's eye, slips the loop off the needle and pushes it through, coaxing it with a little wiggle of her thumb. When it peeks out the other end, she grabs the loop and pulls.

"Wow."

I reach out to accept it. But instead of handing the needle to me, Olympia pulls the thread back out with a flick of her narrow wrist, leaving me where I started. She is treating me like a complete beginner, which stings. But I can't get too angry, since in her eyes I can't even thread a needle right. The only way I'm going to win her over is to show her what I can do. I find the thread's end and repeat what I've just seen. Lips. Loop. Wiggle of the thumb. Magically, the thread goes in. I hold the threaded needle in front of my grandmother like a trophy. She grins and sets the piece of scrap fabric in my lap.

"I don't know where to start," I say, hesitating.

She points to the stone path. I poke the needle up from under the fabric and pull it until the knot I made at the end of the thread stops me. Then I look back at Olympia for guidance. She digs inside her bag again and produces another wooden hoop, which she attaches to the scrap. Now the blue lines of the stone path look like country roads on a gas-station map circled inside a bull's-eye target, waiting for me to take aim.

"Punto cadena," Olympia says.

"Hmm?"

She picks up the hoop and points to the two perfect chain stitches she made a moment ago.

"Oh," I say, nodding, *"chain."*

"Sí, todo esto es punto cadena." She skims her index finger over the portion of the fabric that is stretched tight.

"Cadena," I echo.

Olympia returns her attention to her own work, and when my eyes follow hers, she begins to name each stitch she's made on the tablecloth in Spanish. I strain to follow what she is saying, but her words spill out so fast that my ear can't keep up. Showing me a simple leaf pattern, she says a word that sounds like "Ohio." Then she points to a similar leaf she drew on the fabric scrap in my hands. Next she sets her finger on a pretty peacock tail of knotted stitches and indicates that I should make the same kind of design for the flowers growing on the trellis.

"Yes," I tell her, "I understand. But maybe it would be better if tomorrow we go to the craft store and buy a book of stitches written in English."

She rests her hands on top of the beautiful tablecloth and looks at me quizzically.

"Mañana," I say, searching my memory for a second word to add to my sentence. "Umm . . . *Tienda!"* I say, triumphantly.

Olympia keeps her eyes on mine as I try again.

"Mañana, tienda . . . this . . ." I say, lifting up the needle and thread.

"Oh, no," Olympia answers softly, *"mañana, Diego."* I look into her face, my mood still light from the fun we've been having, and see that her entire expression has fallen. I feel her hand on mine, her skin as powdery as talcum, her fingers flat and strong. *"Por favor,"* she whispers. *"Diego."*

"Of course," I stammer. "I meant before we go to the Rose Tree. *Before."*

When the stroke hit Dad, Mrs. Stevens phoned me and I was out of my front door and headed to the airport in fifteen minutes flat. I spoke to her by cell phone during the entire drive as well as while I parked the car and found the departure gate. She stayed on the line with me while I boarded, and heard me curse the flight attendants when they told me I had to turn off the phone long enough to let the plane scream down the runway. When I got to the hospital, Dad was hooked up to hissing tubes and dripping bags. Machines with glowing green lights monitored every tick of his heart and his face looked so ashen I thought for a moment that he was dead. But his eyelids fluttered, and fat blue veins throbbed at his temples. His good leg twitched.

For years after Mom died, I tried to guess how God was going to take Dad away from me. Would it be in a car accident? A slip down a set of stairs? A snake bite? I prepared myself for anything. At swimming practice, I learned mouth-to-mouth and CPR. At home, I clipped *Reader's Digest* articles describing heroic rescues made by men and women and fearless dogs. I read them over and over so I'd be ready to do the right thing during a raging house fire, a snowy avalanche or a freeway pileup. I collected Red Cross pamphlets and memorized the red-lettered lists of lifesaving advice. *If your car ends up at the bottom of a lake, look for the air pocket near the roof. If a bear is near, act like a tree. Crawl through a fire. Don't fight quicksand.*

In bed at night, I'd listen to Dad move through the house, and as long as I heard the sounds of clipped British accents coming from his regular public television programs, or the liquid tempos of his favorite waltzes by Strauss, I knew it was safe to go to sleep. Every morning, I'd wake up to the sound of his Norelco razor and wonder who in the world decided it was a good idea to put an electric outlet in the light above the sink.

That's why Olympia's plea hits me like a punch. Could she honestly believe I'd forget about him for an entire day? I take good care of Dad, I want to tell her. I take good care of him. You have no idea how hard it will be for you to see him in the condition he's in, I want to say to my grandmother. How deeply it will bruise your heart. But all I can do is look into her face and hope she understands.

I wonder what she remembers about Dad. What memories of her boy does she have locked up inside her? A grin he gave her from his crib? A game of chase he played at a birthday party? Maybe she still has dreams about the last time she saw him. How he said good-bye.

How much does she know about Pancha's run with the rebels? What would she tell me about it if we spoke the same language? Would she defend her daughter? For now, we'll have to let the wordless code of needlework, the push and pull of loops and knots, do our speaking for us. I smooth my scrap of fabric on top of the foldout bed.

"This," I say to her in slow, deliberate English, "early in the morning, and then, of course, Diego."

CHAPTER 17

"*M*y bed's better."

I've got Olympia's large suitcase in my hand and I'm motioning for her to follow me. The needlework has been put away, and she is holding her embroidery bag in one hand and her cane in the other. "I'll change the sheets in a flash, and you'll be all set."

We make our way out of the office and past the kitchen. A quick glance at the microwave clock tells me the night has advanced past eleven. As we make the turn that leads into the living room, I raise my finger to my lips, in case Pancha is still asleep on the sofa. When we get to my bedroom, I step aside and let Olympia enter first.

The first thing that catches her eye is an old black-and-white photograph that hangs over my bed. Encased in a long and narrow frame, it is a vintage print showing the contestants of the 1921 Miss America contest standing in one long row along the Atlantic City boardwalk. Unsure exactly how beauty pageant girls should carry themselves, the pale-skinned beauties are posed square-shouldered and straight-legged, looking directly into the camera. They have droopy white sashes over their knee-length bathing outfits and bemused expressions on their faces. I love the picture because there isn't a single girl in it who looks like she really wants to win.

I pull a set of pink sheets off the bed as Olympia sets down her bag and steps toward my collection of family photos arranged on top of one of the dressers. I watch her peer at a picture of my parents that I took the Christmas before Mom died. I snapped it with the Kodak Insta-matic they gave me as a present that morning. In it, Dad is wearing his favorite terry-cloth robe and his arm is around the slouchy shoulders of Mom's red-checked flannel pajamas. She's got a red-and-green crown of adhesive-backed gift bows stuck to her dark shoulder-length hair, and they are both standing in a sea of torn and crumpled wrapping paper that is ankle deep. I gave her a pair of slippers from Kmart as a present that year because I could buy them with my own money and still have twenty-three dollars left in my savings account.

I step out of the room to get clean sheets from the linen closet, and when I return Olympia has lifted my favorite photograph of my mother from the dresser top. It is a small picture, taken by Dad early one morning shortly after I was born. Mom's hair is pulled into a loose braid that stops at the nape of her long neck. She is seated in a white rocking chair, wearing a pretty yellow nightgown with a dainty smocked top, holding a pink-blanketed bundle in her arms. You can't see my face, but you can see my feet poking out from the bottom of the blanket, lost inside a pair of pink booties that are several sizes too big. Every one of my mother's eyelashes is outlined by the rising sun as she gazes down, mesmerized by me.

There's a picture of the three of us standing by the side of the pool at the first swim meet in which I won a ribbon. I am wet and flashing a toothless grin. And next to that photo, captured in a crystal frame, is an image of me at my college graduation. Snapped by Randy Stevens, the photo shows me waving my rolled diploma in the air while Dad pulls out the empty linings of his trouser pockets and grimaces sarcastically at the camera.

I fluff the two feather pillows and smooth the comforter on top of them.

"There we are," I say as I flip on the reading lamp.

Olympia steps to the edge of the bed and carefully sits herself down. I am about to say good night when she speaks.

"Tu mamá," she says softly, *"y Pancha . . . amigas."*

I wonder if I've heard her right.

"My mother and Pancha were friends?"

"Sí," Olympia says. *"Antes de tu papá."*

"I don't understand."

"Emm," my grandmother replies, trying to recall enough English to make herself understood. "Before?" she finally asks.

"Before?" I ask back. "Mom and Pancha were friends before?"

Olympia points to a slender gold band on her left ring finger.

I think for a moment. "Before Mom and Dad got married?"

"Sí." Olympia nods. *"Pancha y tu mamá, amigas."*

The notion of my mother and Pancha spending time together as young and single girlfriends had never crossed my mind. Mom had painted the picture of her childhood for me in wide, broad strokes. I knew she came from a family with enough money to put her in private schools where she learned to speak flawless French and excellent English by the time she was fourteen. I knew her house had a central courtyard where banana and orange trees grew side by side, and that her pets were parrots and canaries. It seems unlikely that Mom and Pancha's paths would have ever crossed, especially if what Dad told me about his own childhood is true. That he came from the other side of the tracks, the dirt-road and tin-roof section of Guatemala City. His father ran a tiny radio station before he died, and Olympia taught for the public schools.

Mom and Dad told me they first met at a national high school oratory contest, where they were pitted against one another, having taken the top prizes at their respective schools. Mom was sixteen. Dad was seventeen and on the verge of high school graduation. Mom used to say that she let Dad win because the prize was a full scholarship to the university and he needed it more than she did. Dad used to tease that that was Mom's sore-loser excuse.

As a kid, I asked to hear the story so many times that they created a game out of making wild additions to it. Dad would say that a pack of penguins waddled in front of the judges during his speech. Mom would add that her hair caught on fire from the hot stage lights. Every time, the tale got more outrageous and, after a while, I forgot which version was the absolute truth.

Olympia lowers her back onto the pillows and lifts her hand to cover a long yawn. There's no point in asking her about Mom and Pancha now. She needs to sleep.

"Buenas noches," I say after pulling a clean nightgown and a pair of socks out of a dresser drawer. I close the door behind me.

From the hallway I can see that Pancha is awake. Still seated on the sofa, she is concentrating on something perched on her lap, probably the same magazine she was reading when she dozed off earlier. But from where I'm standing, I can't tell for sure. She does not know I am watching, and I use the opportunity to take a long look. The row of polished silver bangles coiled like a spring around her arm is, I have to admit, the kind of jewelry my mother would have loved. And although I have no way to know what kind of clothes Mom would favor these days, I imagine her outfits wouldn't look much different from the flowing skirt and simple jacket that Pancha has on.

"I put her in my room," I say as I approach. "I'll sleep on the pull-out."

Pancha blinks and glances at her wristwatch. She shifts and her bracelets clink. I remain standing, hoping that my body language will show that I'm ready to call it a night. To emphasize the point, I try to coax a convincing yawn from the bottom of my throat, but all I can manage is a quiet sigh. I don't have the energy to get into a conversation with her tonight, and it's just too late to bother with chitchat. The problem is Pancha does not pick up my message.

"You know," she says, "I never saw these."

I see my parents' wedding album spread open across her knees. Even in the dim lamplight, even from as far away as I am standing, I can tell precisely which page she is on. It is the first of six showing snapshots from the reception. Pancha's hands are resting on the black, brittle pages, her thumbs next to the photo of a group of guests I nicknamed The Martinis long ago: three white-gloved ladies in pearls and sleek hats accompanied by two young handsome men. All five of their heads are tossed back in laughter, and the table in front of them is littered with white porcelain cake plates, crushed cigarettes and sweaty cocktails.

Slowly, Pancha turns the page. "I know these people," she says as she studies the faces of my parents' friends. "Or at least I used to know them."

What I feel when I hear this isn't surprise, or anger, or even curiosity. It is more off balance than that. After years of trying to imagine the possible stories behind each of those faces, I have the opportunity to find out exactly who they are. I could sit down right now and ask my aunt whether The Martinis were my mother's artsy friends, as I imagined they were. Or whether they were university chums of my father. She could tell me how the tall, thin man with the horn-rimmed glasses and narrow bow tie, who is pictured dancing with the bride, fit into my mother's life. And I could find out who invited the three straight-faced men in dark glasses who sometimes appear leaning against the walls, solemnly taking everything in.

But I don't.

Pancha moves on to another page, where she sees a shot of Dad playfully closing one eye as he aims a piece of cake at Mom's mouth. I can tell she wants to talk about it, but she is waiting for me to issue the invitation. I'd always wanted Dad to be the one to explain the photos to me. But he never did, no matter how often I asked. As a girl I thought it was because he didn't like being sentimental. But as I got older, I figured out the real reason why. I gazed at the old pictures, but Dad entered them. Every time I set the album before him, he was thrown back to that sunny Sunday afternoon when he believed "until death do us part" would never come. It was too much, so he kept the stories to himself. He told me the wedding was nothing more than friends, and friends of friends, sharing food and a few hours of fun. After a while, I stopped pushing for more.

Now, Pancha is pushing me.

The thing is, I've made peace with the gaps in my family story. I believe the clean slate that my parents handed to me was a gift. No matter what Juno or anyone else says, I know exactly who I am. I'm the girl my parents hoped I'd become, deeply rooted in rock-hard Texas soil and safely distanced from their difficult past. If they didn't want to pass their history down, why should I be digging it up?

Pancha turns another page, and when she does I seat myself beside her, slip my hand underneath the album and gently pull until one side of it is on her lap and the other is on mine.

"Ah," she whispers when she comes upon the snapshot of the wedding guests gathered outside the chapel, waiting for Mom and Dad to emerge.

"That's Olympia, right?" I ask, pointing at the woman I already know is my grandmother. Pancha nods, and when I look up at her, I see a striking resemblance between her face and the one in the picture. Their bodies are not shaped the same, but the curve of their jawline is identical.

"You look like her," I say.

"We both do," she replies.

I'm not sure whether she's talking about my father or about me.

"What did your father look like?" I ask.

Pancha closes her eyes and smiles. "I was fourteen when he died."

My heart skips a beat. I had no idea.

"He was light-skinned," she continues. "Did you know that? So light-skinned that people thought he was American."

I shake my head. "Dad told me that he had a deep voice, a handlebar mustache and a gold ring that he tapped against the dinner table."

Pancha nods. "That's right." She turns to the last page of the album and takes a long, silent look.

"He was a lot older than my mother. You knew that."

"No."

"Unbelievable," she mumbles. "Didn't they tell you *anything*?"

My back tightens and I snap the album shut.

Pancha looks directly at me, expecting me to answer.

"It's late," I say, sliding the photos back underneath the coffee table where they belong.

"Did they at least tell you what happened? Why they left the country?"

I busy myself with the nightgown I pulled out of my dresser drawer, shaking it out and then folding it back up again. I stand and, without asking Pancha if she's ready to go to bed, I start walking toward the office. I hear her following me, her silver bracelets jingling like a gunfighter's spurs.

"You still want the futon?"

"Yes."

I hear her stop in the kitchen, where she turns the faucet on. There's filtered water in the fridge, but I don't bother to let her know. I keep moving, and shut the door to the office bathroom tight. I forgot to bring my toothbrush with me, but to go and get it now I'd have to walk past Pancha. The taste of my tongue is stale and sour, but I'll put up with it until morning. I rinse out my mouth twice and get undressed. As I splash warm water on my face, I come up with a reply. Isn't that always the way it happens? The words you can't find when you need them come floating to the surface when it's too late. I look at my face in the mirror, still wet and rosy, and whisper the answer to my reflection.

"They told me what I needed to know," I say. "That I was their heart and soul and that they loved me."

I dry my face with my nightgown so the guest towel will stay fresh, and I hear the sound of Pancha's ocean-wave machine seep in from underneath the door.

"Good night," I say when I step out.

"Nita," Pancha answers from the middle of the futon in the waiting room.

"I'm really tired."

Pancha won't take that for an answer. She stands and steps between me and the pull-out sofa.

"Look," I snap, "I don't want to get into it tonight. But I know what happened."

"Regina told you?"

Pancha's hair is loose and draped over her shoulders. Her bracelets have been pulled off, and out of her boots she stands several inches shorter than me. I think about the letter that started all this and wonder how many others she and my mother exchanged.

"No," I say. "My father's friends told me. And I've been doing some reading about the time."

Pancha rolls her eyes and runs her hand through her hair. "Which means you don't know anything."

For a moment we look at one another, and without saying a word I step around her.

"It's late," she mumbles as I take the needlepoint pillows off the bed and pull the bedspread down. "No need to get into it now."

I turn off the office light and leave her standing in front of the bathroom door in the dark. The ocean-wave sounds rise and fall as she runs the faucet and brushes her teeth. When she steps out of the bathroom, she makes her way to the side of my bed and I roll over, pretending to be asleep.

I can feel her looking at me. Waiting. I stay perfectly still.

"You know," Pancha finally whispers, "I loved her, too."

CHAPTER 18

I wake up while it's still dim and bang my hip against the corner of the desk before I remember I am in my office. Pancha is sprawled out on the braided rug in front of me, toes turned out, arms slack, and eyes closed, humming like a machine engine each time she exhales. A thin film of incense smoke is in the air, and the spicy, sooty smell of it crawls up my nose.

It takes a moment for the bite of the chilly morning air to filter through my nightgown, but when it does I shiver. The sound of birds exchanging high-pitched calls seems out of sync with the muzzled gray light straining to come through the curtains. It's not until I step over Pancha that I realize she is in a yoga pose and the sunny birdsongs are coming from her sound machine.

When I reach the kitchen I find Olympia sitting at the table already dressed and working on her embroidery. Her hair, which looks to still be damp, is once again pulled away from her face with old-fashioned combs and silver bobby pins. A dark blue mug of something hot is on the table in front of her and she smiles at me over the thin cloud of steam it is making.

My eyes are filmy and still not fully focused. My hair must be a tangled snarl and, despite my billowy nightgown, I feel undressed.

"Good morning," I say. "Did you sleep all right?"

"*Sí, muy bien, gracias.*"

I don't know that I believe her. It can't be much later than nine in the morning, which means in California it is only six.

Following my regular routine, I turn the radio to the all-news station, where a deep-voiced woman is explaining that a jackknifed truck on the Schuylkill Expressway has caused a three-mile backup. I reach for the coffeemaker and see that the pot is already full. I fill a mug and make my way to the table with both of my hands wrapped around it for warmth.

"If you'll excuse me," I say, "I'm going to grab a bathrobe from the closet in my bedroom."

Olympia smiles, unsure of what I've said.

"*Un momento,*" I say as I leave the room.

Olympia has already made the bed and left her nightgown folded on top of the pillows. On the dresser, next to the photos of Dad and Mom, she has set out a tube of lipstick, a paddle-shaped hairbrush, a small round box of face powder and an expensive cake of French coral-colored rouge. Underneath the neatly arranged cosmetics is a crisp white linen tea towel that has a romantic-looking O embroidered near its hem. The monogram is a perfect oval of dark forest green, with the thinnest sliver of sparkling gold thread serving as its outline. Simple and beautiful.

I grab my bathrobe from the hook behind the closet door. Covered with fuzzy rows of pink chenille, furrowed like a farmer's winter crops, it isn't even close to being attractive, but it's warm and functional. I stop in front of the dresser and look at Olympia's things again. My own round plastic hairbrush is inside the top drawer, which I reach down to open, but my fingers land on the polished wood handle of Olympia's brush instead. It is smooth and shaped to fit comfortably in your grip. I run my finger along the length of it, and in the wide bed of dark bristles, trapped between the rows of stiff tufts, I see a few strands of Olympia's white hair. Pulling the brush through my tangles, I feel a pleasant prickle against my scalp. I never got to see my mother's hair grow gray. She was forty-one when she died. Four years older than I am now.

On my way back to the kitchen, I open the front door and see that the morning paper has, miraculously, landed right on the doorstep. The sun has still not broken through the low-lying clouds, and there is a damp thickness to the air that makes it feel heavy. I scan the headlines and see that Juno has made the front page—SUSPECT IN FIVE AREA MUGGINGS ARRESTED—which I know will make him happy. I'll call after breakfast. Maybe he'll come over and help me deal with Pancha. When I close the door, I hear the teakettle whine. After Pancha leaves, I tell myself, that thing is going straight into the trash.

Wrapped in a royal-blue silk kimono, Pancha is squeezing honey from the bear into her tea when I step into the room. I'm about to tell her and Olympia that it feels like snow, but the radio beats me to it.

"So be sure you're prepared," the reporter says pointedly. "The weather bureau is predicting this could be the harshest storm of the season, with eight to twelve inches expected."

"They like to exaggerate," I reassure Pancha, sliding the newspaper onto the table and sitting down.

Pancha tosses her spoon into the sink and joins us.

"I can run out and get some bagels," I offer.

She takes a sip of her tea and shakes her head no. Her cheeks are pink from the yoga exercises and her robe smells of her jasmine incense.

"Mother said you want to take her to a store for thread this morning?"

Olympia smiles as she opens the newspaper and turns the pages without stopping to read any of the articles. "*Y luego, el* Rose Tree," she adds.

"Right," I say. "We'll go straight from there to see Dad."

Pancha sips her tea.

"We need to talk," she says when she sets down the cup. "Whatever you think you know, it isn't true."

"All I know," I answer, using my emotionless counselor voice, "is that I don't want Dad getting upset today." I think of what Olympia told me last night, and I cannot believe it. Mom couldn't have been close to a person as pushy as this woman.

Olympia stops turning pages and gives Pancha a pleading look.

"I'm going to take a shower," I say, rising from the table. "Let's plan on trying to hit the road in, say, an hour?"

On the cordless telephone in the bedroom, I dial Juno's number.

"Come over here and sleep," he says after I tell him about everything that happened with Dad and Olympia and Pancha last night. "There's a whole half of a bed waiting for you."

"I'm serious," I whine. "She's impossible. She told me that everything I've read is untrue. Everything the fullmooners said, too. Can you believe that kind of gall?"

"Well," Juno says, his voice still heavy with sleep, "she's probably a little right."

"What?"

"History is recorded by people who want it told their way."

"Please," I groan.

"Hey," he answers, sounding more deliberate, "that's why it's better to have the whole story."

"I suppose."

"By the way," he adds, "I may be getting somewhere in finding out some more about all of this myself. I've come across some sources—"

"Can we talk about something else?"

Juno sighs and I can hear rustling that suggests he's getting out of bed. I think of his broad back and sturdy legs, and picture him in his undershirt and shorts, blinking at the dull morning light without the benefit of his glasses.

"Saw you made the front page," I say.

"Yeah, froze my butt off standing on the sidewalk while the cops dragged that kid out of his apartment."

"You love it, though, don't you?"

"Not as much as I used to," he says. "It's a young man's game, that's for sure."

"What do you mean?"

"I loved chasing down the breaking stuff ten years ago. I wanted to cover a war someplace, or spend a few years in Africa and China. I felt like the notebook in my hand made me invincible."

"And you don't think that anymore?"

Juno is quiet.

I clear my throat.

"You know why I came here after all those years of working in Miami?"

"Because it's a better newspaper?"

"That's Lauren's version," he says and chuckles. "I came because my best friend, a guy I worked with for fifteen years, was sent to the Middle East for the *Herald*, and I was jealous as hell. He was making the front page every day, and I was stuck on the City Desk covering court cases and city council crap. I told him I was glad for him, but he knew that I wished it was me. Then, one day, while he was out reporting a story on a Palestinian outpost, a stray bullet got him in the chest."

"Why didn't you tell me?"

"I don't know." Juno sighs. "I just couldn't stay there anymore. The editor asked me if I wanted to take over the bureau, like all I'd have to do was clean out his desk and everything would be okay."

"Why Philadelphia?"

"They were the first to offer me a job," he says, "and it's a big enough paper that I thought I might find a safe little beat I could settle into."

"Your family, though."

"It's getting better," he insists. "And, you know, I think I could actually get used to not having them pry into every inch of my personal business."

Should I tell him how I feel? How completely I've fallen for him? How, even though I believe what he's just told me, I can tell by the way he's pursued information about Dad that he still loves the job?

"What's your plan today?" he asks.

"The Rose Tree," I say, feeling my stomach tense.

"Want me there?"

"Yes," I answer instantly. "I do."

I glance through the bedroom window and see fat, fluffy flakes cascading straight down. "Look outside," I tell Juno.

For a moment we both watch, saying nothing.

"How can something so pretty be such a pain in the ass?" Juno cracks.

I don't mention that the forecast is calling for over eight inches. Judging from the way the snow has already picked up speed, the prediction could be accurate.

"We won't stay long," I say. "I don't want to get caught in this when it starts piling up."

"I guess I know what I'm going to be writing about tonight," Juno says. "Traffic accidents and stranded travelers."

After I've showered and dressed, I find both Pancha and Olympia standing outside on the front step with their arms stretched out like scarecrows. Olympia's face is pointed toward the sky, and Pancha's long black hair is covered in a glistening cap of white.

"You need hats," I say, rushing to the closet and digging through the pockets of various coats and jackets for any knit caps or scarfs I can find.

I hand a polar fleece muffler to Olympia and then step up to Pancha.

"We've never seen it before!" she exclaims, her eyes sparkling with excitement. Obediently she accepts the floppy-brimmed wool hat I offer and pulls it over her thick hair. With melting flakes on her lashes, and her nose and cheeks already cranberry red, she actually looks kind. Try harder, I tell myself. Somewhere beneath the sandpaper surface of the woman Pancha has become is the girl my mother once loved. Make an effort to find her.

"Gloves?" I ask.

Instead of stopping at the craft store, I decide we should go to Mega-Mart to buy groceries and some cheap boots and mittens for Olympia and Pancha to use. The lot is jammed with cars and minivans battling for spots, their tires cutting a web of black tracks into the thin veneer of powder that has already begun to hide the parking space lines. Inside the store, people are frantic.

"Grab a bag of that," I order Pancha as I separate from her to claim one of the few shopping carts remaining. Pancha lifts a ten-pound bag of ice-melting salt into her arms and waits for me beside the quickly disappearing pyramid display. Daunted by the crowds, Olympia chose to wait in the car with the heat on and, looking around at the chaos brewing on the shop floor, I am glad. Men and women, young and old, are racing one another to the bread and snatching cartons and jugs of whole and skim and one percent milk, whichever their hands reach first. By the time Pancha and I make it to the bread aisle, every slice of whole wheat is long gone, as is every loaf of white. The woman in front of us, who has a shovel in one hand and a small child in the well of her cart, scoops up the three remaining packets of maple-flavored English muffins and a bag of hamburger buns. Luckily Pancha spots one loan loaf of Jewish rye on the cracker shelf, abandoned, I suppose, by someone who believed Triscuits would taste better.

I have no idea where we should go next, since Pancha's eating habits are so narrow.

"Listen," I say, "why don't you take care of the food while I run to the other side and grab the boots?"

Pancha nods and almost loses her balance when a bald man with a sizable gut elbows his way around her to reach a box of garlic Sociables.

"Excuse me," she says to him accusingly.

Without stopping to acknowledge her, the man continues to wedge himself between Pancha and the cans of imitation cheese spread until his good-size backside rubs against hers. Pancha's eyes widen and we both can't help but laugh. As fleeting as the moment is, it feels nice, as if we might have a chance.

"I'm seven and a half, and she's six," Pancha says, stepping away from the fat man.

"All right, I'll meet you at the checkout."

I make my way to the shoe department, where there are plenty of basic black zip-up boots to be had. I take two pair with good deep treads and walk straight to the hat and glove section. Two women on opposite sides of the twenty-percent-off table are playing an unfriendly game of tug-of-war with a wide green tweed muffler. Assuming both

Olympia's and Pancha's hands are about the same size as mine, I dig through a mound of nylon ski mittens and too-thin-for-warmth dress gloves decorated with delicate lace or shiny satin piping. Finally, on a different table displaying coin purses and leather wallets, I see a few sleek pairs of black leather gloves packed inside flat cellophane envelopes. Imported from Italy, they are more expensive than any of the other pairs. Thirty-five dollars. I grab the ones marked medium and point myself toward the cashier.

Seven long lines of overstuffed carts stretch to the middle of the store, and it looks as if the number of children running around the place has doubled. I find Pancha and wonder what she thinks of the mayhem. She tries on the boots while we wait. Her pair fits and she says she's sure the pair I got for Olympia will do fine.

"Welcome to MegaMart," a voice over the intercom says. "We'll be getting more rock salt out onto the sales floor in just a moment, ladies and gentlemen. But I'm sorry to report that all the snow shovels are now gone."

Pancha glances at me.

"Got one in the trunk of the car," I say, "and one at home."

When we get to the register, I help Pancha place her grocery selections onto the conveyor belt and am genuinely surprised that they are, for the most part, normal. There's a carton of soy milk (which, I imagine, was not running in short supply), a box of shredded wheat cereal, a jar of organic peanut butter, orange marmalade, three boxes of dried pasta and three jars of basil-mushroom spaghetti sauce. She's also selected a head of red leaf lettuce, broccoli and cauliflower, plus half a dozen Granny Smith apples.

"We can bake those," she says, "with a little cinnamon."

"Nice," I say. "It all looks good."

We should just start over. Go back to our first hellos and pave a new road that ends right here. Maybe Pancha would be willing to do that if I asked, to just let go of whatever happened in Guatemala and build a new history from this moment on.

"One hundred sixty-four, seventy-eight," the cashier announces.

"I'll get it," I say, swiping my credit card through the magnetic strip machine perched on the little shelf in front of us.

"I didn't believe you," Pancha says, stopping near the front door of the store to change out of her high-heeled boots into her new ones. "When you said last night that your parents didn't tell you anything about Guatemala. But I guess it's true." She shakes her head as she works the zippers on the boots, as if the thought is still beyond her comprehension.

"If they didn't want me to know, maybe I shouldn't," I say, handing her a pair of leather gloves.

Her bangles clank as she slides her fingers into the snug fit.

"That's not a choice you get to make," she says matter-of-factly, "not when it comes to family history, and not when some people have already filled your head with lies."

I was an idiot to think she'd let it go. Not her. Not ever.

When the store's automatic doors slide open, a rush of freezing wind rolls over us. The snow is falling in a steep diagonal and our shoulders stiffen as we slide the cart through the slushy mix that, by now, has grown two inches deep. The texture of the flakes has begun to change.

"It's turning to ice," I mumble.

"Hmm?" Pancha asks.

"Nothing," I reply, "except if this keeps up, we may have trouble getting home."

CHAPTER 19

At the Rose Tree, Pancha and I help steady Olympia by holding on to her elbows as we make our way into the building. The new snow boots help, but there's enough ice on the ground to occasionally challenge their grip. When the three of us finally step through the front door, a flank of old people who have been watching from the lobby's windows moves back to give us room.

"Nasty!" one woman mutters as we stomp our feet and brush flakes off our shoulders.

The storm has brought every resident who is physically able down to the lobby. There must be at least four dozen men and women clustered in front of the bellowing wide-screen TV. I search the crowd to see if anyone brought Dad out to share the excitement, but I don't spot him.

". . . stalled right over us," the handsome weatherman booms. On the screen behind his head is a radar map with a sea-green swirl flashing over our part of the state. "Let's go out to the roads," the anchorman suggests.

"It's a mess out here, Jim. . . ."

Linda, the front desk receptionist, is using a pencil eraser to punch the seven flashing buttons that are lighting up her telephone console. "Rose Tree, please hold," she says, handing us our badges. "Rose Tree. Yes, ma'am, everyone is fine." Between punches, she slides a small slip of blue paper across the reception desk and points the eraser at me. It's a telephone message from Juno, taken in an obvious rush. *"W'king,"* it says in a broad scrawl, *"C U later."*

I put the note in my coat pocket and begin to pull off my hat and gloves. "Here we go," I mumble as Pancha, Olympia and I begin walking down the main corridor. There's no way to predict how Dad will react when he sees them, and as we get closer, I feel a hot rumble of dread lodge in my gut. When we reach the medical ward, I am surprised to see that Candide is still on duty.

"They asked us to stay because of the snow," she says with a shrug. I can see deep fatigue in her eyes, but her voice tries to mask it. "He knows you're coming," she tells the three of us, standing a few steps away from Dad's room. "But he's still having more trouble than usual swallowing. So take it easy, and if you see any sign of distress . . ."

I look at Pancha, expecting her to translate Candide's instructions for Olympia, but instead of informing her mother, she breaks away from the group and heads straight toward Dad's door.

"Nee!" I hear Dad exclaim as Pancha enters. By the time Olympia and I catch up, she is several steps inside. Dad's wheelchair is parked by the window. Outside, the snow has collected on the dark branches of the skinny tree, making it look like a woman in long evening gloves. I watch as the smile on Dad's face twists into a confused grimace, and I rush to his side to reassure him.

"Here I am, Dad," I chirp, planting a kiss on his cheek and taking his good hand in mine. His eyes dart from my face to Pancha's and back again, and I feel his grip tighten. Olympia, leaning on her cane, remains by the door, and I don't think Dad has even noticed her yet.

"Diego," Pancha says, as if to convince herself.

Still clenching my hand, Dad peers at her skeptically.

"Pansha," he finally answers, astounded.

"And look who else is here," I say softly.

Slowly, Olympia makes her way to her son's side, her face filled with a million combating emotions. Dad simply begins to weep and, the next thing I know, he has let go of my hand and has buried his face in the folds of Olympia's sweater, his strong arm wrapped around her nar-row hips like a vise. Olympia rocks him gently, kissing his hair and whispering into his ear. I think of the picture of my mother holding me as a baby, feeding me limitless love through the devotion in her eyes. At sixty-nine, Dad is still Olympia's baby boy, hurt and scared and grate-ful she's come.

Pancha and I are both wiping away tears when she takes a step toward Dad's wheelchair. Immediately I reach out and stop her. This is their moment, mother and son, and neither one of us has the right to intrude.

A dense silence fills the room, an exhausted calm. Olympia lowers herself into the padded vinyl chair that is next to the bed, and I posi-tion Dad so he is beside her. Pancha steps forward and they exchange a long hug. I find a box of tissues and begin passing it around. Everyone pats their eyes and attempts to pull themselves together. During the lull, I try to gauge Dad's condition, hoping the intense emotions have done him no harm. He is clearly shaken, and his breathing is fitful. But when I ask if he's all right he nods. At that very moment, Candide steps into the room. It's no coincidence, I'm sure. She must have been stand-ing in the hallway, monitoring the situation. Focused on Dad, she checks his pulse, asks him to take a deep breath, and then checks it again. "I'm right outside if you need me," she says, turning to leave.

Pancha is the first to speak. "Why didn't you tell me about Regina?"

Dad averts his eyes and lowers his head. Olympia reaches for his hand and nestles it in her lap.

"You knew about the letters, didn't you? She must have told you." Pancha's tone is stern, but tightly reined.

"Mom didn't tell us anything about you," I say in Dad's defense.

Pancha shakes her head, refusing to believe me.

"And this one," she says, jutting her chin my way, "she says she doesn't know anything."

Dad looks at me, his eyes wide and watery.

"Pancha." Olympia says her daughter's name as if she's issuing a warning, and then goes on to say something in Spanish that I can't make out, but which sounds like a firm command.

Pancha's expression hardens and she begins to pace.

Dad shifts in his chair and straightens his back, preparing himself to form an answer. His lips purse. His eyes squint. He takes his hand from his mother's lap and points his finger at his sister.

She stops and looks at him straight on.

Dad begins, but his words collapse into garbled, guttural sounds. He tries again, and again his body fails him. He jabs his finger at Pancha and then slams his hand on the wheelchair tray in frustration.

I hate her. Hate her so completely that I have to literally sit on both my hands to stop myself from hurting her.

"*Basta!*" Olympia shouts, slapping her cane against the floor near Pancha's feet. "*No más!*"

Again the room is quiet.

Olympia speaks again, her voice soft but firm, clearly trying to redress the situation.

"*No, Mamá!*" Pancha argues. "It's not okay just because time has passed. I won't let this family forget what Regina did."

Now I have had enough. "Don't talk about my mother!" I growl.

Pancha shoots me a condescending smile. "*Mijita*, that's why I'm here. Your mother wanted you to know the truth. And I'm going to tell you. Whether your father wants to believe it or not. Whether you want to hear it or not. I'm going to lay out the truth, because Regina wanted it that way."

I am quivering with anger and waves of hot blood feed my contempt with every beat of my heart as Pancha explains that she kept writing but since Mom never answered she gave up. Dad's expression has turned dark and, again, he mumbles something none of us can understand.

"I already know the truth," I counter. "I know how you turned your back on Mom and Dad and everything they believed in. I know how you bought into the blatant lies and propaganda that wound up getting thousands of people killed. Because your mind is small. Because you're selfish. You should be begging for my dad's forgiveness because you were nothing more than a common criminal."

Pancha crosses her arms and leans against the wall as I speak.

"Is that what you read in your little book?" she asks softly. "Is that what your smart professor friends told you? Ask Diego what his role in that story is. Go ahead, ask him."

I look at Dad, who has clenched his good hand into a fist that I wish he had the strength to swing.

"Por favor!" Olympia sighs as she pulls herself up from her chair and steps toward the bed. Reaching for the yellow plastic pitcher on the nightstand, she pours water into Dad's cup and takes it to him. None of us speaks as Dad takes a sip. Candide is right—he is having trouble swallowing.

I love Olympia's quiet strength, her calm compassion. I wonder what she knows about this, what version of the story she has to tell. I am sure in her younger days she would have been able to keep an outburst like this under control with just a look in her eye. But it's too late for her, or anyone, to stop the situation from breaking wide open now.

Still, Pancha responds to her mother's disapproval by taking a deep breath and holding her hands in a prayer position as she exhales. What a goddamn hypocrite she is, acting like a peaceful Buddha when she's the one thrashing a sword.

"I didn't come here to fight," she says with her eyes closed.

"Right," I scoff.

"Your daughter has no idea who she is," Pancha says to Dad, ignoring me. *"Ella ni siquiera puede hablar español!"*

I look at Dad and he shuts his eyes. Whatever she said to him, it struck deep.

"That's it," I answer. "You're done."

"Oh," she says calmly, "I haven't even gotten started." Sliding her back down against the wall until she is sitting on the floor, and crossing her legs, Pancha refuses to move.

I'm so full of loathing my ears are ringing. To get Dad away from her, I roll his chair toward the door, inviting Olympia to follow.

"Whey," Dad says, tapping my hand.

"You don't need to hear any of her crap," I say to him.

"Whey," he tells me again. "Peez. Stopf."

I hold the wheelchair still and Pancha looks up at us from her place on the floor. Waiting like a spider.

"I don't want to listen to anything she has to say," I tell my father.

"Peez," he replies.

I turn my back to Pancha, praying Dad will change his mind.

"I was wrong about a lot of things," Pancha says softly. "But your dad was, too."

I close my eyes. What good is this going to do anyone? What does any of it have to do with our lives now?

"Dad," I whisper into his ear, "I love you, and I love Mom, and I don't care what happened before."

I see a tear roll down his cheek and his lips begin to move, making the faintest of sounds. Bending down so my ear is next to his chin, I listen as he repeats the same words over and over. "I lie. I lie. I lie."

"Excuse me?" A young nurses' aide I've never seen before has stepped through the doorway. "They're beginning to close the roads, so we need to ask family members to please go home."

Pancha translates as the aide leaves. I turn Dad's wheelchair back toward the bed and take a look out the window. The snow has buried the hedges and shrubs, leaving the lawn looking like a lumpy mattress. Driven by a stiff wind, the snowflakes crash into the corner of Dad's window, where already there is a glistening half-moon of ice.

None of us moves, or says a thing.

In the hallway I hear the voices of other visitors making their way out. Finally Candide walks into the room and repeats what the aide told us. "Come on, now," she says.

"Ess okay," Dad says, rubbing my thumb.

"I love you." I lift his hand and kiss it. "You get some rest."

Pancha stands and, stepping away from Dad's chair, I reach for the coats we draped over his bed.

Candide makes her way toward Olympia and holds out her hand to help my grandmother stand. But Olympia shakes her head and says something in Spanish. Candide and I turn to Pancha.

"She wants to stay."

"I'm sorry, ma'am," Candide says. "The storm is just so bad, we—"

Again, Olympia answers in Spanish.

"She'll sleep in the chair," Pancha says. "She's not leaving her son."

I look at Candide, who has lowered her arm back to her side.

"Por favor," Olympia pleads.

"All three of you can't stay," Candide says sharply. "Absolutely not."

"Can she?" I ask.

Placing her hand on my back, Candide leads me into the hallway.

"This is not the time," she says in a harsh whisper. "Your daddy needs to rest."

"I'll take Pancha," I promise. "She's the one getting him upset."

Candide looks into my eyes, reluctant to agree.

"She's not sleeping in that chair," she finally says. "I'll find her a cot."

"Thank you."

"I'm doing it for your dad," Candide grouses. "You and Pancha get yourselves back home."

"I love you," I say to both Dad and Olympia, giving them strong hugs. "Come on," I mumble to Pancha, grabbing my coat and walking out without waiting for her to gather her things.

The car is covered with an icy glaze that we have to crack with the heels of our hands before opening the doors. Stamping her feet before she climbs in, Pancha settles into the passenger seat with a shudder.

"Don't get comfortable," I snap. Reaching into the foot well of the backseat, I find two ice scrapers and purposefully poke Pancha's arm with one. "I'll do the front windshield. You do the back."

I can tell she's never handled an ice scraper before, but I'm not going to help her. Grateful for the outlet, I slam the sharp edge into the thick sheet of ice clinging to the glass and watch it shatter into a jigsaw puzzle of jagged pieces. With a swipe of my other hand, I brush the pieces aside and continue cutting and jabbing until both the driver and passenger sides are clean.

In the back, Pancha is hopelessly sliding the flat end of the scraper over the slick ice.

"Move," I say, pushing her out of my way and quickly getting the job done.

In the car I turn the defroster on high and then flick on the radio so Pancha cannot talk. I tune in to the news channel and wonder where Juno is right now.

The road is slippery, and as we inch along we pass more than a few cars that have skated off the shoulder and have been abandoned. I keep my emergency flashers on, and every time we approach a stoplight or intersection where there are no other cars, I slide through it because that seems safer than trying to stop. I can tell Pancha is terrified, and if I weren't so scared myself, I'd probably enjoy making her feel even more unstrung.

Luckily the main road home has been thoroughly salted, and once we get onto it the going is easier. Pancha turns off the radio and starts talking about Guatemala again.

"We started out believing the same things," she says. "Your dad and mom and me. Even my mother. She believed."

I reach for the radio knob, and Pancha stops me.

"We all backed Arbenz," she continues. "Until he had a boy I was in love with killed for speaking out against him."

I keep my eyes on the road, where the churning snow and dim afternoon light threaten to erase the outline of the street. The wipers bang from one side of the windshield to the other in a clockwork panic, and the defroster hisses dry, hot air onto our feet and faces.

"I don't care," I say.

"You should," Pancha answers. "Because your father was one of the people who knew my boyfriend was going to be killed. And he didn't do anything to stop it."

I turn off the main road and feel the tires slide. The back end of the car fishtails and I turn the steering wheel in the opposite direction to control it. A plow has cut a narrow furrow through the deep snow, wide enough for only one car to get through. When we finally pull up to the house, I see that my neighbor across the street is outside cleaning his walk with a snowblower. I stop the car in the street and, without saying a word to Pancha, pop the trunk and step out to grab a shovel. My neighbor brings his machine over to help, and in a few minutes we've carved out a parking space wide enough for my Honda.

Pancha follows me to the porch, her boots sinking deep into the white with every step. I slide my house key into the lock and, turning the knob, I say, "You've got to go." Pancha blinks in astonishment, not sure if she should step inside.

"Get in." I step aside to make room. "You can stay tonight. But I want you out of my house and away from Dad by tomorrow."

CHAPTER 20

I hang my coat, step out of my boots and begin walking toward the office.

Pancha follows me, her wet boots squeaking like a rubber toy. "You think you're honoring your parents by living with a white picket fence and an empty page to call your past?"

Yes, I think, I do.

"Ignoring their lives? Pretending your history started with you?"

I refuse to give her my attention.

"Juanita," she says, "families are chains linked together by shared lives. That's what makes them blood. What are you so afraid of knowing? Diego did some things. I did some things. And so did your mother. Things we had to do during a terrifying time. Things you can't help being tied to."

I feel her waiting for an answer, the air between us stretched so tight it's bound to snap.

"Sacrifices were made for you!" Pancha's voice shakes with anger. "Risks were taken so you could live the way you do. Show some respect!"

My muscles tense. Sacrifices? I spent my entire life trying to fill the hole that was ripped into my world when my mother was killed. Not a single day has passed without my wondering what she would think, what she would do. I wake up every morning cursing the person who took her from me. Respect? My father has every ounce of mine, and I show it to him by living his American dream. If history is what forms a family, I've already been through enough to qualify.

I step into the office and see the answering machine blinking. I press the button and hear Juno's voice. The first message says he's been called into work early. The second says he's riding around with a couple of state troopers to get a story. In the third, he asks me to reach him on his cell. I turn to walk out of the room and find myself face-to-face with Pancha.

"It was Olympia, your mother and I who saved your dad's life." Her voice is rigid, her eyes explosive. "Diego was targeted for assassination by the liberation group I was with. I got word out to my mother, and she got word to your mother. Your mom pulled every string she could to get Diego a job in the United States and arrange for the papers they needed to leave Guatemala."

My stomach twists as I think back to the fullmooners' visit and my suspicion that Randy knew more than he was telling me.

"I don't care," I say. Although I do. A million questions are racing through my head. Assassination? Why would Dad be singled out? What would make him a target? Did Olympia know what Pancha was mixed up in? And Mom? Who did she know who could pull strings? Pancha sees the confusion in my face, but I will not give her the satisfaction of asking. I leave her alone in the office and head into my bedroom to call Juno.

"You have lights?" he asks immediately. "Power lines are starting to snap."

I want to tell him everything. What happened at the Rose Tree this afternoon, what Pancha said just now, and how I feel as if I've lost my footing. But before I can start, I hear Pancha's boots crunching through the hallway near the front door. Then the jingle of my keys and the click and thud of the front door opening and closing. Is she going to steal my car?

"Hold on," I say to Juno.

From the front window I see Pancha trudging through the ankle-deep snow, shoulders bent forward, chin tucked into her chest. If I weren't worried that she'd hurt somebody on the road, I'd let her take the damn thing just to get her the hell out of my life. But nothing is that easy with her. I step back into my cold boots as she approaches the driver's side. And, just as I am about to head out the door, I see her step to the trunk of the car, open it and lift out the bags of groceries I'd forgotten about.

I make my way back to the bedroom, boots still on, before she is aware that I'd been watching.

"You all right?" Juno asks.

"Not really."

"It's going to be a hell of a night," he says, stepping over my answer with a rush of words drenched in adrenaline. "Trees down. Ice. You wouldn't believe the accidents we've seen. The governor is about to declare an emergency and close the roads."

I should have stayed with Dad and Olympia. I should be at the Rose Tree. Anywhere but in this house with Pancha.

Finally, Juno hears my silence.

"Bad?"

"She won't let up," I say.

"Listen," Juno replies, dropping his voice. "I found something out about your father that you should know. I didn't want to tell you over the phone, but it doesn't look like I'm going to get to see you tonight."

Whatever it is, I don't want to hear it. Juno hesitates. Maybe he can sense that I'm worn out. Maybe he'll stop right there.

"It took me a while to nail down the facts, but I finally got the full story," he continues. "Nita, your dad lied about his ties in Guatemala. He was a Communist. A Marxist, for at least ten years. He lied about it to become an American citizen."

Beyond Juno's voice I hear the scratchy police radio demanding the state troopers' attention, a woman's voice piercing through the static, reporting one car wreck after another.

"It's a hell of a story," Juno says. "Death and deceit, all that juicy stuff. I'll tell you, that Diego is one fascinating character."

I bite my lip and taste the hot sting of acid rising in the back of my throat.

"You have no right!" I hiss. "You have no right to talk about him like that!"

"I thought you—"

"It's none of your business. None of it is any of your goddamned business. What kind of reporter are you, anyway? Can't you see that it's a lie?"

"I checked with—"

"Did Pancha tell you to do this? Is that what is going on? Did Pancha pay you to dig up dirt?"

"Pancha?"

"What filthy pile of garbage did you crawl through to come up with this, Juno? Did you have a good time rooting through my parents' private lives to get your story?"

"I didn't do it for me," he says, shaken.

"What the hell did you do it for, then?"

"For you."

His words burn. For me? I slam down the receiver and run into the bathroom to vomit. From the kitchen I hear the teakettle squeal. The telephone rings and rings. I can't stay here. Not for another minute.

"It's Juno!" Pancha announces from the other side of the house.

I rinse out my mouth and splash cold water on my face. When I step out of the bathroom, Pancha is standing in the doorway with the cordless phone in her hand and a smug look in her eyes. "Juno," she says again, holding the phone out to me.

I push past her, taking the handset and hurling it against the wall. I yank my coat out of the hall closet, sending its wooden hanger tumbling to the ground. Kicking it down the hallway, I grab my car keys from the table where Pancha set them down and bolt out the front door. Pancha watches without saying a thing. I brush the newly fallen snow off the front and back windshields with four quick swings of my arm, ignoring the cold clumps that fall into my sleeves. By the time I start the engine, my gloves are wet and my fingers are stiff. Instead of moving forward, the tires spin. I slide the stick shift into reverse and hit the gas again. The car jerks and, when I feel the tires achieve the slightest bit of traction, I turn the wheels and back into the slippery street.

It is dark and in the headlights' glare I see nothing but a curtain of whirling white as my car skates through the gully cut by the plow. I look at how the storm has redefined the landscape. All the sidewalks and curbs have disappeared. The lawns and driveways have become smooth, endless meadows. The roofs and chimneys have been draped with icy veils. Nothing looks the way it did this morning, although, I know, underneath nothing has changed.

Why did I let myself believe Juno cared about us? All he was after was a story. Do it for your mother, he said. And I was stupid enough to trust him. Find Pancha. And he made sure I did. He was the one who shoved this family history crap down my throat, insisting it was good medicine. He's been playing his game perfectly since the moment we met. Leading me along.

By the time I reach the main road, I am unable to control the convulsive sobs tearing through my chest. I pull into the parking lot of the first convenience store I can find, fold my arms across the steering wheel and give in to the tears. The engine is still running and the headlights are splashing the store's brick wall with a blue-white light when I look up and see a pay phone. Grabbing two quarters from the ashtray, I decide to call Lauren.

When she answers her cell phone I cannot speak. Every word I attempt dissolves into tears.

"What's happened? Nita? Are you all right?"

I take a jagged breath.

"Where are you?"

"Out," I manage.

"Out?" I can tell Lauren is working; her voice is taut and exhilarated.

"Juno . . ." I mutter.

"Is he with you?"

"No."

"Nita, where are you?"

I take another breath and, finally, words form. "I'm trying to get to the Rose Tree," I say as the wind bites my wet nose and cheeks.

"Where are you right now?"

"On Lancaster. At the 7-Eleven."

"Stay right there," Lauren commands. "I've got a company SUV. I'm not too far away."

"I need to talk."

"Can't right now," Lauren answers in a rush. "Just wait in your car. I'll be there in a little bit."

I hang up the phone and step into the store. The air is warm and moist.

"I'm closing," the man behind the counter barks before the door swings closed behind me.

"Do you have any coffee?"

He points to two pudgy glass pots with plastic lips and handles that are sitting on a hot plate in front of the cash register. I pour myself a cup before I realize that I've walked out of the house without my purse. The man watches me as I pat the pockets of my coat and then the pockets of my pants.

"Forget it," he grouses. "I just want to get out of here."

I can feel the heat of the paper cup stiffening my damp gloves, and the steam rising from the small opening in the white plastic lid warms my chin. In the front seat of my car, I sip the bitter coffee slowly and try to decide whether I should wait for Lauren or head out for the Rose Tree on my own. There are no other cars on the road and, although the snow is still falling heavily, I probably could get there before it gets too deep to negotiate.

I think of Pancha and what she said to me. I think of Juno and what he's done. And when I think of Randy and the fullmooners, my eyes land back on the pay phone. I get out of the car and call him collect.

"It's true," Randy says and sighs, sending a shudder through me.

"And you didn't bother to tell me?" What the hell is the matter with everyone?

"You didn't want to hear it," he says sharply. "You made that very clear when we were there."

I take a gulp of coffee and let it singe my tongue. I surrender.

"Tell me," I say.

I hear Randy take a deep breath, trying, I think, to figure out how he can soften the story. "Do you know who your mother's parents were, Nita?"

I shake my head, assuming Randy already knows my answer.

"They were friends of Arbenz," he explains. "Your grandfather was his speechwriter."

I hold the receiver closer to my ear and lean against the store's brick wall, stretching the telephone's metal cord as tight as it will go as Randy goes on.

"During the coup, he sent your mother away to art school in France. You knew that, right?"

"Sort of," I reply.

"Well, anyway, your father had gotten involved in campus politics at the university in Guatemala. He was an Arbenz supporter and became president of the student body, and your grandfather liked what he saw. Your granddad became your father's mentor and brought him into the Arbenz circle as a student liaison."

"Was Dad a Communist?"

Randy clears his throat. "Lots of people were."

I know Randy wants to tell the story slowly, but I don't have time to wait. I ask if Dad knew about Arbenz having people killed for speaking out against him.

Randy stays quiet.

"Pancha says he did."

"Both sides were involved in awful things," Randy says.

"What happened?"

"I don't know the whole story."

"What do you know?"

"Your father was hired in Dallas sight unseen. We all knew it was a political thing, an order from the chancellor. There were theories and whispers, but nobody knew what his story was for sure. And after a while, Nita, none of it mattered because he was a fine professor. Everyone could see that."

"How did he get into the country?" I ask. "How did he get past the border?"

"I suspect somebody bribed the right immigration officials in Guatemala to get them to fix his papers."

My feet are numb and my knees hurt when I bend them. I switch the telephone from my right ear to my left and plunge my cold hand as deep into my coat pocket as it will go.

"He didn't tell me about any of this until after your mother died," Randy continues. "He felt her death was somehow connected to his deceit. He was consumed with guilt. Never got over it, Nita. No matter how many times we tried to tell him there couldn't be a connection. He was convinced his lie had something to do with her murder. That somehow God was evening the score."

Hearing Randy, I remember how, as a girl, I told Dad that I hoped the police would kill the person who hurt Mom. I said I'd like to watch them shoot the guy right in front of me. And I remember how Dad said that wouldn't make me feel better, even if I believed with all my heart that it would. Back then, I thought he meant that the robber's life could never be worth as much as Mom's. Not that he blamed himself for the crime that killed her.

"For a while he considered going to the INS and confessing, but he knew he would be deported if he did," Randy says. "And nothing was more important to him, or to your mom, than raising you as an American."

The wind whips a cloud of snow from the ground into my face and I feel the tears that are streaming down my cheeks harden into ice. I wipe them away and step back toward the telephone box.

"Is Diego all right?" Randy asks.

"I don't know," I answer. "There's a snowstorm here and I haven't been able to get to the Rose Tree."

"Nita?" Unexpectedly, I hear Mrs. Stevens's thin voice on the line. "We love you. Don't you ever forget that."

I lean my forehead against the pay telephone's metal casing and close my eyes tight.

"Do you hear me?" she asks. "We will always love you."

I mumble thank you and hang up the phone.

"You stuck?" the man from the store asks as he pulls the glass door shut and locks it.

"No. I'm fine."

"Better get home," he says, rubbing his hands together. "It's getting worse."

I start the car's engine and get back on the main road. The man was right. It is worse. Even at their highest setting the wipers can't keep up with the rush of flakes. Shots of stiff wind rock the car back and forth, and furious squalls of ice and snow cloud my field of vision. The fastest I can travel is ten miles per hour, and a few minutes into my trip I hear a police siren wailing behind me. If I try to pull to the side of the road I will careen into a snowbank, so I tap the brakes and slowly come to a stop in the middle of the lane.

The officer gives me a callous stare when I hand him my registration and tell him I left my driver's license at home. I have to get to the Rose Tree, I say, and he shakes his head. We look at one another for a long moment and then he says, "You need to get off the road, ma'am."

"I will, as soon as I get—"

"Now," he insists.

"It's just a couple miles up the road."

"Is this your address?" he asks, looking at the registration card.

I don't answer.

"Ma'am?"

"Yes."

"You're going home, and I'm going to follow you," he says sternly.

I extend my hand so he can give my document back to me.

"I'll hold on to it," he says, "until we get you back home."

CHAPTER 21

*P*ancha comes to the door with a candle in her hand.

"Thank God," she says as the officer leads me inside. "Juno's been going nuts. And Lauren is out looking for you."

Pulling my arm free of the policeman's grip, I walk past Pancha and into the living room, where she has at least a dozen candles burning.

"If I see her out again, I will arrest her," the officer warns, as if I am some wayward teenager.

"Yes, sir," Pancha replies, shaking his hand.

When I try to turn on a lamp, I find that the power has gone out. On the coffee table, lying open between the same candlesticks I took to the Rose Tree for the fullmooners' dinner, is my parents' wedding album. Next to it is a box of tissues, my mother's address book and Pancha's letter.

"She's fine," I hear Pancha say into the telephone. "We'll be here." She steps into the dim candlelight, her long hair falling over her shoulders like a shawl. "Juno says he'll tell Lauren that you're here."

My coat is still on and my hands are still cold as I turn my back on Pancha and look out the front window. The storm has not let up and, with the electricity out, the lustrous mounds of snow look purple and eerie. I have never felt as deserted by my mother as I do right now. Why isn't she here to hold me? To tell me how I'm supposed to feel?

Letting my coat fall to my feet, I brush past Pancha and walk into the dark kitchen, where I reach across the counter, feel for the telephone, and punch in the number to the Rose Tree.

"Please hold," the receptionist says the instant she picks up. I wait, listening to a maddeningly upbeat recording of "American Pie."

"Rose Tree," she says, halfway through the song.

"I need to speak to Candide."

"I'm sorry, ma'am."

"This is Nita DeLeon."

"The lights are flickering here, Ms. DeLeon, and things are a little crazy."

I don't reply.

"Can I have her call you back in a minute?"

"Is my dad all right?"

"I'm sure he's fine," she says, not bothering to say good-bye before cutting me off the line.

Pancha walks into the kitchen with one of the candlesticks in her hand. The flame bathes her face in yellow light and between the flickering shadows I see her eyes are swollen and red.

"Will you let me tell you?" she asks softly. "The whole story?"

I stare at her, too numb to resist. She takes my hand and leads me into the living room and we both sit on the floor as Pancha recalls the past.

When Jacobo Arbenz became president of Guatemala, Pancha tells me, my mother's father, Arturo Acosta, rose in the government ranks. He traveled around the country with the new president, talking to farmers and housewives and shopkeepers to gather material for the speeches he wrote. He met Olympia at a function for schoolteachers and was so impressed by her that he recommended she be hired by Arbenz and his wife as a private tutor for their children.

"That's how Regina and I met," Pancha says. "As part of my mother's payment, the president arranged for me to attend the same private school that Regina went to."

"What about Dad?"

"He had a scholarship to the university. Regina had one year of high school left to go. I had two."

I tell Pancha what Randy told me over the phone. How my grandfather Acosta liked Dad's political leanings and brought him into the president's inner circle.

She nods. "The thing is, Arbenz never really had a chance. He was too eager to challenge the Americans, who never intended for him to succeed. He had moral goals, but immoral men working to achieve them. Diego was so devoted to Arbenz's ideals that he couldn't see the shades of gray that separated the practice from the principles."

"But *you* knew," I ask skeptically, "at sixteen?"

Pancha responds to my remark with a brusque look.

"Olympia," she says pointedly, "warned Diego and me to never trust a man of power blindly."

"Was Dad a Communist?" I demand.

"Yes," Pancha replies. "Lots of students were. The Communists were the ones fighting for labor unions, for the peasants' rights. That's what communism meant to your father. Equality rising from the people."

"What about you?"

"At first I believed in Arbenz with all my heart. He was like a Franklin Roosevelt and Santa Claus rolled into one."

Pancha tells me that every day after school she and my mother would walk to the national palace, where they'd meet up with Olympia and Arbenz's kids and do their homework.

"We ran around the place like it was our own house. We heard things we weren't supposed to hear. The president and his staff treated us like we were their own and, I guess because we were girls, they never worried about the topics they discussed in front of us. It was right around that time that your mother and father started to date."

I try to picture my parents as teenagers, walking hand in hand, sneaking kisses in the president's garden.

"Everyone expected them to get married, and it probably would have happened sooner if things had gone more smoothly."

I tell Pancha that I know the basic story behind the coup.

"Your grandfather Acosta sent your mother to France when things started getting bad. And things turned ugly fast. Conservatives accused Arbenz of being controlled by the Soviets, and the fact that he had Communists in his ranks only fed their suspicions."

"What about you?" I ask.

"I wanted Arbenz to be the hero I'd built him up to be. An honest savior. But he turned out to be just like the others when he found himself backed into a corner. He closed his eyes to what his men said had to be done, and like lots of followers, Diego talked himself into looking past the ugly particulars to see the lofty goal. But I couldn't. Not when one of the so-called particulars included the murder of my boyfriend."

I look at the deep lines around Pancha's mouth and eyes and wonder how long the memory has plagued her.

"So, you turned against Dad?"

She nods.

"What about Olympia?"

"I didn't tell her where I'd gone because it would have put her in danger."

"But you weren't any better," I argue. "You joined people who killed and kidnapped to overthrow Arbenz."

Pancha shakes her head. "Nita." She sighs. "We weren't the ones who overthrew Arbenz. America did that. I joined a group that saw what was coming and tried to do what we could to keep it from turning into a bloodbath. My mistake was believing that any of us could change the direction of events, when the truth was that we were being used as pawns in a power struggle that had nothing to do with us. The bloodbaths came," she whispers, "and they were more horrible than any of us could have ever imagined."

"So who was good and who was bad?"

Pancha rolls her eyes. "The only place that sort of thing is clear is in church."

I expect to feel angry at her, but instead I feel sorry. Sorry that my father felt my love for him was so fragile that he couldn't share his past with me. And sorry that Pancha hasn't been able to let it go.

"After the coup most of Arbenz's supporters were put in prison or shot," Pancha says, pulling the wedding album toward us. "Your grandfather Acosta was arrested and put in jail, but was let out after a few years."

We both look at the photo of Mom smiling alongside her parents.

"How come?"

Pancha shrugs. "I think somebody agreed to let him see his daughter get married. But not long after the wedding he and his wife both died in a fire at their house."

That much Mom had told me. But I'd always assumed it was an accident.

"Diego survived the coup by lying low and quietly working on his graduate degrees, praying the new regimes would leave him, Regina and Olympia in peace."

For a while it worked, Pancha says. In public Dad stayed silent, but in private he attended secret meetings of former Arbenz supporters.

"What he didn't know is that Regina and I had never lost touch," she says. "We'd written to one another while she was in Europe, and mailed letters to the house of an old school friend of ours so we could keep corresponding while I stayed underground after the coup."

"Why didn't you and Dad work things out?"

"After the fire, your mother was a nervous wreck," Pancha tells me. "We both knew that Diego was in danger if anyone found out about the meetings."

Pancha closes the album and looks at me.

"We weren't the only family that was split apart, Nita. It was a horrible time when nobody knew who to trust. Talking to the wrong people could get you killed. Can you even begin to understand that? People were dying so fast that news reports of bodies being found in ditches and rivers stopped leaving us shocked. We had no idea which police officers or schoolteachers or even priests were spies. Your father believed that I'd betrayed him by joining the other side, and your mother knew that reconnecting with me openly could lead to trouble for him."

Pancha places her hand on mine and I feel it trembling.

"Regina miscarried two babies during all this," she says hesitantly. "She was pregnant with you when they left."

Her words make me feel faint, and the room is so quiet that Pancha and I both jump when the doorbell and telephone simultaneously ring. Pancha heads to the door while I run to the kitchen to answer the phone.

"Nita," Candide says, sounding exhausted.

"Oh," I say, feeling guilty for wasting her time. "I just wanted to—"

"He's having trouble," she says bluntly.

I wait, expecting Candide to assure me that she's got everything under control. But instead she says, "You need to get over here."

"We have to get to the Rose Tree." I take Lauren's wet parka out of Pancha's hands and give it back to Lauren without saying hello. Lauren shakes her head and is about to argue with me when she recognizes the panic in my eyes.

"Come on," she says, slipping her jacket back over her shoulders and swinging open the front door. Pancha opens the closet, grabs her jacket and hands me mine.

The wind is blowing so strong the snow is flying sideways. Inside the SUV, a police scanner beeps and screeches. I think of Juno as we buckle ourselves in.

"Call him," Lauren says, handing me her cell phone.

I shake my head. "Not now." Instead I dial the Rose Tree and tell Candide that we are on our way.

"Good," she says. "I've called Dr. Gorman. Nita, you need to get here as soon as you can."

"Drive faster," I say to Lauren as we set out.

She revs the engine, but eases off the gas pedal when the back of the truck starts to shimmy.

"Go!" I shout.

Lauren downshifts and turns the volume of the police scanner down low so the only thing we hear is the engine wrestling against the storm. I know Lauren is doing her best, but my muscles are jumping out of my skin. We need to get there. Now.

Pancha begins filling Lauren in on the story of Mom and Dad, and hearing it a second time doesn't make it seem any more real to me. Secret meetings. Rebel forces. Fires. Miscarriages. Were my parents ever the people I thought they were? Or was the life we lived in Dallas a long, defensive lie?

"The rebels found out that Diego was meeting with other former Arbenz backers, and they decided he was trouble," Pancha explains.

"Why would they tell you?" Lauren asks. "Didn't they know you're his sister?"

"Diego hated me. And they had no idea Regina and I were still friends."

Outside, the squalls have obscured the traffic lights and road signs, making them impossible to read. With hazard lights blinking, Lauren rolls through each intersection without even touching the brakes. The SUV has no problem cutting through the slush accumulating on the street, but every now and then the tires hit a patch of ice and the three of us hold our breath as they slide.

"I knew they were going to go after Diego," Pancha continues, more, I believe, to keep us calm than to retell the tale, "and I had to get word to Regina."

Pancha says that she told Olympia to wrap her letter of warning in tinfoil and bake it into the bottom of a casserole. Olympia then left the dish on Mom's doorstep, covered with a red-checked napkin, which was Pancha's signal that a crucial message lay inside.

We pass the hotel where the fullmooners stayed, which means we are halfway to the nursing home. I glance at the speedometer. We're moving just under twenty miles per hour. My foot presses against the floor and I slam the dashboard with the heel of my hand.

"I can't go any faster," Lauren responds curtly.

"Friends of Regina's father helped her find a teaching position for Diego," Pancha proceeds. "And my mother bribed the immigration officers to get the papers in order."

My mind stops. "Olympia?"

Lauren's cell phone rings.

"Here," she says, tossing the telephone into my lap. "I'm sure it's Juno."

"Listen, I'm sorry—" he begins.

"Dad." That is all I manage to say before I begin crying so hard that my lips go numb.

Lauren takes the phone from me and tells Juno that we're almost at the Rose Tree.

CHAPTER 22

*T*he Rose Tree glows like an oasis.

"Emergency generators," Lauren says as she pulls into the parking lot.

Inside the center, the wide-screen television is silent and dark but the lobby and the dining room are bathed in a strained, vibrating light. Men and women whose skin looks as gray as their hair sit at the card tables and stand near the front desk listening to radio updates about the storm. Every telephone in the place is ringing.

I don't bother to sign in, and the receptionist waves me along as I rush past her.

Running down the main corridor, I beg God to make Dad be all right. *Please.* I hear Lauren and Pancha right behind me, our boots landing hard and wet against the clean linoleum, Pancha's bangles jangling.

When we reach the medical wing, I stop in front of the wide door. Lauren and Pancha stop, too. Lauren takes my left hand and Pancha takes my right, our fingers throbbing and gripping tight.

"Come on," Lauren says, pushing the door with her shoulder.

When I see Candide, my knees buckle. I know that look. I saw it on Dad's face twenty-five years ago. Pancha and Lauren try to steady me but I let go of their hands and sink.

"I'm so sorry," Candide says, sitting on the hallway floor beside me. "So, so sorry." I don't try to stand. I just let Candide's solid arms hold me, her honey voice ache for me. I should have been here. As Candide rocks me, my tears splash against the polished tile. I watch them fall, one after another. When Mom died, I felt like somebody had stabbed me with a knife. Now I can't feel a thing. I can't hear the telephones ringing anymore. Even Candide's voice sounds distant. My hands are burning hot and I set them flat against the cold tile. Suddenly my back tenses and my mind clears. It's so plain. So obvious. This is just a scare. A horrible mistake.

"He's fine," I say to Candide, straightening myself up and wiping my face. "It'll just take him a minute."

She loosens her embrace and, when she tries to speak, I set the tips of my warm fingers on her lips to stop her.

"You'll see," I say. "He's waiting for me."

I stand and see Dr. Gorman, Lauren and Pancha flanking Dad's door.

"Nita," Dr. Gorman says.

In Lauren's eyes I see defeat. In Pancha's, naked sorrow.

"He's fine," I tell them. "Give him a few minutes."

Inside, Olympia is holding Dad's hand.

"Talk to him," I say, rushing to my grandmother's side. "Wake him up!"

She whispers something to me in Spanish, brushing hair away from my face.

"Dad!" I shout, moving Olympia's hand away and furiously slapping the back of his wrist. "Daddy, I'm here. Wake up."

He is so handsome. His smooth dark eyebrows. His elegantly frosted temples. So very refined. "I'm here, Dad," I say into his ear. "I'm here."

Olympia sets her hand on my shoulder.

"No," I flinch. "Don't touch me!"

Dad's arm is limp, his face pale. I press my fingers into the curve of his neck and wait to feel the beat of his heart.

"Cardiac arrhythmia," Dr. Gorman explains softly. "I'm sorry."

I look over my shoulder and see that Pancha has entered the room. Dr. Gorman steps out, leaving us alone. Just family.

Olympia says something. "It was quiet," Pancha interprets, sitting herself on the arm of Olympia's chair while trying to swab her tears with her thumb before they fall.

"*Tranquilo,*" Olympia repeats.

I look into Dad's face and see that he's gone. With Pancha's help, Olympia stands and pulls the bedsheet over him. She takes my hand, presses her lips against the tips of my fingers and then places both her hand and mine against the middle of my chest.

She speaks a few words in Spanish, her voice low and strong.

"You were his life," Pancha translates. "Every breath of it."

Lauren steps into the room, her face red and blotchy. Juno follows.

The fire inside my head explodes at the sight of him. "Get the hell out of here!" I scream.

He looks down, shifts his feet, but does not move.

"Get the hell out!"

"Nita," Pancha gasps.

Lauren exchanges a long glance with Juno and, without a word, he leaves.

"It's his fault," I shout, feeling my heart pounding like a jackhammer in the veins of my neck. "His goddamned fault."

Lauren looks at her hands.

"This would have never happened if he hadn't pried. It was too much. Too much."

"Nita," Pancha says.

"No," I snap, glaring at her. "I don't want to hear anything else you have to say."

"*Mija,*" Olympia soothes, stroking my hair, patting my back.

"Why didn't Dad tell me?" I ask her. "Didn't he think I'd understand?"

Pancha translates my questions for Olympia, then translates for me when Olympia says, "Love. He loved you. He loved Pancha."

I shake my head. "How could he? He had no idea what Pancha and Mom did to save him."

Olympia looks at Pancha and says a few words.

"She told him," Pancha says. "Tonight. She told Diego everything."

Despite the snow and ice and the impassable roads, the newspaper hits the front door just after the sun comes up. Olympia is asleep in the easy chair, but Pancha, Lauren and I are still awake.

"I'll get it," Lauren says.

The power came back on sometime during the night. We heard the refrigerator rattle and hum, but none of us reached for a light switch. The burned-down candle stubs provided as much light as we needed to call Carla and Randy Stevens and the rest of the fullmooners.

"Look." Lauren sets the paper on top of the coffee table, where rivulets of wax have hardened against the stems of the candlesticks like white lava. There, on top of the obituary page, underneath Juno's by-line, is a long article about Dad.

> *Professor Diego DeLeon, who fled his native Guatemala to spare his wife and daughter an uncertain future filled with life-threatening terror and political strife, and who embraced his new home in the United States with the inspired fervor of a truly grateful citizen, died yesterday at the age of 69.*

There are gracious quotes from Randy and Dr. Carver, a mention of Mom's art, and a line about how near the end of his life Dad was happily reunited with his mother and sister. There is no mention of communism, nor of Mom and Pancha's long-held secret.

The expression on Lauren's face is full of questions. Am I going to call him? Do I regret what I said at the Rose Tree? Am I still angry that he got his story? I hand the paper to Pancha, who quietly begins to cry again as she reads. The truth is I don't know what to think. And I don't have the energy to try to figure it out.

The telephone rings and, assuming it is Juno calling, I go into the kitchen to answer it. Instead of Juno it is someone from the agency where I used to work, offering condolences.

Ever since Olympia and Pancha arrived, I've lost all track of time. I stop to look at the calendar on the kitchen wall and realize Patrick will be at the stage design program in a few days. I place my finger on yesterday's date and slowly slide it over to the day I'm supposed to get Dad's ashes back and head down to Dallas for the memorial service the Stevenses have already started to plan. That, I note, will be right before Easter.

"I need yoga," Pancha says, stretching her arms over her head as she enters the kitchen.

"Will you show me?" Lauren asks, following behind.

I watch them file into the studio. Nothing that has happened since the Rose Tree seems real. I don't remember the drive back to the house, although clearly we are here. I can't remember what any of us said along the way. Did we talk? I don't even know what any of the fullmooners told me after I said Dad was dead. The only thing I can recall is Mrs. Stevens saying she'd take care of things, and Candide handing Lauren a packet of forms concerning Dad's remains.

Pancha's noise machine sends the sound of springtime songbirds floating into the kitchen. But when I look out the window I see nothing but dunes of white. I decide to take a shower. The hot water feels good. I let it soak into my hair and trickle down from my nose to my chin. I close my eyes and pretend I'm in a swimming pool, my hands slapping the surface, my arms tensing as I push through each stroke, steadily making my way to the other side. I imagine the soles of my feet pressing against the hard tile and my lungs filling with clean, new air each time I inhale. I don't know how long I stay like that, but when I open my eyes I find myself wedged into the corner of the shower stall, cold and crying.

Tying the sash of my bathrobe tight, I look at myself in the mirror and wonder who is looking back at me. Using Olympia's soft-bristled brush, I begin smoothing the tangles out of my wet hair. Dad and Mom must have believed that starting over with a clean slate was the only way they'd make it here. After all, what was the point of weighing our little family down with painful memories of people they never expected to see again? They wanted to protect me, to keep me from falling into the dark, bottomless canyons of their pasts.

But why didn't Dad tell me about it when I got older? Was he afraid I'd hate him for lying? Would I have? Without meeting Pancha and Olympia, would I have even understood?

I think about my parents' wedding album, and how I'd pestered Dad to tell me the stories behind the photographs. Now I know why he refused. It was too hard for him to remember how the future he and Mom had hoped for fell apart. How strongly he had wanted to believe that he'd be able to change things. I wonder how many of his friends, those pretty, smiling people in the pictures, were killed during the upheaval. When Dad looked at the pictures, I'm sure the same question filled his head. Who was alive and who was dead?

I'll never be able to page through that album the way I used to. I'll never be able to look into the bright eyes of the wedding guests and believe in a happily-ever-after. That's the problem with knowledge. Once you know something, you can't go back to not knowing it. Up until now, I thought the important events that shaped my life happened in front of me. Mom's death. My marriage. The divorce. But I was wrong. My life has been shaped by people and events that happened long before I even got here. The same sort of remarkable events I'm sure are part of every family's history. I am just the latest link in the DeLeon chain.

Carefully I fish my stray hairs out of the bristles of Olympia's brush before I set it down on the embroidered tea towel. Then I take a closer look at the monogram, so finely stitched by a natural needleworker's hand. Funny what traits get passed down.

Olympia clears her throat to let me know she's standing in the doorway. When I look over at her, I see deep circles under her tired eyes and almost no color in her lips. The tortoiseshell combs that usually hold her silver hair neatly away from her face have lost their grip and dangle like fallen twigs from a few stiff strands. Taking her elbow, I help her to the bed and gently pull the combs out as I sit down beside her. Using the tip of her cane to help slip off her shoes, Olympia settles herself against the two pillows I've propped against the headboard.

"*Gracias*, Juanita," she whispers.

Unable to hold back my tears, I drop my chin and begin to cry again. "I'm sorry," I say, my voice cracking. "I'm sorry you didn't get to really know him."

Olympia lifts my head with her finger and holds my gaze until she, too, is overcome with emotion. Her dark eyes close for a moment and I notice that her lashes have the same lazy curl as Dad's. Slowly, she shakes her head.

"Juanita," she says, her rich accent embracing every word. "Already, I know him. Now, you know him, too."

CHAPTER 23

From the room at the funeral home where we've been told to wait, Pancha, Olympia and I can hear the fullmooners welcoming people, their voices distant and hushed. I'm not sure what the funeral director expects us to do in here, although the vanity tables and makeup mirrors give me a hint.

Pancha and I haven't gone near them, and after Olympia sat herself down on one of the velvet-tufted stools, she turned her back to the looking glass. What's the point? We look like we feel, and there isn't enough powder or lipstick to mask that.

Still, Randy and Carla Stevens have done a beautiful job with everything. There are spring flower arrangements and several pieces of Mom's pottery next to the photograph of Dad as a young professor. The music is Bach. They've lined up the speakers for the service and, kindly, have spared me from having to try to say anything myself.

After the service, we'll scatter half of Dad's ashes at the sculpture garden in the arboretum so he can rest with Mom. And then Pancha and Olympia will fly down to Guatemala tonight. I'll join them Thursday and we'll finish the heartbreaking chore.

Last night I pulled out the same plastic globe that Mom once used to show me where our family came from. I still can't picture how

Guatemala will be. But I know Olympia will be relieved to finally get her son home.

Outside, it's a beautiful day. The live oaks are flush with new leaves, the azaleas are exploding bright pink and the breezes are lusciously warm. I wish Lauren could have come. The fullmooners would have loved seeing her again. But, always levelheaded, she said she'd be of more help to me after the funeral, when I decide whether to sell Dad's house and stay in Philadelphia or keep it and move back to Texas. Either way, Lauren has promised to take time off from work to help me get the job done.

"We're ready," Randy tells the funeral director.

Taking Olympia's arm, Randy helps her stand and carefully escorts her down the aisle of the softly lit chapel. The director hands Pancha and me a sheaf of white tissues as we step out of the anteroom and follow. I see the president of the university, my former high school principal, my old swim coach. People of a certain age. But, surprisingly, at least half of the pews are filled with much younger faces, men and women who are at least a decade younger than me. Students, I suppose. Dad's other kids. I think back to the dinner at the Rose Tree and all the notes of gratitude inside the scrapbook the fullmooners made for Dad. These must be the faces behind the words. My heart swells.

I take a seat in the front row, between Olympia and Mrs. Stevens. Randy positions himself at the end of the pew, next to Pancha. The rest of the fullmooners and their wives are directly behind us. Once we've settled, the organ music stops, leaving the room humming with the delicate sound of muffled crying and whispers. Randy stands and walks to the small platform at the front. Mrs. Stevens takes my hand. I hold Olympia's.

"Diego DeLeon was my best friend," he begins.

My throat closes and my nose burns. This is going to be hell.

Leaning close to Olympia's ear, Pancha quietly translates every speaker's comments. I see my grandmother's face fill with pride as Randy speaks about Dad's exceptional teaching abilities and lists the numerous awards I never even knew he'd won. Then I see her expression slide back into grief when Randy talks about the unremitting pain that Dad and I felt when Mom was killed.

He goes on to describe Dad's less-than-stellar housekeeping abilities and his colossal handyman disasters. He tells a story of the time Dad built a carport to protect his brand-new Pontiac from the brutal summer sun and came out the next morning to find nothing but a pile of nails and heavy lumber covering the car.

It feels right to laugh.

Dr. Carver is next. He pulls a piece of paper out of his suit pocket and holds it less than an inch away from his thick eyeglasses.

"Death, be not proud," he begins, reciting the John Donne poem in a beautiful baritone voice vibrating with emotion, "though some have called thee mighty and dreadful, for thou art not so."

When he is done, Dr. Carver walks to the edge of the platform, judges its height with his toe, and carefully makes his way toward me. With a tender kiss to my forehead, the professor hands me the paper he's just read from and whispers, "There's a hole in my heart."

My lips quiver and Mrs. Stevens grips my fingers tight.

Ted Lansky, dressed all in black, climbs onto the platform with a Bible in his hand. His white hair, sweeping up to a peak, looks like a candlewick.

Olympia makes the sign of the cross over her shoulders and bows her head as he opens the book, and it dawns on me that Dad must have been raised Catholic. By the time I came along, Mom and Dad had stopped going to church and the only way I knew we were Christian was that, come December, we put up a tree.

"Psalm Eighty-four," he says, clearing his throat and lifting his chin. "How lovely is thy dwelling place O Lord of hosts . . ."

As soon as I hear the words, I remember Dad saying once that poetry isn't poetry unless it's read aloud.

"Even the sparrow finds a home, and the swallow a nest for herself, where she may lay her young, at thy altars, O Lord," Dr. Lansky continues. "Blessed are those who dwell in thy house, ever singing thy praise."

I shut my eyes and whisper, "Amen."

When I look up again, I see Juno standing on the platform.

"He got in late last night," Mrs. Stevens says in my ear. "He's a good man, Nita. Your mother would have thought so, too."

In his eyes I see both pain and comfort, and beyond that I see love.

"Professor DeLeon and I had just met," he says, shifting his gaze from me to the congregation. "But I knew he was an exceptional person long before I even shook his hand. Because I've gotten to know his daughter, Nita. And there is no finer testament to him than her."

I hear Pancha translate for Olympia, who turns to look at me and nods. It is too much. I bury my head in my hands, and when there are no more tears I keep my face covered and listen to my own uneven breaths. For a moment I feel mercifully removed from what is happening. Juno's voice sounds muted, his words unrecognizable. I picture myself sitting at Dad's bedside, watching old movies with him. I think of the day he and Juno met and the happiness I saw in his eyes.

Juno's voice pulls me back and, as he continues, I realize he's not speaking English. In a voice that is perfectly paced and metered, he is reciting Spanish poetry. The kind Dad taught. The kind he adored.

Why don't I know the language? I should have insisted. Out of respect, if nothing else. I should have done so many things differently. Now, how will Mom and Dad ever know that I understand what they went through? How much they gave up to raise me in ignorant bliss. How can I ever repay them?

Juno lowers his head when the poem comes to an end and again our eyes meet. I'm glad he's here and, from the way he sets his jaw before stepping back into the pews, I know that he understands.

After the service, I look for him as Randy ushers Olympia, Pancha and me into the lobby to shake hands with the dozens of people who came to pay their respects. I see him but not before a long line of wellwishers has formed and one person after another begins to graciously tell me they're sorry.

Finally I see Juno in the line hugging Olympia, patting Pancha on the arm. When he touches my hand, my heart ignites. I pull him toward me and hold him tight.

"I'm sorry," he whispers in my ear. "I'm so very sorry."

I don't let go. His neck is warm against my cheek, and all I can think of is being with him.

"I love you," I say, making myself step away.

His face is flushed. "I love you, too," he answers, gently wiping away my tears.

At the airport, Olympia pulls Juno and me aside while Pancha arranges their boarding passes.

"It's good you are bringing him home," Juno translates. I'm not sure if she's talking about Dad or Juno, but I say yes as she hugs me. "It's good he's with your mama," she continues, "but it's also good that he's in Guatemala, too."

Now I know Olympia is speaking about Dad.

I nod. I need to learn Spanish so I can tell her how much I love her. How safe I feel around her.

"You come back," I offer, "whenever you want."

Pancha steps up beside us.

"It's time to go," Pancha says. "Nita, this has been a difficult visit. Let's hope the next one is under better circumstances."

Juno slips his arm around my shoulders. I'm still not sure how I feel about Pancha, or how she feels about me. But I believe what she told me is the truth, and she did what she thought was right.

"Thank you," I say, holding my hand out to her.

"We're family," she answers, her silver bangles clanking, "first and forever."

Juno embraces them both and, as they begin to walk away, Olympia stops and points the tip of her cane at us. She asks something in Spanish, and Juno modestly shakes his head.

"What?" I ask him.

"Nothing," he mumbles.

Olympia repeats herself.

"She wants to know if he's coming with you," Pancha explains.

"To Guatemala?"

Olympia nods.

Before any of us can answer, the attendant announces that the flight is boarding. A young man in a blue blazer takes Olympia's arm and says he'll help her to the gate. Pancha, who has the same scarf on her head that she wore when I first saw her, trots off behind them.

"Do you want to?" I ask Juno after they've disappeared from sight.

"She was just being polite," he answers.

Maybe, I think. But I'm not. "I want you there," I tell him. "I really do."

When we get back to Dad's house, Juno calls the newspaper to get a few more days off. Then he phones his landlord and asks if he'll open Juno's apartment and pull his passport out of his desk drawer.

"If you send it by overnight mail, I'll get it in time," he says. "Would you throw in an extra sports shirt, too? Add the charge to my rent."

I tell him that before I left Philadelphia I met with immigration officers to get a special document allowing me to travel under my married name, Nita Nile.

"It's the one official document I forgot to change after the divorce," I say, feeling again as if I may start to cry.

"Nita Nile?" Juno repeats. "That name doesn't fit you at all."

"No," I say, "not anymore."

The Stevenses call to see if there's anything I need, and I thank them again for everything they've done.

"We'll pick you up Thursday at noon to take you to the airport," Mrs. Stevens says. "Do you want me to come over and cook breakfast, or would you like to sleep in?"

I look at Juno, surveying Dad's literature collection.

"I'll manage," I say. "Um, Mrs. Stevens?"

"Yes?"

"Juno's coming to Guatemala with me."

There is a slight pause. "Yes," she answers. "Yes, that's a good idea."

When I step back into the living room, Juno has my father's old Herb Alpert album in his hand.

"Shall we?" he asks.

I try to remember the last time I watched a stereo needle settle into the groove of a vinyl record. When it touches, we hear pops and scratches before the lonely trumpet slides in. Together on the sofa, we listen.

"You were right," Juno finally says. "It was none of my business."

My eyes fill with tears, and once again I am weeping.

"I meant what I said, at the service," Juno goes on. "So forget all that crap about you not knowing who you are. Okay? Your parents passed their love and courage down to you, and that is what makes you an amazing woman, Nita. Not the coup or the secret Pancha kept."

"Shhh," I protest. "I'm glad I know. I wish Mom and Dad could have told me. But I guess they thought it was a burden they didn't want me to carry. And, to be honest, a year ago I would have agreed. But look what the past brought me, Juno. It brought Olympia, and Pancha, and you."

Juno grins. "I'm not sure I want to be on the same list as Pancha."

"You know what I mean."

"Yes," he whispers more seriously, "I do."

"Dad thought Mom's murder was his fault, and that I'd be ashamed of him if I knew that he'd lied to get into the country. When I was younger, I probably would have been. And Mom. I'll never know how much she intended to tell me. All I know is that I feel different now."

Juno rubs my hand as my tears fall. I turn my lips toward him and, gently, he responds, kissing my salty lashes, my nose, my mouth.

"I want to make you feel good," he says, "but not here."

The music has stopped, and the needle lingers at the raspy end of the record for a few moments before the arm lifts.

"Do you want to spend the night at my hotel?"

I want to say yes. I want to lie next to Juno's body and soak in his strength. I want to lose myself for a night and wake up to a brand-new day.

But instead I blurt out, "I can't have children," surprising even myself.

Juno rises from the sofa and pulls me up to meet him.

"What does that matter?" he asks, nuzzling my ear.

"It does," I say, pulling away. "I know it does."

"We'll deal with it," he answers, holding both my shoulders, looking me straight in the eyes. "We'll figure something out when the time is right."

"You sure you want—?"

"*Mi amor,*" Juno interrupts. "Grab a change of clothes and get in the car. I love you, and it's time to go."

CHAPTER 24

The outside of Olympia's house is the color of butter.

Its dark wooden door, flanked by shuttered windows and smooth painted plaster, opens directly onto the uneven sidewalk that banks the narrow and noisy cobblestone street. In the middle of a long city block, it hides its charms behind its plain exterior.

Once inside, Juno and I step into a tropical dream, a glorious court-yard crowded with jungle flowers and flamboyant greens. From some-where in the middle of the thick vines, I hear the call of birds I cannot see and the buzz of cicadas being carried by the humid breeze. My grandmother herself looks like an orchid in the open-air patio, her olive skin and splendid gray hair playing off the russet tiles underneath our feet.

We have arrived in Antigua near the end of Holy Week, and during the hour-long drive from the Guatemala City airport it looked as if everyone in the nation was out running errands. There were lines streaming out the door of every tiny grocery store that we passed. Women in limp summer clothes were carrying heavy tote bags, or ba-bies, or both on their hips and backs. I saw men in short-sleeved shirts and well-worn pants cramming themselves into already overcrowded buses. And in the thick crowds, I saw the Mayan Indians I'd read about, barefoot and obviously poor, small and sturdy native people in outfits that looked like needlepoint come to life. Their clothes praised life. The women's skirts and blouses radiated the bright reds and blues and yellows of the rain forest, and the men's embroidered trousers looked like carved ivory. The bold designs woven into the fabrics are the same chevrons and zigzags my mother etched into her pottery. Exotic birds in a stark setting.

Beyond the city, the landscape is green. Not the blue green of the Pocono Mountains, or the shamrock green of suburban lawns in summer. It is a fierce jungle green, the color of unpolished jade. The road that goes from Guatemala City to Antigua is curvy and steep, cutting through mountains filled with stair-stepped crops of coffee and sugarcane. And the land is so fertile that even the twigs pushed into the ground as fence posts have sprouted.

As Pancha drove us out of the bustling capital city, I saw the deep disparity of wealth that fed political differences. Houses along the street were either rambling fortresses of stucco, marble and heavy timber or broken-down shacks with rusting tin roofs and walls made out of corrugated steel. I tried to picture Mom living here as a girl, going to her fancy private schools. And Dad, working hard to create equity between the classes. I can see why they each believed that change was needed, and how hard it must have been to figure out whose method to believe.

On every street corner I saw soldiers with guns. Young men with dark eyes and nervous expressions, prepared to pull the trigger on practiced insurgents or spontaneous young troublemakers. I think of Pancha's friends, dragged away and murdered in the jungle. Of Dad facing death at the end of one of those rifles, and Mom carrying me over the border in the safety of her womb.

Everything looks foreign, but still, somehow, familiar, like a dream I'm having with my eyes open.

"You should visit the cathedral today," Olympia tells Juno, who translates for me. "Because tonight and tomorrow it will be so crowded you won't be able to move."

On the plane, I read about the Holy Week traditions. In Antigua, thousands of people come to watch the religious processions that snake through the town's narrow streets on Good Friday. But the solemn parades of men and women carrying enormous wooden statues of Jesus and Mary on their bare shoulders aren't the only attraction. People come to see the elaborate *alfombras* covering the streets. In English, the word means "rugs," but the *alfombras* really are mosaics made by ordinary citizens out of painted sawdust, flower petals, fruits and nuts. The travel book offered a few pictures showing entire families kneeling over wide, intricate creations that looked as sophisticated as the flower show displays that Lauren photographed in Philadelphia. The mosaics, it said, are offerings to Jesus, things of beauty provided for Him to walk over on His way to the crucifixion. Street by street, the murals are destroyed by the feet of the faithful participating in the processions, which begin at dawn and continue until the evening.

There is a break to commemorate the hour of Jesus' death and then, just after sunset, there is one final procession, carrying Christ in a crystal coffin through the streets. People line the sidewalks, holding candles, to watch the slain Savior pass.

"You can see the *andas* at the cathedral today," Olympia says, talking about the heavy wooden floats the paraders will carry on their shoulders. "You'll be amazed at how big they are."

Pancha leads us to the living room, where thick roof beams and windows encased in wrought iron show off the house's colonial Spanish heritage.

"The processions have been the same since the 1600s," she explains. "And most of the *andas* are at least two hundred years old. The whole thing has become a tourist attraction, but it's a serious day for the people who walk the routes. Carrying the *andas* is an honor bestowed on them by the church and, you'll see, it's not a pleasant thing to do."

Olympia tells us she will take a nap while we are out, so she'll have enough energy to go with us tonight and watch the mosaics being made.

"They'll start building them at sunset," Olympia says. "And stay up all night until they're done."

"Our plan," Pancha says, "is to let Diego's ashes go in the hours between the crucifixion and the night procession. If that's okay with you."

I feel Mom and Dad so strongly here that the pain I felt in Dallas seems cushioned by a tender stroke of love. I nod to let Olympia know that her plan is all right. And when our eyes meet, I see that she feels she's finally brought her family back together.

"You two go and take a look around town," Pancha says. "And we'll have dinner ready when you come back."

Outside, Juno kisses me.

"I know this is hard," he says. "But you look so right here. So beautiful."

I wave off his compliment with my hand, but inside I feel it, too. My face looks like everybody else's on the street. My dark eyes and dark hair. My generous curves. They blend right in, which they have never done before.

"Remember when I said you are a classic Latina beauty?" Juno asks as we approach the town square.

I squeeze his hand to answer.

"Now, do you see?"

"I wish my parents were here," I whisper.

"They are, *mi amor*," Juno answers. "Everywhere you look."

Inside the church it is cool and dark. The floor is made of stone that has been polished and smoothed by the feet of people who have knelt before the same gold-gilded altar for four hundred years.

Somehow this beautiful town has survived through hundreds of years of upheaval and sorrow. The sturdy buildings built by the Spanish invaders have been passed down to families with deep Guatemalan roots. And the unchanged streets and the stately architecture attest to the healing power of time.

Alongside the simple wooden pews, glorious *andas* with statues of Jesus and Mary line the sanctuary beneath the stations of the cross. The floats of the hauntingly lifelike wooden saints sit on top of dozens of sawhorses, waiting to be lifted and carried out of the cathedral by believers tomorrow morning. There is one displaying a life-size Jesus sitting on a rock, his head forlornly in his hand, his shoulder-length hair lovingly combed over his slumped shoulders. There is another of Jesus praying on his knees and yet another of him on an eight-foot-tall cross.

At the base of each *anda* worshipers have laid down offerings of bread, bananas, mangoes, pineapples, corn and apples, spread out like a beautiful cape on a bed of raw white rice.

Olympia was right; we are astounded at the size of the floats. They are at least forty feet long and ten feet wide. And, according to my travel book, they weigh between two and three tons.

At the altar I see people who look as if they own nothing but the clothes on their backs kneeling next to plump American tourists with expensive cameras around their necks, and I wonder what the Guatemalans see when they look at Juno and me.

Back outside, the sun floods our eyes and across the street the town square is bustling. Vendors with insistent voices call out to passersby, selling balloons and shoe shines and rainbow-colored popsicles from rickety carts. Children in their Sunday shoes dash around adults' knees and dip their outstretched hands into the water cascading from the central fountain. Beds of carefully tended flowers separate the rows of whitewashed wooden benches, which are already filled with teenage couples holding hands and anxious parents keeping close watch on their sons and daughters.

The little girls with silky dark hair and coffee-bean eyes look like walking baby dolls, and the rambunctious boys with dusty scuffs on the knees of their pants challenge you to try to hold them back. I feel the familiar ache of longing as I watch them play.

Juno slips his arm around my waist and tugs me closer to his side.

Farther down the main street, in the yard of a much smaller church, a dozen food vendors have pitched tents and set up portable grills, offering roasted chicken, fresh sliced fruit, tortillas and pastries. At one stand there are paper cups filled with what look like thick french fries but turn out to be fried bananas. The air is thick with the music and smells of a carnival, and everyone seems to have collectively agreed to set their worries aside long enough to breathe in the rapture of the afternoon.

"I'm going to stay," I say to Juno. "In Philadelphia, I mean."

"I'm glad." He hands the man selling the fried bananas a coin and tells him to keep the change. The fruit tastes warm and sweet. I think of the fullmooners and, as if he's read my mind, Juno turns and adds, "We'll make a visit with the professors a yearly thing."

"I'd like that," I say, silently relishing the notion of "we."

For the rest of the afternoon, we stroll through town stopping at little shops selling books and paintings and knickknacks. Juno's perfect Spanish wins warm smiles from the shop owners, who are just as quick to offer me a friendly handshake when he tells them I'm Olympia DeLeon's granddaughter.

"Tell him that the next time I come I'll be able to speak Spanish," I say when we greet the owner of what must be the best jewelry store in town.

"Good," the owner answers in English. "I'll help you practice. Now, how about a ring for you two?"

I feel my face begin to blush.

"No," I tell him quickly.

"Not quite yet," Juno adds.

The man frowns and slides his hand to the other end of the glass case that is between us.

"How about a bracelet, then?"

Juno leans over to take a closer look, and the man pulls out a tray of shiny gold bangles.

I shake my head. Too much like Pancha, I think.

"Look at this." Juno points to a gold link bracelet with one large charm.

"It's an antique coin," the jeweler says as he places the bangles back in the case and pulls out the link bracelet. "One hundred quetzales. Pure gold. Our money is named after this bird." The jeweler shows me the image of a little parrot with long tail feathers on one side of the coin.

"Look," I say, pointing to the date pressed into the base. It is from the year my parents left Guatemala.

"We'll take it," Juno says. This time I don't argue.

The shop owner smiles and begins arranging the bracelet inside a pretty box.

"No." I hold out my wrist. "I'll wear it out."

"Yes, for today," the man says and smiles. "But tomorrow the street is filled with thieves and pickpockets. So be careful."

Juno and I step out of the store and I thank him with a long, deep kiss.

After supper, Olympia takes Juno's arm and the four of us set out to watch the *alfombras* being built.

Two doors down, Olympia's neighbors have laid a bed of sand over a patch of the cobblestone street as big as a queen-size bed. The sun has not yet set, but they've already lined four standing lamps along the sidewalk, using a chain of extension cords that disappears underneath the house's front door.

"This is Alfonso Rojas." Pancha introduces us to an old man in baggy khaki pants and a paint-stained sweatshirt. "He's been making the best *alfombras* in town for more than forty years."

Olympia gives the man a hug and tells him who I am. He puts his hand to his heart and sighs.

"*La hija de Regina y Diego?*" he asks, looking me straight in the eye.

I nod.

He and Olympia exchange comments and Juno calls me to his side. "She told him that your father died," he translates. "And now he's saying that you look just like him."

"*Sí,*" Olympia agrees, struggling to hold back a wave of tears. I step to the other side of her and plant a kiss on her cheek.

Pancha introduces Juno.

"*Mucho gusto,*" the man says, shaking Juno's hand and, finally, shaking mine.

"What he'll do first is draw his design in the sand," Pancha says.

Mr. Rojas smiles and pulls a small prayer card out of his pocket. Its corners are frayed, and it is no bigger than the palm of his hand. The picture is of Jesus in a bright red robe, holding a tall staff as he shepherds a flock of fluffy white sheep.

Mr. Rojas kneels on a wide plank of wood that's supported above the sand by a line of bricks on either side of the sand.

"The bricks keep the wood off the sand," Pancha explains. "After he draws the design, the rest of the family will put down more planks and start filling in the picture with flower petals."

Mr. Rojas pulls a pencil out of his pocket. He sets the prayer card on the sand and dips the pencil tip into the very center. With long, graceful strokes he sketches the body of Christ in perfect scale. I think of Mom and the Saturday-morning art lessons I sat through at the museum.

"Did my mother ever come to see this?" I ask Pancha.

"Every year," she answers. "Alfonso was her favorite."

"Tell him he's my favorite, too."

Pancha makes a face. "You haven't seen any of the others yet."

"It doesn't matter. I already know."

Juno tells him for me and, for a moment, Mr. Rojas stops his pencil and bows his head.

"*Gracias a Dios . . .*" he says, looking up at me as he finishes this thought.

"He says thanks to God he's lived long enough to see our family back together," Pancha tells me.

Mr. Rojas goes on, his face full of emotion.

"He's going to make this year's *alfombra* especially for you," Juno translates.

I kneel down at the edge of the sand and hold out my hand. When Mr. Rojas takes it, I feel the same strength I used to feel in Mom's fingers. He wraps his thumb around mine and threads the pencil between both our fingers. Effortlessly, his hand guides mine over the sand. With the pencil tip we draw letters that flow diagonally across the bottom corner of the mosaic. *Para la familia DeLeon,* they say.

"*Gracias,*" I whisper when he lets go of my hand. "*Muchas gracias.*"

When I stand, I notice that a crowd has started to form. Tourists and townspeople are toeing the edges of Mr. Rojas's creation, squinting and snapping photos.

"Let's go look at some others," Pancha suggests. "We'll stop back on our way home."

Every street we walk down is paved with mosaics in the making. Some run the length of two cars; others are as small as a bathroom rug. Men, women and children scoop brightly colored sawdust out of knee-high burlap sacks and sprinkle it over cardboard templates of flowers and butterflies and every kind of geometric shape imaginable. Neighbors stop to chat with one another, and the glow of lamps and lanterns lining the sidewalk casts a blissful yellow tinge over all of them.

We spend almost two hours winding our way through the narrow streets, and although I wish I had brought my camera, it seems wrong to treat this like a show. None of the mosaic builders complain when the tourists lean over their shoulders and aim long lenses down at their work. But I'm sure they'll feel more at ease when the sightseers have all gone back to their hotels and the quiet of the night belongs only to them.

When we arrive back at Mr. Rojas's place, the rest of his family is out working on the *alfombra* while he stands back and watches. Two young girls reach into a laundry basket filled with red carnations and carefully set each blossom into the area of the drawing depicting Jesus' robe. Three other women carry out plastic tubs of yellow mums and burgundy daisies and begin pulling the petals off of the stems. Carefully they scatter the delicate flakes along the rim of the mosaic. Following behind them are two teenage boys holding trays laden with tiny pink rosebuds that Mr. Rojas himself sets one by one into the sand. At Jesus' feet I see three puffy sheep made out of cotton bolls, coffee beans for their hooves. Mr. Rojas winks at me from the other side of the mosaic, and I raise my eyebrows to tell him I'm impressed.

"*Hasta mañana,*" Olympia says to him.

"*Sí, Doña Olympia,*" Mr. Rojas replies. "*Muy buenas noches.*"

Much later, when everyone else is asleep, I get up and go to the patio, using my cotton bedspread as a shawl. I climb into a wide rattan chair and pull my knees up to my chest. The sky is as black as I've ever seen it, and the stars look like pinpricks letting in the light from someplace else. It's just cool enough for my nose to feel a nip. I never thought I'd want to be here, but now I can't imagine anyplace else I'd rather be.

$\mathcal{A}$t dawn, the bray of an off-tune trumpet wakes me and, when I swing open the window shutters, a cloud of biting smoke drifts in.

Outside my room, I hear Juno and Pancha saying good morning to one another.

"Nita?" Juno raps on the door. "Pancha says we need to hurry if we want to see Mr. Rojas's *alfombra* before it's stepped on."

"Be right there!" I pull on a pair of blue jeans and a faded sweatshirt, rub my eyes and pull back my hair. The trumpet keeps calling and, when I peer out the window again, I see at least one hundred boys and men clad in deep purple satin robes and pointed wizardlike hats lining the sidewalk. Some are swinging chains that have smoldering, egg-shaped incense burners at the other end of them. The white, ashy smoke lodges in my throat and I have to close the shutters before it fills my room entirely.

"Where's Olympia?" I ask when I meet up with Juno and Pancha in the patio.

"Asleep," Pancha answers. "We'll come back for her later. But if you want to see Alfonso's *alfombra*, we need to leave right now. It's always the first to be walked on."

Pushing our way through an already thickening crowd, we hurry to Mr. Rojas's door. There, a few steps from the curb, is his prayer-card mosaic looking like a priceless Renaissance painting in the clear morning sun. Christ's red robe has folds that have been shaded with hundreds of dark maroon petals. His face, His hands and His feet have been sculpted out of a smooth bed of putty-colored moss. The borders of the *alfombra* are an elaborate jigsaw puzzle of pink rosebuds and thousands of threadlike pistils glowing gold with moist beads of pollen. It looks like a perfect piece of needlepoint.

Over my shoulder I hear the trumpet growing closer and the slow steady beat of drums. The next thing I know, the one hundred men and boys in purple are stopping in front of us, forming lines along both sides of the street. The incense balls belch a thick pungent fog that lingers low in the morning air.

"They're the *cucuruchos,*" Pancha says. "The brotherhood of the church who usher in the *andas.*"

In the middle of the smoky haze, I see the dark outline of an *anda* slowly swaying down the street. The trumpets stop blaring but the drums continue to pound out a heart-thudding funeral march. The *anda* looks like a huge wooden ship inching its way toward us. The *cucuruchos* stand at attention as it nears.

It's hard to say which sight is more impressive, the forty-foot-long *anda* with life-size saints on top of it rocking from right to left or the four dozen men in black robes walking in step to the drumbeats with the heavy float on their bent shoulders. The enormous weight of their burden is evident in the pained grimaces on their faces as they trudge over Mr. Rojas's gorgeous *alfombra*, obliterating the intricate image with each slide of their shuffling feet.

"They're called the *penetentes,*" Pancha explains. "The penitents."

After they pass, the purple-robed men stay at attention and wait for the next, smaller *anda* to arrive.

"The second one carries a weeping Virgin Mary, and it's always shouldered by the women," Pancha says.

Also dressed in black, with gauzy veils over their heads, the women cart a tall, beautifully robed Mary, whose eyes point sorrowfully to heaven, a crystal tear on her cheek. When I look down to watch the middle-aged women step on the *alfombra*, I notice that every single one of them is wearing high heels.

Once they've passed, the *cucuruchos* scurry down the street to line up in front of the next *alfombra* half a block away.

"This is how it is all day," Pancha says. "Until the hour of the crucifixion."

"It's not the same people carrying the *andas* all day, is it?" Juno asks.

"No. Different churches carry different *andas*. They come from all over to march, and they each take different routes."

As she speaks, we hear the sound of trumpets a few streets away, and once again the slow beat of drums.

"Go have a look," Pancha suggests. "I'm going back home to make breakfast for Mama."

"What time do we need to be back?" Juno asks.

"Around one."

This is the perfect day to scatter Dad's ashes, when everything from the *alfombras* at our feet to the incense being carried by the wind is a reminder that no matter how beautiful or precious a life might be it will not last forever. I look at the exotic mosaics stretching as far as I can see and realize they are testaments to the unpredictability of life, as well as to an unfaltering faith that joy will win out. I'll never be able to change the decisions Mom and Dad made here, or the silence they chose to keep. But I can agree to lift the burden off of their shoulders, and be grateful for where the truth has led me.

By ten o'clock the processions are in full swing. American tourists, prayerful Guatemalans and colorfully dressed Mayan Indians crowd the sidewalks seven or eight deep as the *andas* pass. Children with Easter baskets on their arms dash into the street afterward, collecting the flowers that have been strewn all about.

"Amazing." Juno sighs as the fourth float we've seen goes by. "It's like Mardi Gras and a state funeral rolled into one."

At one o'clock the town falls silent.

"Everyone takes a nap, or goes to mass," Pancha says when we see her at Olympia's house again.

After we've showered and changed, Olympia meets us in the court-yard wearing the same sort of black veil the women carrying the *andas* had on. Pinned underneath her chin, it makes her look frail and sad. Suddenly I realize that for her this is Dad's true funeral, not the service we held in Dallas. Her face is full of pain, and while the empty look in her eyes sends a dart through me, I feel surprisingly at peace.

Juno is wearing the same dark suit he wore in Texas, and Pancha steps out of her bedroom in a flouncy white peasant blouse belted over a billowing black skirt made of crushed velvet. I cradle the brass urn in my arms, pressing it against the snug waist of the simple black dress I packed. Pancha takes Olympia's arm and we head for the door.

The streets are empty except for the crews of city workers in white jumpsuits sweeping away what's left of the mosaics. The smell of sulfur from the spent incense settles on our skin and our clothes. We walk the same route that the early-morning *penetentes* took, and Pancha stops to pick up a few stray blossoms that have been swept to the curb. When we reach the edge of town, Olympia asks Juno to take her other arm.

"We're going down to the stream," Pancha says, pointing to a shady green valley at the bottom of a steep hill.

"There's no road?" Juno asks.

Olympia shakes her head and takes the first step. It is slow going, with Olympia digging her cane into the soil every few inches and Juno stomping on the grass to make sure she won't slip. The afternoon sun is high in the sky and it doesn't take long for beads of sweat to slide from my forehead into my eyebrows. When we finally get down to the creek, Olympia pulls a handkerchief out of the cuff of her sleeve and hands it to Pancha, who dips it into the clear, rushing water. My grandmother dabs her temples and the back of her neck and then gives the hanky back to Pancha, saying something that I assume means, "Pass it around." The cold feels good, and after we've all cooled down, Olympia begins.

"Diego loved Guatemala like no one else I've ever known," Juno translates. "He wanted to believe that people with good hearts could save it, and he felt not only hurt, but ashamed when the man he believed in turned out to be as ruthless and corruptible as the dictators who came before him."

Pancha and I lock eyes and, with the bright sun filtering through her long hair, I can see what she looked like as a girl. High-spirited and idealistic, she must have adored Dad, the way any little sister would. Carefully I set the urn down and hold out my hand. She takes it. I look at Juno, who answers me with an approving nod, and then turn my attention back to Olympia, whose voice is trembling with emotion.

"When he and Regina left Guatemala, I knew I would never see them again," she says. "My heart soared when Pancha got that letter from Regina so long ago. I prayed and prayed, but we didn't hear from her again."

Flowers on sinewy vines snake from the tree branches down to the water. The blossoms are a virulent orange and an alarming yellow, colors I've avoided in my needlepoint because they seemed so unnatural.

When Olympia says that she told God she refused to die without seeing her son again, I believe her. From the distance we hear a single church bell calling. The mass of the crucifixion has begun. Olympia closes her eyes and pauses.

Six months ago, I never would have pictured myself standing on the same ground that my parents fled. I never could have imagined how powerfully connected I would feel to people I had not even met. I look at Olympia's tiny, dignified frame and Pancha's defiant chin and see so much of Dad in them. I feel the intensity of Juno's tender love every time he glances at me.

"My life has been long," Olympia continues, "and now that I have met you, Juanita, I can say it has been good."

Pancha clears her throat and steps closer to the creek bank. Juno helps Olympia, and I follow. The church bell continues to beat like a slow pulse as I open the urn and tip its mouth toward Olympia. Silently, she removes a handful of ashes and holds them tight. Pancha takes some, too. Then Juno gently takes the urn out of my grasp so I can reach inside it. But I cannot move. Back in Dallas, the fullmooners let Dad's ashes go. I couldn't do it then, and I can't do it now. I don't want to feel the nothingness of what's left. Juno closes the urn and Olympia turns toward the water.

"In here," Juno translates as Olympia speaks, "Diego will flow through every corner of his beloved Guatemala."

"In here," Pancha adds, "the blood and tears will wash away."

Like black snowflakes the ashes sift into the stream as Olympia and Pancha rub their hands together. A few stray flakes land at my feet and I bend down to touch them. First with one finger, and then with all five, I rub the dirt until the ashes have dissolved. With tears streaming down my face, I place my other hand on the ground and begin to wash my hands with the cool, dark soil. I rub it deep into my skin, hoping some of it will seep into my blood.

The church bell stops keeping time, its last ring fading into the cloudless afternoon sky. When I look up, I see Olympia standing over me, holding out her black-stained palm. I set my hand in hers and together we walk away.

"Tell her I'm leaving the urn with her," I say to Juno. "So she and Dad will never be apart again."

At the airport the next day, Pancha makes us promise to come see her in California. Olympia hands me a package wrapped in Christmas paper and tied with string.

"Open it on the plane," Pancha translates.

The four of us hug, and then we hug again.

"I'm coming back," I have Pancha tell Olympia. "And when you see me again, I'll be speaking Spanish."

She kisses my cheek and smiles.

"For that," she says, "I wait."

Juno and I leave them in the lobby and walk to the security station, where the armed guard orders me to open the package.

"It's a gift," I argue.

Without another word, he reaches over and tears the string off the bundle.

"Take it easy," Juno protests. "We'll do it."

I set the present down on the inspection table and carefully unwrap it. It is the embroidered tablecloth Olympia had been stitching. The guard orders Juno to unfurl it, and when he does, I see that Olympia has embroidered her initials and those of her late husband in one corner, Pancha's in another, my parents' in the third and mine in the fourth. The guard points the tip of his rifle to a note pinned to the fourth corner. Juno reads it in Spanish, and then turns to me and translates. "It says she left enough room for you to stitch the initials of your children."

The security guard grunts and gestures for us to move along, but I take my sweet time folding the tablecloth back into a neat square, letting my fingers linger over Olympia's beautiful stitches, taking care to keep the note from falling off. Holding it against my chest, Juno and I continue down the marble hallway until we reach the gate.

On the plane, I use the tablecloth as a blanket and sleep all the way back home.

"Thank you," I tell Juno as we wait in line at customs in Philadelphia.

"For what?"

"For finding Pancha, for coming with me, for liking Dad."

"Oh, it's going to cost you," he says and chuckles, "believe me."

"It is?" I say, playing along.

"Oh, yeah. Easter with your family means Christmas with mine. And, if you think the fullmooners are characters, wait until you meet *tía* Concha and *tío* Chente!"

He slips his arm around my waist, and together we approach the immigration desk and set our passports on the counter.

"Mr. Juno Herñandez?" the blank-faced officer asks, keeping his eyes on Juno's passport picture.

"Yes."

The officer looks up, squints at Juno and then looks down again and snaps the passport shut. "Welcome home, sir."

Juno takes a step to the side and waits for me.

"Mrs. Nita Nile?"

"Oh," I say, remembering the special document in my purse. "Just a minute."

I smooth the piece of paper out and the immigration officer leans closer to read it.

He looks at me with his narrow eyes and then looks at the paper again.

"Ms. Juanita Del-YONE?" he asks.

I listen to the name and, for an instant, consider correcting him.

"That's right," I finally say. "That's me. Juanita Del-YONE."

"Fine," he answers. "Welcome home."

Over the next week, Lauren says she's going to call *National Geographic* and ask them to send her to Antigua next year to take pictures. Juno begins searching the Internet for information about visiting Guatemala again, and the fullmooners call to see how I am faring.

In the pile of mail that accumulated while I was gone, I find a card from Joy Taggert offering her sympathy. In the postscript, she tells me that her visit to Atlanta has been extended indefinitely and she's looking for an apartment. I also find a card from Aaron, signed with nothing but his name.

I take a few days to settle back in, and on the night before Patrick's next appointment, I finish needlepointing the profile-and-goblet pillow.

When he arrives he gives me a strong hug.

"My parents told me about your dad," he says.

"Thanks," I say. "But let's not talk about that. Let's talk about you. How did the stage design workshop go? You look terrific!" And he does. His face is bright and his posture is brimming with newfound confidence.

He laughs. "Oh my God. It was so awesome!" For forty-five minutes Patrick races through stories about one particular boy he met, the techniques he learned in class and the plays and films he and his new friend have already planned to create together.

"So you felt like you found your group?"

"Totally!"

"And this guy, David, you keep mentioning. He was special to you?"

Patrick frowns, weighing the implication of my question. "You're not going to tell my parents, are you?"

I shake my head. "No," I say softly. "You are, but only when you're ready."

"That will never happen." He sighs.

"Hey," I say, "I've got something for you. A little present I want you to have."

Patrick looks confused but relieved that, for the moment, the conversation has moved on.

"Close your eyes, and hold out your hands."

Patrick holds out his hands and waits.

I set the pillow in his hands and he wiggles his fingers underneath it.

"Okay, open," I say.

Patrick looks at the pillow and runs his palm over the stitches. "Faces," he says. "It's nice."

"Is that what you see?" I ask. "The two faces?"

He nods his head.

"Anything else?"

He looks again and shakes his head.

"Set it over here," I tell him as I rise from my chair. "Put it here and stand back a few steps, next to me."

Side by side we look at the pillow.

"Look in between the faces," I tell Patrick. "Clear your mind."

"Oh!" he catches on. "A wineglass. Cool."

"It's about things, and people, not always being what you see."

Patrick shifts his weight and crosses his arms.

"You need to be honest with your parents about who you are, Patrick."

He looks down at his feet.

"And I know how difficult that can be."

I put my arm around him, and feel his back stiffen.

"There's no rush," I assure him. "We'll take it slow, and when you're ready, I'll be there with you, if you want."

"Thanks," he mumbles.

"I promise you, it'll feel good to finally be comfortable in your own skin."

Patrick looks into my eyes.

In the waiting area, we hear his parents walk in, and I tell him we're done for today. He tucks the pillow under his arm and takes a deep breath before opening the office door. As he turns the knob, I want to tell him more.

Take it from me, I want to say, the truth may seem terrifying right now, but in the end nothing is more powerful than knowing exactly who you are.

PHOTO BY JACK BOOTH

Tanya Maria Barrientos, a journalist for more than twenty years, is a staff writer and columnist at the *Philadelphia Inquirer*. Her fiction was awarded a 2001 fellowship by the Pennsylvania Council on the Arts and the 2001 Pew Fellowship in the Arts. Born in Guatemala and raised in El Paso, Texas, she currently lives outside Philadelphia with her husband, Jack.

Tanya Maria Barrientos

FAMILY RESEMBLANCE

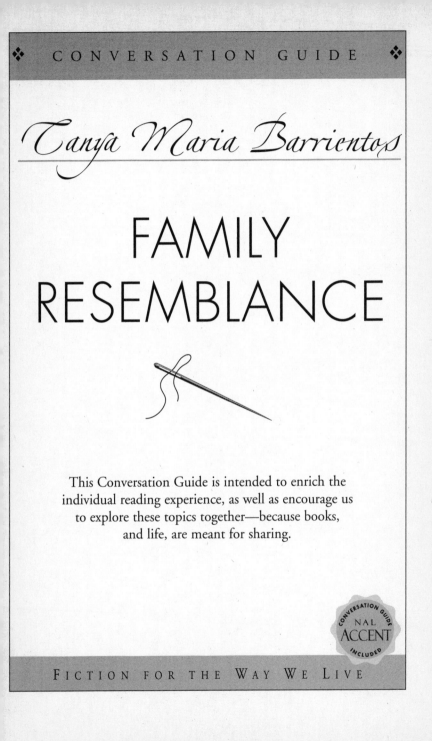

This Conversation Guide is intended to enrich the
individual reading experience, as well as encourage us
to explore these topics together—because books,
and life, are meant for sharing.

CONVERSATION GUIDE
NAL
ACCENT
INCLUDED

A CONVERSATION WITH TANYA MARIA BARRIENTOS

❖

Q. What inspired you to write about a family split apart by the 1954 coup in Guatemala?

A. I was born in Guatemala and came to the United States with my parents in the early 1960s. Like Nita, I grew up knowing very little about the place where my family is from. I wanted to write a novel about a character coming to terms with a family history she didn't realize would affect her so deeply.

Q. How much of Family Resemblance *is drawn from your own life?*

A. The basics are from my life. My parents left Guatemala for political reasons. We embraced American culture with gusto, especially since back then there was considerable societal pressure to assimilate as quickly as possible. Still, most of the novel's details—the long-lost sister, the political rift, the murdered mother, the stroke—are pure fiction. I don't actually know much about my parents' lives in Guatemala. They don't often discuss it. Maybe that's why I decided to make up my own plot with my own characters. Of course, I plan to get the true story from my parents one day. But to be honest, I didn't want them to feel like I was invading their privacy.

Q. Have you ever been to Guatemala?

A. A few times, but I don't go regularly. The last trip I made was with my father, who had not been back in over forty years. We traveled to Antigua to see the Holy Week processions, and he showed me where he was born and told me a lot about my grandparents. (It turns out that one of my grandmothers actually wrote speeches for Jacobo Arbenz.) It was a very moving trip for both of us.

Q. Family Resemblance might be described as a story about three generations of women. Do you find female characters more interesting to write about?

A. I like writing about women because I believe they are often the backbone of the family. They are the ones who nurture family tradition by teaching their kids about cultural holidays, passing down family recipes, putting together scrapbooks, organizing the family get-togethers. I know that's the case in the Latino community, and I suspect it's somewhat universal. It's hard to know if Nita's mother would have eventually told her about the events in Guatemala if she hadn't been killed. But I like to think that she would have because she and Pancha were already, secretly, trying to keep the family together. I certainly don't dislike writing about male characters. But I think the emotional connections that exist between women are a rich vein to explore.

Q. What do you consider the major themes of Family Resemblance?

A. Identity and forgiveness. To me, the book is about how honest people are willing to be about who they really are. Nita struggles with her cultural identity. Diego and Pancha struggle with their family identity. Patrick struggles with his sexual identity, and so forth. It's also about setting aside old grudges and looking at love with fresh eyes.

I think Juno and Olympia are already comfortable with who they are, and they end up being the ones who lead the other characters through the transition. Juno believes in facts and he teaches Nita that knowing the truth, no matter how unpleasant, can empower you. Olympia believes that love can heal deep grievances, and she never doubts the power of family.

Q. Olympia and Nita share a love for needlepoint. Why did you choose this?

A. Art is a recurring element—Nita's needlepoint, Regina's pottery, Patrick's films, the *alfombras* in Guatemala. I started out writing about needlepoint because that is one of my own hobbies. As the novel progressed I realized that these characters created their own visions of themselves and their different worlds through art. I also used art as a nonverbal form of communication between the characters, because it often says more than words ever could. And in Nita and Olympia's case, it was the way they connected.

Q. This is your second novel, following Frontera Street. *How was the writing process different?*

A. I wrote *Family Resemblance* in just over one year, while it took six years to write *Frontera Street*. I felt more confident in my storytelling abilities this time around, and I found the rewriting and editing process much less daunting. The one big challenge involved in this book was the historical research. I spent many weeks reading about the 1954 coup in Guatemala and the horrible violence that spread through the country afterward, which, of course, gave me a new appreciation for the risks my parents took getting our family to the United States. I'm also discovering that, when I run into a plot problem, I often end up dreaming about it and working the details out in my sleep. It's a strange technique, I know, but I'm learning to trust it.

Q. What are you working on now?

A. I have a few ideas for a third novel, but nothing specific yet. I'd like to continue writing about the lives of women and the issues surrounding cultural identity.

QUESTIONS FOR DISCUSSION

❖

1. On coming to America, Diego and Regina decided to start over. Do you think they had an obligation to tell Nita about their lives in Guatemala? Would Diego eventually have told her? Is it ever acceptable to lie to spare the feelings of loved ones? What do you know about your own family's origins? Do you feel that we, as a nation, are more or less tolerant of immigrants than we once were?

2. Discuss Nita's desire to be all-American. She says that America is made up of discarded pasts. Is this true? Can you ever discard the past? Have you ever misrepresented who you were in order to fit in? In what ways do Nita's issues with identity mirror those of her clients?

3. Do you think Nita truly changes over the course of the novel? Talk about the factors that encourage and discourage her to accept her family history. Would she have made the same decisions without Juno? Without the fullmooners? How much influence did Olympia have? Was their language difference a hindrance or help? How is the bond between grandparent and grandchild different than the one between parent and child?

4. How does the passage of time impact betrayal? How does it affect the keeping of a secret? Should Pancha have made more of an effort to

track down Diego over the years? Should Diego have tried to contact his mother in Guatemala? Do you think he knew about the address book or the letters from Pancha all along? Do you know anyone who has handed down a grudge or misconception from one generation to another? Do you think you have to forgive yourself before others can forgive you?

5. Pancha and Diego were both idealists when they were young. In what ways did they suffer for their beliefs? Is the sacrifice of human life justified in the name of a greater cause? What do you think it means to be patriotic today? Can you assimilate into a group without losing your sense of self? Can cultural or ethnic identity ever become more harmful than enriching? What balance do you think Nita finds in the end?